ALSO BY DAVID BLACK

NOVELS

The Extinction Event
An Impossible Life
Peep Show
Minds
Like Father

NONFICTION

Medicine Man
Murder at the Met
The King of Fifth Avenue
Ekstasy

PLAYS

An Impossible Life

POETRY

Mirrors

FILMS

The Confession
Legacy of Lies

TV

Bluebloods
CopShop
CSI: Miami
The Bedford Diaries
The Education of Max Bickford
Sidney Lumet's 100 Centre Street
The Cosby Mysteries
EZ Streets
Law & Order
The Nasty Boys
H.E.L.P.
Gideon Oliver
Miami Vice
Hill Street Blues

DAVID BLACK

FAST SHUFFLE

A TOM DOHERTY ASSOCIATES BOOK • NEW YORK

This is a work of fiction. All of the characters, organizations, and events portrayed in this novel are either products of the author's imagination or are used fictitiously.

FAST SHUFFLE

Copyright © 2015 by David Black

All rights reserved.

A Forge Book
Published by Tom Doherty Associates, LLC
175 Fifth Avenue
New York, NY 10010

www.tor-forge.com

Forge® is a registered trademark of Tom Doherty Associates, LLC.

ISBN 978-0-7653-6612-2

Our books may be purchased in bulk for promotional, educational, or business use. Please contact your local bookseller or the Macmillan Corporate and Premium Sales Department at 1-800-221-7945, extension 5442, or by e-mail at MacmillanSpecialMarkets@macmillan.com.

First Edition: July 2015
First Mass Market Edition: May 2016

Printed in the United States of America

0 9 8 7 6 5 4 3 2 1

For Barbara,
Susannah, Toby, and Hadley

PART ONE

In fine, having quite lost his wits, he fell into one of the strangest conceits that ever entered the head of any madman; which was . . . that he should commence knight-errant, and wander through the world . . . in quest of adventures.

—Miguel de Cervantes
Don Quixote
Translated by Charles Jarvis

CHAPTER 1

The hand holding the unfiltered cigarette was long, narrow.

Smoke curled up from the cigarette tip in a movie poster arabesque. The ash was half the length of the cigarette, gray speckled with black, wiry-looking like the knuckle hairs.

From a record player, not a CD, came Frank Sinatra's 1959 version of "Stormy Weather." The version he recorded before the Kennedy assassination. The song's sorrow conventional, dramatic not tragic, not specific, not full of tears like the version he recorded after Dallas.

Don't know why—Sinatra sang—*there's no sun up in the sky* . . .

The hand shifted.

Stormy weather.

The ash fell off the end of the cigarette. A man—Harry Dickinson—cleared his throat.

Since my gal and I ain't together . . .

Harry sang along with Sinatra, coughed, and again cleared his throat, letting Sinatra sing alone.

Harry lay the cigarette in a chipped clear glass

ashtray, found the tumbler half full of Jack Daniel's—from the way his hand moved cautiously half an inch one way, then half an inch the other, the pinky extended ahead of the rest of the hand like a blind man's cane, it was clear Harry wasn't looking at the side table where the glass stood—wrapped his hand around the tumbler (Harry would have called his hand a *mitt*) and brought the tumbler to his mouth.

He drank half the booze, his eyes shadowed, the light from under the old vanilla-colored paper lamp shade illuminating his upper lip, his mouth, his chin, his two-day-old beard.

He lowered the glass. Licked his lips.

With the back of his other hand, he wiped his mouth as the doorbell rang.

"*It's raining all the time,*" Harry sang.

Harry's office was a mess, a low-rent, dusty hole-in-the-wall. Brown-and-white cardboard bankers' boxes were stacked along the baseboard of one wall. On top of them were back issues of the Springdale *Union, The Boston Globe,* yellowing magazines from the 1930s and 1940s—*Black Mask, Dime Detective . . .* Shelves were crammed with *Forensics, Criminalistics, Shadowing and Surveillance, Gun Digest, Emmanuals's Evidence, Correction Law of Massachusetts, Penal Law . . .*

On the walls hung framed movie posters: *Where Danger Lives, Rogue Cop,* and *The Killers.*

Dusty daylight filtered in through the slats of crooked venetian blinds, bathing the office in a sepia glow.

Harry was thirty-five with a long, seamed face,

sleepy eyes, and a mouth crimped up on the right in a semipermanent, dubious grin.

He was tilted back in his chair, his feet crossed on his desk. Next to his feet was the bottle of sour mash.

His baggy brown suit was cut with wide lapels. His white shirt was starched. One collar tip was bent up like the corner of his mouth. His maroon tie was wide, and he wore it short, a hand span higher than his belt. His brown brogans were polished.

Harry, the room, the whole atmosphere, evoked a 1940s hard-boiled detective movie.

"*Life is bare,*" Harry sang.

The doorbell rang.

From an alcove, a kettle whistled.

"Harry!" a voice called.

A female voice, low, throaty, coaxing.

Friday's voice.

"*Keeps raining all the time,*" Harry sang.

The doorbell continued to ring.

Friday—whose real name was Linda Chapin—appeared in the entrance to the alcove, holding a copper tea kettle and a jar of Chase & Sanborn instant coffee.

She was a few years younger than Harry. With something doll-like about her eyes—as if they closed when she lay down and flipped open when she was upright.

That was the only doll-like thing about her.

Friday was a savvy, tough-talking, angular brunette whose hair always seemed on the verge of escaping from the knot on the top of her head.

"Harry," she said.

"Gloom and misery everywhere," Harry sang.

"Harry!" Friday repeated.

"Stormy weather," Harry sang.

"Hey, Chief," Friday said,

"Hold the phone," Harry said, and he finished singing.

"The door," Friday said.

She glanced significantly at the kettle in her hand.

Harry took a drag on his cigarette and flipped it toward the ashtray. It fell short. Harry let it lie.

The doorbell rang.

Friday sighed, turned back to the kitchenette, and put the kettle back on the hotplate.

"I'll get it," she said. She went to the door separating Harry's office from the outer office. "You make the coffee."

"Happy birthday," Harry said.

From the kneehole of his desk, Harry took a brown paper bag, which he held out toward Friday.

Friday said, "Oh, Harry . . ."

The doorbell rang.

Friday put the bag on Harry's desk, smiled at him, and said, "I'll be right back."

She disappeared into the outer office.

When Harry stood, he seemed to be unwinding, not just rising but growing.

From his desk, he took a dirty coffee cup.

Whistling "Stormy Weather," he crossed to the kettle. He emptied the dregs from the cup into the wastebasket and wiped the inside of the cup with a cotton handkerchief he pulled from his right hip pocket. He found a spoon on the table and scooped some instant coffee into the cup.

Friday came back into the room.

"Client?" Harry asked.

"Your favorite kind," Friday said.

"Rich?" Harry asked.

"Female," Friday said.

From the paper bag, Friday took her birthday present. As she unwrapped it, Harry picked up the kettle and poured hot water into his coffee cup.

"*Don't know why . . . ,*" Harry sang under his breath.

"Not again!" Friday said, holding up an army surplus ammo box, fastened with a lock.

"Can't crack a lock," Harry said, "can't be a detective."

"I don't *want* to be a detective," Friday said.

"Of course you do, Friday," Harry said. "Everyone does."

Friday tapped the lock and asked, "What's the combination?"

Harry sipped his coffee.

"It took me two hours to open my Christmas present," Friday said.

"This is a cheaper lock," Harry said.

Friday sighed and turned the knob on the combination lock.

"Anyway," Harry said, "you're getting better."

The lock didn't open. Friday scowled.

"I'll send in Miss Mysterious," she said.

Carrying the ammo box under her arm, Friday went into the outer office, where she put the ammo box on her desk.

A woman stood just inside the door. She wore a severe beige suit with a wide leather belt—vaguely military—as though she were fighting a war with her voluptuous figure. Her lipstick was a little too red. And smudged on her upper lip.

Friday jerked her head in the direction of the office.

"Boss'll see you," she said.

The woman—Carol LeGrange—entered Harry's office.

Friday sat at her desk. From her pocketbook, she took an emery board, which she used to file her fingertips. Like Jimmy Valentine. Then, she blew on her fingers. Eyes closed in concentration, leaning close to the lock so she could hear—as well as feel—the tumblers drop into place, she turned the lock's knob.

Carol hovered in the doorway of Harry's office, a little impatiently.

"What do private eyes always say in novels?" he asked. "'A hundred dollars a day plus expenses. And I don't do divorce work.' Well, it's one-fifty. And I'll take any case you got."

"Seven-thirty," Carol said.

"Address?" Harry asked.

Carol started for the door.

"I don't have time for this," she said.

Harry called after her, "What's your address?"

Carol didn't turn around. She sighed. "Twelve Crescent Hill."

"A hundred-fifty now," Harry said. "I'll bill for expenses."

Carol slammed out of Harry's office.

Harry followed, entering the outer office just in time to see the door swing shut after Carol.

Friday was still trying to crack the lock on her birthday present.

Not glancing up, she said, "What did Miss Mysterious want?"

"The usual," Harry said.

Friday got the last number. The lock snapped open. Harry glanced at his watch.

"Fifteen minutes," he said.

"I *am* getting better," Friday said.

"But," Harry asked, "can you do it when there's a guy with a gun coming down the hall?"

Friday opened the ammo box and took out her birthday present: an old book in mint condition.

"*The Thin Man,*" she said.

"Pick you up at nine," Harry said.

"You do," Friday said, "and I'll call the cops."

Imitating Jimmy Cagney's nasal voice and flat vowels, Harry said, "You threatening me? Are you threatening me? Don't threaten me. I'm in the threat business."

"*I'll* pick *you* up," Friday said. "I don't like driving in cars older than my mother."

Harry blew her a kiss and headed out the door.

Friday opened the book and read the copyright: "Nineteen thirty-four. A first edition."

Harry re-opened the door and grabbed his battered slouch hat from the clothes tree.

"Harry," Friday said, "it must have cost a fortune."

He fit his hat on his head at a rakish angle and left.

Hefting the book, Friday smiled.

CHAPTER 2

April twilight. The smell of new-mown grass and gasoline from the cars on nearby Route 91. Springdale, Massachusetts.

The Art Nouveau lamps along the paths in the town common were lit. Their glow illuminated the green buds of the maples. One side of the common was flanked by two copies of the Parthenon: Symphony Hall and City Hall. Between them, a clock tower that looked like it should be in the Piazza San Marco in Venice. The marble was covered with spray-painted graffiti: *CAM 1, SCOOP, OZ-52* . . .

Opposite Symphony Hall and City Hall was a block of old-fashioned office buildings—the kind with gilt letters arching across dusty second-floor windows.

Harry came out of one of the office buildings. He turned right toward Main Street. Everyone he passed— a newspaper vendor, a man in a gray suit, two middle-aged women carrying Kmart shopping bags—greeted Harry with affection and enthusiasm: Hey, Harry! Harry! How you been? Harry returned the greetings cordially, with a courtly formality. He tipped his hat.

Very 1940s. Their contemporary look made Harry seem odd and out of place. But there was something lovable, exuberant in Harry's anachronistic style, something that cheered the people he passed.

A man—Frank Emholdt—came along the sidewalk. He was about Harry's age. But, unlike Harry, Emholdt seemed beaten down, depressed. He walked with a slump.

"Hey, Harry," Emholdt said. "See any suspicious characters around?"

"They're all suspicious, Frank," Harry said. "That's what makes life interesting."

Emholdt nodded noncommittally.

"Take you, for instance," Harry said. "Now, you're an interesting fella."

"I'm a dentist," Emholdt said.

"You and I . . . ," Harry said. "We don't know each other very well."

"We don't," Emholdt agreed.

"But just about every night for the past . . . what? A dozen years. I've seen you on your way to the garage there," Harry said. "We say, *Hi,* whatever, pass on our way. And just about every night, instead of going right into the garage . . . Instead, you walk half a block out of your way so you can pass the florist shop."

"That's right," Emholdt said.

Under Harry's gaze—and interest—Emholdt began to straighten up, to look more cheerful, more confident.

"And just about every night," Harry said, "*before* you get to the florist shop, you straighten your shoulders, adjust your tie."

"I do?" Emholdt asked.

"I've wondered about that," Harry said.

"You have?" Emholdt asked.

"There's a mystery there," Harry said.

"There is?" Emholdt asked.

"That's what I tell myself: 'Mr. Frank Emholdt . . . He's a man of mystery,'" Harry said.

"I am?" Emholdt asked.

Emholdt straightened up even more, became even more cheerful and confident.

"Sure," Harry said. "At least, it's a mystery to *me*. Why *do* you do that? Go by the florist. With the . . ."

Harry mimicked Emholdt adjusting his tie. Cautiously, Emholdt looked around to make sure no one could overhear.

"I've never told anyone this," he said, "but . . . Rhonda Tripp. The woman in the florist shop."

"The blonde?" Harry asked.

Emholdt nodded.

"The one who always wears her hair in a ponytail," Emholdt said. "When I was in fifth grade, I had a crush on her."

"And still do," Harry said.

Again, Emholdt nodded.

"Harry," Emholdt said, "I've been married for almost twenty years. And no one knows. No one has ever known. Not my wife."

"Not even Ponytail," Harry said, "what's-her-name, Rhonda?"

"I haven't talked to her since fifth grade," Emholdt said.

"A mystery," Harry said. "What did I tell you!"

Harry headed up the street.

Emholdt watched Harry leave.

"Me," Emholdt said. "A man of mystery. How about that?"

He smiled.

CHAPTER 3

The hallway outside of Harry's office was lit with only three sixty-watt bulbs, each on hanging wires, which reflected from three angles onto the pebbled-glass pane of Harry's door.

Friday, a short red jacket under her arm, locked the door. At the end of the hall, the old-fashioned elevator whirred into motion.

Friday started down the hall, which smelled sweet. Of insecticide.

The elevator stopped. The door opened—and out came a man Harry's age, but as different from Harry as he could be. Sonny Plante.

Plante wore a Ventile hunting jacket, pre-washed jeans, and three-hundred-dollar sneakers. Working-class clothes no one in the working class could afford.

Seeing Plante, Friday said, "Oh, shit!"

She bolted down the stairs.

Plante ducked back in the elevator, hit the "down" button. The door closed. The elevator whirred.

In the lobby, yellow-stained white tile on the walls and floor, Friday rushed from the stairway just as the elevator door opened, disgorging Plante, who chased Friday out of the building.

Plante hit the sidewalk in time to see Friday slipping into her car an old, battered Tercel—which she was having trouble starting. The motor ground and ground.

Plante ran to the car.

Friday locked all the doors, rolled up the windows, and again tried to start the car as Plante peered through the window, knocking on the glass.

The motor started.

Friday pulled away.

Plante ran after her for a block and then stood, breathing heavily, watching the car roar off. Angry, frustrated, he kicked over a trash can.

CHAPTER 4

On Main Street, Harry passed a shoe-shine stand.

The shoe-shine "boy," Diogenes Nunez, mid-seventies, ash-colored hair, wearing a stained apron, leaned against the wall of his stand, gazing out at the street, as he had done every evening at this time for the past sixty years.

"Nikes, Reeboks, Adidas, Etonics, New Balance, Saucony . . . ," Nunez said.

Shaking his head, Harry said, "Sneakers. Terrible."

Harry entered the stand and sat on one of the raised wooden chairs. Nunez spritzed Harry's shoes with cleaner.

"Lawyers, salesmen, bankers," Nunez said.

Harry nodded and said, "Even doctors wear them."

"Used to be," Nunez said, "a man could make a living shining shoes."

Harry picked up a nine-by-twelve manila envelope from the seat next to his.

"Someone forgot something," Harry said.

"Must of been the guy with the boots," Nunez said. "In here about an hour ago. Red boots. Had me polish the whole thing. Uppers and lowers. Then stiffs me, like he was wearing a pair of loafers."

Harry turned the envelope over.

"No name," Harry said,

"Boots must of cost, what?" Nunez said. "Six, seven hundred? More? Lots more, probably."

"No address," Harry said.

"Wearing dirty overalls," Nunez said, "white painter's cap, you understand . . ."

Harry opened the envelope and took out a bank statement for Marian Turner.

"All his money on his feet," Nunez said.

"She just closed out her account this afternoon," Harry said. "Three hundred thousand dollars."

Harry got up.

"I haven't buffed the left yet," Nunez said.

"You got a phone book?" Harry asked.

Nunez grunted as he stood, pushing his left hand against his left thigh for leverage. He went into the back of the stand and came out with a tattered city directory, which Harry flipped open to the *T*'s.

Harry ran his finger down the page.

"Turner, Alan," Harry said. "Turner, Carl. Turner, Daniel. Turner, Daniel, Jr. Turner, Leonard. Turner, Marian. One twenty-eight Sumner Avenue."

CHAPTER 5

One twenty-eight Sumner Avenue was a four-story 1920s yellow-brick apartment house two blocks from Forest Park.

Harry parked his 1936 purple Packard touring car in front of the building. In the immaculate hallway, Harry checked the names next to the buzzers: *Marian Turner 3A*.

He rang the bell for 3A and waited.

No answer.

He jerked the door toward him and rapped the heel of his hand against the doorjamb, popping the lock.

Scalloped lights were mounted on either side of a large wall mirror. Threadbare Oriental runners carpeted the stairs, which Harry climbed to the third floor.

At 3A, Harry knocked.

No answer.

Harry took a long, thin, flexible metal strip—a slapjack—from his inside coat pocket and slipped it between the door and the door frame, loiding the lock.

The door clicked open.

Marian Turner's apartment smelled of lavender. Living room: a cream and blue rug. A large blue Chinese vase on an oak side table with dried roses. Browning petals were scattered on the dusty tabletop. Farther into the room, a lamp illuminated part of a couch, a footstool, a mustard-colored easy chair. . . . Everything else melted into shadows. A ginger cat rubbed itself against Harry's ankle.

The room had the feel of having been empty for days.

There was dust on the coffee table, on the top of the piano, on the closed laptop, which he stared at but didn't touch

Harry leafed through a stack of magazines— *Harper's, Wired, the New Yorker, Mother Jones, Vanity Fair, Rolling Stone, Bride, Architectural Digest*—and picked up an alumni magazine from the University of Massachusetts.

" '*Turner, Marian, '10,*' " Harry read from the address label.

Harry put the mail back, from the floor picked up a newspaper, and looked at the date.

"Week ago Monday," Harry said to the cat, which stood on its hind legs and pawed Harry's pant leg.

Harry tossed the paper onto the table.

The cat dug its claws into Harry's leg.

Harry bent to scratch the cat behind the ears, along the jaw, under the chin.

In the kitchen, the overhead light was on. On the table was a plate with the remains of a spaghetti dinner, dried to a crust. A half-empty glass of red wine. A dried purple circle ringed the glass. The refrigerator wheezed.

On the stove was more spaghetti in a pot, a solid clump. In a pan tomato sauce had patches of mold.

The cat meowed.

The pet bowls next to the refrigerator were empty. The food gone. The water evaporated.

Harry filled the water bowl at the sink. He opened the cupboards with difficulty. The paint was so thick, the cupboard doors stuck. He searched the crowded shelves until he found a bag of dry cat kibble, which he poured into the food bowl.

The cat attacked the food—one paw in the bowl, growling as it ate.

In the bedroom, a streetlight shone through the window on the bedspread, which had pockets of shadows in the indentations where the cat had slept. It didn't look as if anyone else had slept in this bed for a while.

Harry picked up an empty coffee cup from the bureau. Dust was everywhere, except where the coffee cup had been.

The digital readout on the answering machine had twenty-three messages.

Harry straddled a chair, took out a pad and pen to copy down the messages, and hit the "replay" button.

CHAPTER 6

Friday's apartment building was modern. Clean. But, like many new buildings, already falling into disrepair. The rugs were prematurely worn. The cheap light fixtures were speckled with rust. The lobby mirror was blotched, branched where the silver backing had worn away.

Friday unlocked her mailbox, took out a handful of letters and catalogs, locked the mailbox, and was leafing through the mail as she crossed the lobby when a shadowy figure slipped from behind a dying potted palm: Plante.

"Linda," Plante said.

Startled, Friday dropped the mail.

Harry stood at the open door to the apartment next to Marian Turner's place. Marian Turner's neighbor, a woman in her mid-fifties named Sharon Lahey, wore a sweatsuit and was wiping her hands on a small blue-checked towel. Her apartment, behind her, gave off a smell of fried onions.

"So," Lahey said, "the second, third time I'm out

running and some guy gets in my slipstream, figuring he's got a free look during his run, I decide the hell with giving a show to these yo-yos and I get a Nordic Track."

"Your neighbor . . . ," Harry said.

"So," Lahey continued, "I figure, I'm running in place in my own home, what's to worry?"

"The last time you saw her . . . ," Harry said.

"What I forgot," Lahey said, "is the gas man, the electric man, the mailman, you. . . ."

"I'm sorry I disturbed you," Harry said, "but—"

"Morning, night," Lahey said, "doesn't matter, the minute I put on my sweats, the doorbell rings. . . ."

"Ms. Lahey," Harry said, "this is important."

"Is there a light," Lahey said, "an alarm somewhere, goes off: Lahey's in her sweats?"

"I'm investigating—" Harry began.

"Garter belts, I can understand," Lahey said. "But what is it, this thing about men and sweatpants?"

"Your neighbor," Harry said, "Marian Turner—her answering machine's got a week's worth of messages."

"Maybe she took a vacation," Lahey said.

"When you go away," Harry said, "don't you call in for your messages?"

Lahey shrugged.

"These kids," Lahey said. "Move in, move out. Odd hours. Who can keep track?"

"She didn't say anything about a business trip?" Harry asked. "A vacation? A family emergency?"

"Never talked to her," Lahey said. "Hardly ever saw her."

"Anyone visit her recently?" Harry asked.

Lahey shook her head no.

"Far as I can tell," she said, "she's got nobody."

"Friends?" Harry asked. "Family?"

"Except for the carpenter," she said. "Guy, mid-thirties, coveralls, impressive red boots. Should of asked where he got them. Working in her apartment a week ago Saturday. His truck was parked out front all morning. Pillette Construction."

CHAPTER 7

Winchester Square was a slum. Holiday Street was lined with slum shops. *Lincoln Pawnshop. Checks Cashed. Tropical Products. Hardware-Houseware. Goodwill. Auto Parts.* Failing businesses and small-time operations.

Pillette Construction was a hole-in-the-wall with a light showing through a dirty window. Still open. It stood next to an old theater turned into a dollar store. On the marquee, instead of the names of movie stars and feature films, was an advertisement: *Everything you need under $1.*

The first *E* was missing: *verything you need . . .*

As Harry entered Pillette's, a bell over the door rang. Over the counter hung a cheesecake calendar, 1940s style: A busty woman in a one-piece striped swimsuit leaned forward, holding a huge beach ball, her bottom stuck out. The store smelled of sawdust and oil—a smell that gave Harry a taste of tin.

A man came out of a back room, carrying a roll of construction plans. He was heavyset, unshaved, dressed in a faded blue work shirt, carpenter's coveralls, a white painter's cap, and red boots. Newly polished.

"Pillette?" Harry asked.

The man nodded.

"Bookcases, loft beds, roofs, decks, maintenance, renovations," Pillette said. "I don't do masonry, electrical, mechanical, or plumbing, but I got good subcontractors. Any job two hundred dollars or more, there's ten percent overage."

"Marian Turner," Harry said.

Pillette didn't react.

"You did some work for her?" Harry said.

"You got a job for me?" Pillette asked.

Harry took out a twenty-dollar bill, folded it lengthwise, and tented it on the counter.

"Yeah," Harry said, "tell me about it."

Pillette took the twenty.

"Kitchen cupboards," he said.

"Really?" Harry said. "I saw her kitchen. You have an interesting way of painting. Lots of coats. Making it look like the work is at least twenty years old."

"It's late," Pillette said. "I'm only here 'cause I was going over plans for a redwood deck."

"You have a copy of Marian Turner's plans?" Harry asked. "Estimate? Bill?"

Pillette came from around the counter, opened his door for Harry to leave.

The bell rang.

"You want some work done," he said, "give me a call, okay?"

He waited.

"Your job for this gal Turner," Harry said. "Is that why you had her bank statement?"

Pillette wrinkled his nose as if about to sneeze.

A tell? Harry wondered. Or a tickle?

"She withdraws a lot of money today," Harry said, "but doesn't seem to have been home for a week."

Pillette sneezed.

Maybe the sneeze is the tell, Harry thought.

Pillette rubbed his nose with a knuckle.

Harry nodded at the twenty Pillette still held.

"Apply that to my deposit," Harry said.

CHAPTER 8

Friday's living room was furnished with secondhand pieces, which Friday had improved. She had stripped and Butcher's Waxed a pine cabinet. Draped a couch with red and gold cloth. One wall was dominated by a Georgia O'Keeffe lily. Another wall was covered with photographs of Springdale—pictures she had taken. A few showed Harry, some when he was much younger: playing softball in Forest Park, on a picnic at Tanglewood, clowning with friends, trying out a super-soaker at the Eastern States Exposition.

One showed Harry on the steps of Classical High School around 1997 with his arms around two friends: a huge beefy guy in a football sweatshirt—Brian Rossiter—and a guy in a sand-colored lamb's wool sweater better groomed than either Harry or Rossiter—Plante. A little too well groomed.

Friday circled the room turning on every light. Plante followed her, holding the mail she'd dropped downstairs.

"Harry's never going to marry you, Linda," he said.

"Which means I have to marry *you*?" Friday asked.

"You could do worse," Plante said.

"Only if I really worked at it," Friday said.

"Eight hours a day in that dingy office," Plante said, "waiting for Harry to come through with a paycheck you and I know is never going to arrive."

"Is this a marriage proposal," Friday asked, "or a job offer?"

"You and Harry," Plante said. "I don't get it."

"You wouldn't," Friday said. "It's called love."

From the wall, Plante took the picture of himself, Rossiter, and Harry.

"Even in high school," Plante said. "The police scanner Harry kept in his locker. He'd hear a call, liquor store burglary, stolen car, whatever. . . . Cut class, show up at the scene of the crime. What is it with him?"

"You were ready enough to cut school," Friday said, "jump in the car . . ."

"Kicks," Plante said. "And I stopped—when I grew up."

"Now you get your kicks stalking me," Friday said.

"Stalking?" Plante laughed. "You know how many women would be flattered?"

"How many?" Friday asked.

"Stalking," Plante repeated. Not laughing.

"When are you going to stop that?" Friday asked. "I can't stand it, Sonny!"

"Eighteen rooms," Plante said. "Heated swimming pool. Private tennis court."

"I've seen your place," Friday said.

"It could be yours," Plante said.

Friday took the mail from Plante and gestured to the still-open apartment door.

"A whole new life," Plante said.

Friday didn't answer.

"Do you hate me that much?" he asked.

"Sonny," Friday said, "if I hated you, it would be easy."

Given this encouragement, Plante approached Friday, who backed away.

"In high school," Friday said, "I used to pray that Harry would call me up before you to ask me out on the weekend. Because I knew if you called first, I'd accept. We'd go out. A soda. A movie. We'd do what everyone does. And I *wanted* to do that. I still want to do what everyone does. Get married, have babies, watch late-night TV together. Turner Classics. *30 Rock* reruns."

"If you *want* that—" Plante said.

"Chances are," Friday said, "Harry's never going to sit around watching late-night TV."

"Then?" Plante said.

Friday said, "I could be so easily tempted."

Plante leaned in to kiss her.

Friday shook her head no and said, "So be a pal, Sonny, and don't tempt me."

CHAPTER 9

Harry followed Pillette's pickup truck from Winchester Square to Agawam, staying three cars behind, sometimes four. The truck was easy to spot ahead in the traffic. Pillette turned onto an industrial strip—NAPA Auto Parts, Best Value Hardwoods (*Floor Laying, Refinishing & Resurfacing*), Tri-State Show Stock, SecureCo Alarm Systems, SESBG (*Dedicated to Serving Small Business*), Affordable Self Storage (*Friendly, Fences, Gated, Paved, Well Lit, Cameras*), a small cement-block envelope factory. (The sign: An envelope the size of a town car. Below it, an LED running display: *Business envelopes. Everyday mailing needs. Economical, security tinted, gummed, self-sealing, strip flap. Plain, window, double-window . . . Through our windows, you can see the future.*) He pulled into a chain-link-enclosed parking lot for a strip club, Angel's Lap. A blue and pink—nursery colors—neon sign showed a naked, winged, pouting woman straddling a faceless male figure.

Harry parked across the street, halfway down the block.

He let Pillette enter Angel's and listened to two

songs on John Pizzarelli and Jessica Molaskey's Radio Delux—"They Can't Take That Away From Me" and an old recording of Slim and Slam's "Tutti Fruitti"—before he followed Pillette into the strip club, ducking to get through the basement entrance and shouldering through the clacking beaded curtain.

Harry paused to survey the room as he grabbed a handful of white mints from a bowl by the cash register.

"People use the urinal," the Bouncer-Greeter said, "don't wash their hands, then stick their paws in the mints."

The mints had a blue stripe around the middle. Harry spilled the mints into his jacket pocket.

"They did a study," said the Bouncer-Greeter, a spherical man, his belly the size of a medicine ball. "You don't want to know what's in the mints."

"Who's *they*?" Harry popped a mint into his mouth. "People always say *they* did this, *they* did that. . . ."

The beads clacked as someone entered and passed behind Harry.

"Haven't you wondered if *they* might be *us*?" Harry asked. "*Us* if we took another path in our past. If *you*, for example, got interested in mints, candy, free candy—maybe when you were a kid, maybe when you—you know, all kids do—pinched a Sky Bar. Which section did you like best? Caramel, vanilla, peanut, or fudge? The peanut always seemed out of place. Like a food. Peanut. The rest were strictly candy. Fudge, vanilla, caramel. But peanut . . . Yellow wrapper, red letters. I loved Sky Bars. You had your people—maybe they're the *people* who people always say *people say*—your people who preferred Trudeau's

Seven Up. 'Seven Delicious Varieties in One Bar.' Seven. Too much, right? Who can remember the seven. Caramel, yeah, that's easy. I think they had caramel. Fudge? Maybe. Seven's too many choices. Too many choices leads to paralysis. You think it had anything to do with 7UP, the soda? There's something to think about. How many candy bars shared a name with a soda? Seven Up, Sky Bar, when you ate them did you start at one end and work your way through? But then which end to start with? Or did you break the sections apart and eat them in some other order? Or no order at all? Or did you only get them when you could share them? Different sections, seems like you should be sharing. You definitely had to share a Three Musketeers. 'All for one' and that. But Three Musketeers—you didn't have the problem of choice. All three sections tasted the same. Sky Bar, Seven Up—they were *existential* candy!"

"Yeah," the Bouncer-Greeter said, grinning. "Sky Bar. You the man."

The dim room was damp and smelled like a locker room. Despite the No Smoking signs, smoke swirled in the colored lights. Men sat alone or in small groups along the runway or at small tables, some mesmerized by the stripper who hung by her legs upside down from a pole, one knee akimbo, her hands caressing her body, others arguing about the Sox or the Celtics. One guy sat, back to the stage to get the light, working on a newspaper Sudoku. In front of every guy were half a dozen empty glasses and one or two full ones—two-drink minimum.

"You know the first stripper to caress her own body?" Harry asked, his head tilted, smiling at the stripper, who smiled upside down at Harry. "Hinda Wausau. In the twenties. Claimed she invented stripping. One of the three great arts invented by America. Stripping, the cartoon strip, and jazz."

"No shit?" the stripper said, flipping upright. "Art, huh?"

"Put your hands together for Janine," the disk jockey said, stifling a yawn. "Janine, at the back bar. Sarabeth, main stage. Let's show Janine how much we liked her dance. On deck—Shady Sadie."

The manager—Doreen, thirties, a face with sharp planes as if sheared from shale, leopard-print bra and panties, tattoos of snakes and vines down both arms, tattooed tears below her left eye—hurried over to Harry.

"Behind the VIP curtain," Doreen said. "Poor dope can't get the flag up the flagpole. Blames the stripper. Refuses to pay. Refuses to go."

"What's he waiting for?" Harry asked.

"A miracle," Doreen said.

"People come out to have fun," another Bouncer said, short, square, "and we end up cleaning up their mess."

"You *are* PD, aren't you?" Doreen asked Harry.

"Private," Harry said.

"We have a deal with you?" Doreen asked.

"'Down these mean streets . . . ,'" Harry quoted Raymond Chandler.

"Whatever," Doreen said. "As long as it doesn't come off the top. The cops aren't here. You are. My gorillas look tough, but one is too pilled up to fight and the other has a glass jaw. A love tap—and he's down for the count. My third guy doesn't want to tear a fingernail. New manicure. Why are they in the business? Bottom line: We need the help. And you can take your fee out in trade."

Harry crossed the club with Doreen. The flashing lights made it seem as if the tattooed snakes slithered up Doreen's arms. Turning a corner into a dogleg hallway, they came to a crowd—strippers in easy-off dresses, a few waitresses, a third bouncer—hanging around outside the door to a VIP room.

Harry ducked into the small space. Doreen lagged behind him, trying to see around him. A stripper in a turquoise chemise.

"Chevy," Doreen said, "this is—"

"Harry," Harry said.

Doreen squeezed into the room, standing close enough for Harry to feel the brush of her breasts.

Pillette sat, naked except for his red boots, on a burgundy velvet couch. His cock, uncircumcised, hung between his thighs. He had the biggest, hairiest balls Harry had ever seen.

"Geeze," Pillette said, eyeing Harry. "Perfect."

"Rat grabbed me so hard," Chevy said, "I got a bruise."

She showed her upper arm.

"Okay, Lazarus," Harry said, "you're not going to rise from the dead tonight."

"Bait-and-switch is what we got here," Pillette said—to Doreen, not to Harry, whom he ignored.

"She gave you what she promised," Doreen said. "Not her fault you didn't take advantage of the opportunity."

"That's some bruise," Harry said.

"She had it when I met her," Pillette said.

"You got two choices," Harry said. "You leave nicely or—"

Pillette lurched up, dragged on his pants—which got stuck on his boots—and, trailing his shirt, pushed his way out of the room.

"Can I buy you a drink?" Doreen asked Harry.

"A lap dance?" Chevy asked.

Harry shook his head no.

"A girl," Chevy said, "can dream."

PART TWO

I wrestled with reality for over thirty-five years, Doctor, and I'm happy to state I finally won out over it.

Elwood—my mother always called me Elwood by the way—Elwood, in this life you must be oh so smart or oh so pleasant.

For years I was smart. I recommend pleasant.

—Mary Chase
Harvey

CHAPTER 10

As he sat at his desk in the bullpen, phone cradled between shoulder and cheek, Brian Rossiter, SPD detective, pushed his hat back on his head.

Rossiter was a giant, six foot seven, 350 pounds of muscle. Hair as red as raw meat, cut so short his white scalp showed through on the sides. He got married the year he graduated from Western New England College, the same year he became a cop. Twice, he had left Springdale: once to go to a required cop function in Boston, the other on a trip with his family to Lake George.

His trench coat collar turned up, Harry stood at the pay telephone on the corner of Webster and Clay streets. An old-fashioned walk-in folding-door box phone booth. One of the last in the city. Harry knew them all. He refused to get a cell phone.

"Rossiter," Harry said, "all I'm asking is—"

"—a favor," Rossiter said.

He leaned back precariously in his old walnut rolling chair, his feet propped on his desk. As he talked to Harry, he folded a sheet of eight-by-ten paper into an airplane.

"Harry," Rossiter said, "you're a pest."

"A lovable pest," Harry said.

"But a pest," Rossiter said.

It was an old routine.

"When I hear your voice," Rossiter said, "why do I know you're going to say, 'All I'm asking . . .'"

Anti-Crime Unit officers passed in and out of their cramped office across from Rossiter's desk. Noisily.

Holding the phone handset away from his face, Rossiter shouted, "Can the chatter, you mooks give me a headache."

Next to the Anti-Crime office was the holding cell. Next to the cell was a bench to which two hookers, one black, one white, were handcuffed.

"We lucky to be in a business where we can make some money," the First Hooker said.

"Yeah," the Second Hooker said, "go out and sell my body."

"I mean," the First Hooker said, "*real* money."

"*Your* body?" the Second Hooker said. "You want me to hold the quarters?"

Rossiter closed one eye and aimed the paper plane at a wastebasket three desks away.

"For old times' sake," Harry said.

"One, I'm busy," Rossiter said. "Two, it's an infraction of the rules."

"Which," Harry said, "you've broken before."

"Three," Rossiter said, throwing the paper plane with a snap of his wrist, "you still don't have a PI license."

"A technicality," Harry said.

The plane missed the basket, hit the wall, and landed on the floor near a half-dozen other paper planes.

"Anyone got a phone book?" George "Moose" Dulebond, arrested for drunk-and-disorderly, leaned against the bars of the holding cell. "Anyone got the white pages? For Longmeadow?"

"That where your lawyer live, Big Guy?" the First Hooker asked. "Longmeadow?"

"It's where my Jennie lives," Dulebond said. "Where she lived when I shipped out."

"You in the service?" the Second Hooker asked.

"Merchant Marine," Dulebond said. "Wiper on a bulker."

"When did you ship out?" the Second Hooker asked.

"Six years ago," Dulebond said.

The hookers exchanged a glance.

"Six years ago," the First Hooker said. "That the last time you seen her?"

Rossiter's immediate boss—Sergeant Edgar Valet, a stooped man in his mid-forties with a greenish complexion, ancient acne scars, and beautiful blue eyes—stopped at Rossiter's desk.

To Valet, Rossiter said, "It's Dickinson."

"That nut!" Valet said.

Two patrolmen hustled a suspect, Fritz Donis, to the holding cell.

"I didn't steal no sweater," Donis protested.

"That sweater you wearing?" the First Hooker said. "That the one you didn't steal?"

"He *got* to be innocent," the Second Hooker said. "No one would be dumb enough to steal those threads."

Valet took the paper plane Rossiter was making, finished folding it, and sailed it across the bullpen, without aiming at anything.

Rossiter said, "Wants to know if there's a missing person out on Turner, Marian, Caucasian female." Into the telephone to Harry, Rossiter asked, "How old?"

"Graduated college five years ago," Harry said into the pay telephone.

To Valet, Rossiter said, "Early twenties."

"Could have been adult education," Harry said. "That would make her older."

"You always complicate things," Rossiter said.

"Am I wrong?" Harry asked into the phone.

"How much did Dickinson give the Benevolent Association this year?" Valet asked.

"Five hundred," Rossiter said.

"Next year, he doubles it," Valet said. "Run it for him."

Into the telephone, Rossiter said, "I'll get back to you, Harry."

CHAPTER 11

The street lamp reflected in the telephone's fake chrome trim. Harry hung up.

A young woman in her late twenties sauntered over. She was wearing a translucent rayon blouse, a blue push-up bra, a red pleather microskirt, so short you could see the curve of her ass cheeks in red lace panties, and a dirty white waist-long fun-fur jacket.

"Looking for a good time?" she asked.

"Can't afford it," Harry said.

The hooker gave Harry a *You kidding me?* look. Head pulled back. Chin tucked, eyebrows arched.

"You got to be at least two, two-fifty a pop," Harry said.

Amused and pleased, the hooker said, "You think so, huh?"

"Sure," Harry said. "A classy lady like you?"

"Sixty," the hooker said. "Full hour."

"You're selling short," Harry said.

"Round the world," the hooker said.

Harry took a few steps toward his purple Packard.

"France," the hooker said, "Greece, Lebanon . . ."

"Lebanon?" Harry said.

"You don't want to know," the hooker said.

"Anyway," Harry said, "I got an appointment with Miss Mysterious."

"Who?" the hooker asked.

"But," Harry said, "if I had the time and the money . . ."

Harry winked. Got into the car and drove off.

The hooker looked at her reflection in a storefront window.

"Hundred an hour," she said to herself. "At least."

CHAPTER 12

The smell of the rotisserie chicken made Friday's mouth water. Steam rose from the paper shopping bag she hugged to her chest and warmed her chin. She climbed the two wooden steps to the back porch of the single-story cottage where her father still lived. Pressing her right elbow tight against the bag, she opened the unlocked door and passed through a small mudroom, jackets and sweaters and scarfs and hats on pegs, boots and flowerpots and plastic wrapped six packs of bottled water on the floor. She entered the kitchen, where she put the shopping bag on the counter next to the sink.

"Lee," she called. "I've got your dinner."

From the paper bag, she took the plastic sack holding the chicken, a white cardboard container of mashed potatoes, another of steamed broccoli, and a baguette.

Her father, Lee, came into the kitchen. Tall, jeans and white T-shirt, sleeves rolled all the way up, sinewy, a seamed face, and cobalt blue, almost black, eyes. His hands were large with prominent veins and knuckles; the skin silvery and puckered.

"I was trying to fix the big press," he said. "It keeps jamming."

He smelled of the benzene he used to clean the printers' ink.

"I got your latest broadside in today's mail," she said, preparing the food on a plate.

"Multinational corporations," he said, getting a Heineken's from the refrigerator and twisting off the cap with a *hsst*. "Multinational unions."

"You're just an old Wobblie," she said, putting his plate on the table.

"How's your crazy boyfriend?" he asked, sitting.

"No crazier than you are," she said, sitting across the table from him.

"'*Workers of the World . . .'* the sanest political platform." he said.

"A century ago."

"For the century to come."

From outside came the rising and falling whine of a chainsaw.

"You going to eat?" Lee asked.

"Got a date," she said.

Lee held a forkful of brass-colored glistening skin. "It's one thing to care about him—" he said.

"We're not going there," she said. "I'll get the laundry."

She left the room.

"You need a life," Lee called after her.

"Dry cleaners put too much starch in your shirts last week," she called back from the hall.

Lee looked at the chicken skin dangling on the end of his fork and parked it reluctantly—his cholesterol was high—on the side of his plate.

Friday went down the basement steps, into the familiar dank and oily smell of cellar and machinery. A basket of the week's dirty laundry stood on the mottled cement in front of an old-fashioned deep slate sink. To the left was her father's small nine-by-fourteen Kelsey printing press and the large flywheel press run by a motor bolted to the floor. Beside it stood a double-width type rack with room for thirty California type cases, fifteen and fifteen side by side. All that Lee had rescued from his letter press print shop that had gone out of business twenty years earlier. The type case on top, which Lee had been using, was ten-point Bodoni.

Mechanically, Friday touched a finger in the type compartments, *A, B, C,* playing a kind of hopscotch as she identified where each of the letters were stored, knowledge from childhood, part of a secret lore she shared with her father. A composing stick with three rows of type in it sat tilted on the case. A galley held two columns of matter. Lee's next week's broadside.

Reading upside down and backward—a skill Harry told her would come in handy when she became a detective—Friday scanned the text. Nothing new. The same impractical compassionate socialism she had grown up with, dreaming of "Joe Hill," and trying to be a good Rebel Gal.

No wonder I have a soft spot for a guy who won't let go of the past, she thought.

CHAPTER 13

Harry drove, left elbow propped in the open window, right forearm twelve o'clock on the steering wheel, controlling the car by moving his arm. A tape player sitting on the seat beside him played Georgie Fame and Annie Ross, singing Hoagy Carmichael's "Hong Kong Blues." Harry sang along: *"And now he's bopping a piano just to raise the price of a ticket to the land of the free . . ."*

A car approached, its brights on. Harry blinked his lights. The approaching car did not dim its brights. Harry kept his lights on low as the cars passed each other.

Harry stopped the Packard at two granite pillars, which flanked a path to the front door of a white Victorian house. He killed the ignition, got out, and, crouching, ran around the side of the house. Easing a gun from his shoulder holster, he tried the knob of a side door.

The knob turned.

Harry entered a laundry room. Keeping to the wall, he moved through the door into a modern kitchen. Multiple sinks. A Garland eight-burner range. A wood-fired pizza oven. A twenty-four-cubic-foot stainless steel Sub-Zero refrigerator. A Pavoni four-station espresso machine. A Sunbeam Mix Master. A Cuisinart Pro. Copper-clad stainless pots and pans hung over a butcher block preparation table. Henckel knives were lined up on a magnetic bar. On a shelf, all by itself, stood a silver-plate duck press from Christofle.

On the walls behind the shelves were trompe l'oeil paintings of what the shelves held: a blue-and-white pitcher stood in front of a duplicate blue-and-white pitcher, a cream-colored mixing bowl stood in front of a duplicate cream-colored mixing bowl; if an object were removed, from across the room it looked as it were still there.

From the dining room beyond, Harry heard the sound of a dinner in progress. Two voices, a man's and a woman's.

The woman was saying, "We can't just get rid of him."

Her voice was familiar.

The man, his voice raspy, a smoker's or ex-smoker's voice, replied, "You make it sound like murder."

"Well," the woman said, "*you* make it sound like a vacation!"

Harry prowled through the butler's pantry and slowly pushed open the swinging door, his gun ready.

From the dining room ceiling hung a Provençal hand-painted chandelier. Under the chandelier was an imitation Italian Directoire dining table. Art Deco, hand-carved chairs. A good copy of a Louis XIV console serving table. On one wall, a bright-colored fourteenth-century hunting scene tapestry. On the facing wall, a large gilt Chippendale mirror with matching sconces.

At the dining table sat the man and woman. The two Harry had overheard from the kitchen.

The woman was Harry's Miss Mysterious, the same woman who had come to Harry's office: Carol.

The man was impeccably dressed: Brooks Brothers blue blazer with enameled Williams College buttons, blue dress shirt, blue bow tie with white polka dots (not a clip-on; free-style, jumbo-butterfly), chinos. Harry couldn't see his shoes, but what else could he be wearing but cordovan tassel loafers. He face was thin with a pinched-looking expression, as if he were suffering from a chronic headache: Carol's husband, Phil LeGrange.

Carol had no discernible scent.

Phil smelled of a floral aftershave. Not cheap, Harry figured. Not too sweet. But with enough of an afterscent to indicate it wasn't too expensive either.

There was a third setting at an empty chair.

Carol noticed Harry standing in the doorway and said, "You're late."

Without glancing at Harry, Phil told Carol, "Your brother's always late."

Carol nodded to Harry's gun and said, "Put that away and sit down. We started without you."

"Sure, Toots," Harry said.

He tucked his gun back into its holster and sat at the empty place.

"Lentil soup," he said, peering first into Carol's then into Phil's bowls. "Great!"

"How come you weren't at work today?" Phil asked Harry.

"I *was* at work," Harry said.

Half-rising, Harry leaned over the table and ladled soup into his bowl.

"I mean, real work," Phil said. "Selling cars. Remember!"

"Harry," Carol said, "you can't expect Phil to keep you on salary if you never show up at the lot."

"I'm busy on a case," Harry said between spoonfuls of soup.

"Make-believe, Harry," Phil said.

"Phil—" Carol interrupted.

Phil talked through his wife's word.

"Just because your brother lives in a fantasy," Phil said, "doesn't mean I have to."

They'd had this conversation before.

The doorbell rang. "I'll get it," Harry started to stand.

Carol and Phil both got up.

"No," Phil said, "I'll get it."

Carol said, "Finish your soup, Harry."

Phil went through the archway into the front hall.

"So," Carol said, clearly not interested, "you have a case?"

"Two," Harry said. "One, a missing person. The other, some dame. Came in, just gave me her address and a time."

Carol's spoon hovered halfway between her bowl and her lips.

"Harry," she said, "that was me."

Without looking up from his soup, Harry said, "I wondered about that."

Phil entered with a UPS man, who carried a

clipboard, a pen, and a long cardboard tube, the size of a rifle.

"You're working overtime," Phil said to the UPS man.

"The rules say," the UPS man explained, "it's addressed to this Harry Dickinson, and Harry Dickinson got to sign for it."

Throwing himself sideways out of his chair, Harry pulled his gun and rolled across the floor, aiming at the UPS man.

"Drop it," Harry said.

The UPS man dropped the cardboard tube, the clipboard, his pen, and froze.

"Gun's not loaded," Phil told the UPS man.

The UPS man didn't move.

"I said," Phil repeated, *the gun's not loaded.*"

The UPS man still didn't move.

"You slow?" Phil asked the UPS man. "Or just hard of hearing?"

Phil picked up the package, clipboard, and pen, and held them out to Harry.

"Sign here," Phil said.

Harry tucked his gun away, took the package, clipboard, and pen.

"My brother," Carol explained to the UPS man, "has this idea—"

"Delusion," Phil said.

"—he's a detective," Carol finished.

Harry signed the manifest on the clipboard

"You know," Phil said, "Dashiell Hammett."

The UPS man still didn't move.

"Raymond Chandler," Phil said.

The UPS man still didn't move.

"Humphrey Bogart," Phil said. *"The Maltese Falcon . . ."*

Harry ushered the UPS man to the front hall. The UPS man stared sideways at Harry.

"You married?" Harry asked.

The UPS man nodded.

"Kids?" Harry asked.

"Two and a half and a little over a year," the UPS man said.

"Going to have more?" Harry asked.

"*I* want to," the UPS man said.

"But three'll wear *her* out?" Harry said.

"Not just her," the UPS man said.

"You're working, what?" Harry asked. "Double shift?"

"Had engine trouble this morning," the UPS man said. "Stuff backed up. Figured I'd deliver what I could."

"Usually you work late at the depot?" Harry said.

The UPS man nodded.

"Every night?" Harry asked.

"Almost," the UPS man said.

"And your wife," Harry asked. "She thinks you're stopping off to have a beer, two, on the way home?"

The UPS man nodded.

"Avoiding, you know, the kids screaming," the UPS man said, "diapers . . ."

"But," Harry said, "you don't want to tell her how hard you're working."

The UPS man nodded.

"If she knew," he said, "she'd get a job . . ."

"To help you out," Harry said.

"And she works hard enough with the kids," the UPS man said.

"So," Harry said, "this overtime. It's your little secret. Your little mystery."

"You might call it that," the UPS man said.

"The heroism of everyday life," Harry said.

"Huh?" the UPS man said.

"That's what *I* call it," Harry said. "Working hard for a family. Not asking for any pity. Just doing the right thing."

Harry handed the clipboard and pen to the UPS man.

"*The heroism of everyday life,*" he repeated.

The UPS man stood up a little straighter, put his shoulders back, held his head higher.

Phil entered the front hall.

"What are you waiting for?" Phil asked the UPS man. "An invitation to dinner?"

The UPS man scowled at Phil and slammed out of the house. The evening air was mild. A block away an owl hooted. On the front path, the UPS man passed Friday.

"I wouldn't go in there," the UPS man said.

"There's a guy acting strange?" Friday said.

"A real son of a bitch," the UPS man said.

Friday looked at the UPS man.

"The guy who thinks he's a detective?" she asked.

"No," the UPS man said. "The other one."

PART THREE

Every society gets the kind of criminal it deserves.
What is equally true is that every community gets
the kind of law enforcement it insists on.

—Robert F. Kennedy
"Free Enterprise in Organized Crime,"
The Pursuit of Justice

CHAPTER 14

Friday closed the door behind her, as Carol came through the archway, holding a half-unrolled poster of *The Naked City* and the empty mailing tube in the other.

"Harry went up to change his shirt," Carol said. "He'll be right down." From the foot of the stairs, one hand on the newel post, she called, "Harry, you're late."

"Doesn't matter," Friday said. "Half the time, we never get to the theater, anyway."

"Clues?" Carol asked.

Friday nodded and said, "The world's full of them."

"If only I could figure out what he's trying to solve," Carol said.

"After all these years," Friday said, "whatever it is, the trail's pretty cold."

"Don't you ever . . . ?" Carol started to ask.

She didn't finish her question.

"Think of leaving Harry?" Friday asked.

Carol nodded.

"It's not much of a life for you," she said.

"You know how slow the days are with Harry,"

Friday said. "I have plenty of time. And as long as people need a freelance researcher, whatever . . ."

She shrugged.

"I get by," she said.

"I didn't mean the job," Carol said. "Phil and I . . . We've been talking about—"

"*More* therapy?" Friday asked. "*More* cures?"

"You know how I hate the idea of an institution," Carol said, "but . . ."

"Carol," Friday said, "every six months, you go through this, and every six months you—"

"They're discovering all these new drugs," Carol said. "Neuroleptics. Antipsychotics."

"Harry's *not* psychotic," Friday said.

"What *is* he?" Carol asked. "Twelve years old, playing cops-and-robbers in the backyard?"

"Maybe that's *exactly* what he is," Friday said.

Phil came in from the dining room.

"How long are we supposed to put up with Harry's shenanigans?" he asked.

"As long as you're living in his house," Friday said.

Phil turned to Carol and said, "Why your mother ever left the house to him . . ."

"She assumed," Carol said, "*you'd* be able to earn enough to get one for *us*."

"Maybe I could," Phil said, "if we weren't supporting him."

"If *we* don't support him," Carol asked, "who will?"

"The state hospital's got great lawns," Phil said, "a terrific rec room—"

Carol didn't answer.

"He'll be happier," Phil said.

"Harry *is* happy," Friday said.

"I just can't make up my mind," Carol said.

"We could get our own place!" Phil said.

"I grew up here," Carol said. "I want my babies to grow up here!"

"With Harry around," Phil said, "any babies—if and when they arrive—will be wearing sharkskin diapers, tiny fedoras, and, instead of pacifiers, they'll be sucking on stogies."

To Friday, Phil said, "You've been stuck on Harry ever since high school."

"Junior high," Friday said.

"Take him away somewhere," Phil said, "anywhere."

"If I could," Friday said, "I would."

"At least," Carol said, "she takes care of him during the day."

"Great!" Phil said. "That leaves twelve hours *we've* got to put up with him."

"Do you know what a nurse—working Friday's hours—would cost?" Carol asked.

To Friday, Phil said, "If you *don't* get him out of my hair . . ."

Imitating Harry imitating Cagney, Friday said, "You threatening me? Are you threatening me? Don't threaten me. I'm in the threat business."

Phil threw up his hands and said, "You're both crazy!"

Carol followed Phil back into the dining room.

"At least," Carol said, "she knows it."

Harry turned onto the landing between the second and first floor and came down the stairs.

Quoting *Farewell, My Lovely*, Harry said, "'I was

wearing my powder-blue suit, with dark blue shirt, tie and display handkerchief. . . . I was neat, clean, shaved and sober. . . . everything the well-dressed private detective ought to be.' "

Harry grabbed his hat from a chair, put it on his head, tugged the brim over his right eye, and headed out the door.

From the arch between the dining room and the front hall, Carol sighed.

To Friday, Carol said, "He's all yours."

CHAPTER 15

An old part of town. Near the railroad station. A seedy area.

Above the railroad arch was a neon sign advertising *The Charles,* decades ago an elegant hotel, now a flophouse. Half the letters in the sign were either out or fizzing and half lit. They reflected red on the street's cobblestones. The gutters reeked of garbage and gasoline.

Two blocks down the block was an old theater—the Paramount, a grand movie palace left over from the thirties and forties. Now, its balconies closed, it was being used as a community center. The marquee advertised *Film Noir Festival—April 19, 20, 21.*

Half a block in the other direction was a tobacconist shop and newsstand. Through the plate glass window, Harry noticed a few shabby men standing around, flipping the pages of magazines.

Harry got out of Friday's Tercel—tires the most valuable part of the car—which she had parked at the curb.

"Harry," Friday said. "Your brother-in-law and sister are thinking about—"

Harry took Friday's arm and led her along the sidewalk. *Away* from the theater. Toward the newsstand.

Harry said, "Pretend we're just walking along the street."

"We *are* just walking along the street," Friday said.

"Look down the block," Harry said.

"Harry . . . ," she said.

"Look toward the theater," he said.

"Carol and Phil—" Friday began again.

"The alley," Harry said.

"They're talking about an *institution* again," Friday said.

"See the shadow?" Harry asked.

In spite of herself, Friday looked for the shadow. Annoyed at having fallen for one of Harry's fantasies, she stopped and turned toward him.

"Harry," she said, "you're not a detective. You're a used car salesman."

"They're lying in wait," Harry said.

"And I'm not your girl Friday," Friday said, "I'm—"

"Pretend we're just chatting," Harry said.

"—so hopelessly in love with you I put up with your craziness, but—"

"We don't want *them* to know *we* know they're watching us," Harry said.

"—I don't know how much longer I can take it," she said.

"Look over my shoulder," Harry said.

"This is *just* the kind of thing they're going to use to get you committed!" Friday said.

"What do you see?" Harry asked.

The shadow of a man detached itself from the darkness in the alley and moved along the wall.

"There *is* someone there!" Friday said.

"Go into the newsstand," Harry told Friday.

"What about you?" she asked.

Harry jerked his head toward the newsstand.

"Go," he said.

Friday took a few steps, turned . . .

"Go!" Harry said.

Friday ran into the newsstand.

The only other people in the place were the three old men, looking at skin magazines; one of them, the clerk, obese, the other two scrawny, not a bunch of heroes.

"Help!" Friday suggested.

The three men glanced at Friday—uninterested.

CHAPTER 16

On the street, Harry saw a kid, not more than eighteen, move out of the alley and into the pool of light cast by a street lamp.

He wore a ragged gray topcoat and—oddly—unfastened rubber snow boots.

Behind him, two other muggers, about the first kid's age, maybe younger, slinked along the closed-up shops toward Harry—who waited for them, in his 1940s fedora, his open trench coat and open suit jacket, revealing his suspenders, looking quaint, ineffective against their unromantic poverty.

"Spare change," the First Mugger said.

He circled Harry, blocking any retreat toward the newsstand.

"Someone stole our condo," the Second Mugger said.

The second and third muggers blocked any advance toward the theater.

"Nice hat," the Third Mugger said.

"I wish I had a hat like that," the First Mugger said.

"Who sent you?" Harry asked.

"Huh?" the First Mugger said.

"Which mob?" Harry asked.

"Mob?" the Third Mugger asked.

"He thinks we're part of a mob," the Second Mugger said.

"A mob . . . ," the First Mugger said, trying out the idea.

He stood up straighter—flattered.

"Yeah," he said. "*That's* what we are."

"A mob?" the Third Mugger asked.

"Okay, Pops," the First Mugger said, "empty your pockets."

With Bogart's aplomb, Harry flicked his cigarette at the first mugger's feet.

"Tell your boss," Harry said, "he wants to talk to me, he can make an appointment."

"The man *asked* you for some spare change," the Second Mugger said.

The first mugger took out a knife.

Harry said, "All I got in my pocket is—"

Harry pulled his gun.

"Oh, shit," the Third Mugger said.

CHAPTER 17

In the newsstand, Friday stood in front of the old men and the clerk, who were still holding the skin magazines.

"Please," she begged. "My friend's being mugged."

The old men looked at each other, at the clerk.

"They're going to *kill* him," she said. "Call nine-one-one!"

The old men and the clerk went back to their magazines.

"My cell's out of juice," Friday said.

No one looked up.

"Where's the phone?" Friday asked.

She glanced outside, trying to get a glimpse of Harry. No luck.

She sidled up to the first old man.

"What're you reading?" she asked.

She took the magazine.

"*Leg Parade*," Friday said.

She turned a page and looked at one of the porno photographs.

"She's very nice," Friday said. "A little out of proportion. But you'll never need a hot water bottle."

Carrying the first old man's magazine, she went up to the second old man and took *his* magazine.

"*Underage Cuties,*" Friday said. "Shame on you."

She flipped through the magazine, stopping at one picture.

"Does she look underage to you?" Friday asked. She shrugged. "Hard to tell from that angle."

Carrying the two magazines, Friday went up to the clerk and took *his* magazine.

"*Flic!*" she said.

She glanced at one of the pictures.

"How do you think she gets herself into that position?" she asked.

She tossed all the magazines on the counter.

"Now, do I have your attention?" Friday asked. "Good. There's a man outside being attacked by a gang."

The old men and the clerk still did not move. The old men looked at each other. The clerk looked at the ceiling.

Friday took a deep breath and went into a bump-and-grind, singing, "*Dear, when you smiled at me, I heard a melody.*"

She sang and did a bump-and-grind out the door.

The old men and the clerk—mesmerized by this erotic display—followed.

Like a seductive Pied Piper, Friday led them into the street, singing and grinding away.

The three muggers goggled at Friday.

"Shit," the First Mugger said.

To the old men and the clerk, Friday said, "*Do* something!"

"Looks like your friend doesn't *need* any help," the clerk said.

Friday looked past the knot of muggers at Harry, who had them covered with his gun.

"Guy pulled a gun on us," the First Mugger said to the clerk.

Harry tossed his gun onto the ground.

The three muggers looked on with amazement.

"He's nuts," the Second Mugger said to his friends about Harry.

"Let's *go*, man," the Third Mugger said to the First Mugger, who seemed to be the leader.

"Who you most afraid of?" the First Mugger asked. "The joker? The lady? Tons-O-'Fun? Or the two grandpas?"

The First Mugger lunged at Harry—who side-stepped him, tripped him, and rabbit-punched him as he went down.

Watching his friend hit the sidewalk, the Second Mugger hesitated—just long enough for Harry to slug him. The Second Mugger stumbled back. Harry hit him again, knocking him down.

The Third Mugger ran off.

The other two staggered to their feet—and followed their friend.

One of the old men picked up the gun and handed it to Harry.

"Why didn't you use it?" he asked.

"They didn't have a gun," Harry said.

The old man didn't get it.

"They didn't have a gun," Harry repeated.

"His code," Friday said.

The old man still didn't get it.

"Like in a detective novel," Friday said. "You don't shoot an unarmed man."

The old man shook his head.

To Harry, he said, "You're either very brave or very stupid."

"I wish I knew which," Friday said.

PART FOUR

All men's faces are true.

—William Shakespeare
Antony and Cleopatra

Rossiter and his partner Deborah Sears drove through the side streets of the Meatpacking District. Warehouses and expensive lingerie boutiques. Young club crawlers—some local, some from the Five College area to the north: Smith, Amherst, Mount Holyoke, UMass, Hampshire—swarmed through the area, threading their way in between drunks and bums. A tall hooker wearing nothing but a G-string darted in front of their car.

Rossiter squealed to a stop. The tall hooker gave him the finger. "I hate Third Platoon," Rossiter said.

"Yeah?" Sears said. Sears had a gymnast's body and a face with misaligned eyes. Like a bad Cubist portrait. "You like eight to four, never see your kids off to school?"

Rossiter shrugged, shifting his bulk. He was so big, he had to keep his head ducked to fit under the car ceiling.

"'Course Third Platoon," she said, "you never see your kid in the class play."

"Third graders doing *Guys and Dolls*?" Rossiter said. "Pass."

"I like eight to four," Sears said.

"When you got your malefactors," Rossiter said, "your drunks, a gangbanger or three, some squawk woman, and Ten-Percenters, some poor sap checking out St. Jude's poor box, your debutante shoplifter, your pedigree crook or a habitual, who can't keep his hand out of your pocket or stop from checking whether or not you left your kitchen window unlocked or your Escalade motor running. Your Ford F250 four-door. Your Dodge Charger HEMI. Why do they boost those big cars? What you *don't* get eight to four is your degenerate, your weenie-wagger, the sexpert cooze-hound, who always chooses the crowded bus, ding-a-lings like our young lovers two o'clock high," nodding at a young couple, fumbling in each other's clothes, stumbling into the middle of the street.

Rossiter hit the siren.

"In the City," Rossiter said, "this early, kids would still be home, putting on lipstick and smoking crack."

"At least," Sears said, "you're not a C-Pop."

"Foot patrol?" Rossiter said. "You got to be kidding."

"Or DV," Sears said. "Like I was too many years. Going into some family squabble, guy slapping his wife around, you try to help, the wife whacks you upside the head. What I want . . ."

"I know," Rossiter said. "Warrant officer."

Sears grinned and said, "Kicking down doors. Arresting fugitives."

"Or SNEU," Rossiter said. "Taking out the drug dealers."

"Whatever," Sears said.

"We can't really complain," Rossiter said. "The work is steady, the check clears the bank."

"You still in hock?" Sears asked.

Rossiter sighed.

"Into a Shylock?" Sears asked.

"I wish," Rossiter said. "Their vig wouldn't be anything compared to the credit cards'."

"It's not against the law to be broke," Sears said.

Again, Rossiter hit the siren. Another couple, stumbling in each other's arms, headed toward Jackie's, a club with a neon silhouette of a naked woman lying in a champagne coupe, one leg raised.

"'You are like a wild donkey in heat,'" Rossiter said. "Jeremiah two: twenty-four."

Sears sucked on a back tooth: *This again.*

"'I made a covenant with my eyes, so how could I look at a maid?'" Rossiter said. "Job: Thirty-one: one."

"Your parents really did a number on you, Rossiter," Sears said.

"'Better to marry than to burn,'" Rossiter said.

"Even I know that one," Sears said. "Paul, right?"

"First Corinthians, seven: nine," Rossiter said. "The Bible was the only book in the house."

"We had the *Encyclopedia Britannica,*" Sears said. "With its own bookcase."

"You use it much?" Rossiter said.

"Only to look up the human reproductive organs," Sears said.

The squawk-box crackled into life.

"Rossiter," the tinny voice on the other end said, dispensing with police protocol. "Your pal's in trouble. Again."

When their car pulled up in front of the newsstand, the sidewalk was crowded with a dozen bystanders—a couple of hookers, a drunk—their faces bathed in the rotating red and blue police light Rossiter had put on the dashboard. They gazed at the old men and the newsstand clerk, who were no longer spectators in the drama, but actors: witnesses.

At the center of all this attention were Harry and Friday.

"Looks to be half a riot," Sears said.

Ducking, Rossiter emerged from the car.

"Who's operating around here, Rossiter?" Harry asked.

"This is the third time this month you've gotten into a scrape, Harry," Rossiter said.

"It's a tough town," Harry said. To Friday, he said, "Tomorrow, see if we can get a make on the mob those mugs are part of."

Rossiter turned to Friday—who raised her hands, palm out.

"Don't look at me," she said.

"You recognize any of the kids?" Rossiter asked the newsstand clerk.

The clerk shrugged.

"Kids is kids," he said.

To the old men, Rossiter asked, "You?"

"One of them sounded like he had the flu," the first old man said.

"The eighty-proof flu," the second old man said.

"Sniffing snow," the newsstand clerk said.

"Snow," Rossiter, eyebrows raised, said to Sears.

"You coulda been killed," the second old man said.

"Death isn't the mystery," Harry said. "Life is the mystery."

"A philosopher with a solid right," the second old man said.

"On that missing person?" Harry asked Rossiter.

"No Turner," Rossiter said. "Nothing even like Turner."

"Any DOAs?" Harry asked. "Jane Does?"

"Harry," Rossiter said, "remember the year your dad died and you dropped out of law school, came home, started hanging around the station?"

"The year you joined the department," Harry said.

"People go through . . . phases," Rossiter said. "But eventually they have to—"

"That was the year we broke the pickpocket ring," Harry said.

"It wasn't a pickpocket *ring*," Rossiter said. "It was one guy, a drunk, who tripped trying to snatch some lady's purse while you were following him. And *we* didn't *break it*. *I* ran the guy in for D-and-D. And *you* almost got busted for interfering with a police investigation."

"His gang—" Harry started.

"The guy was seventy," Rossiter said. "He didn't *have* a gang! Harry, people *like* you . . . put up with you. But . . ."

Harry waited.

To Friday, Rossiter said, "Linda?"

"What do you want me to do, Brian?" Friday asked.

"*Talk* to him," Rossiter said.

"I do," Friday said. "I have. Every day. You know that."

Rossiter started to leave, stopped, and turned back to Harry.

"Just don't get into any more fights," Rossiter said. "You keep climbing into bed with mugs like this, one day you're gonna get kissed."

CHAPTER 19

Harry and Friday strolled up Main Street until they reached a classier stretch—Sephora, J. Crew, Bay Bank . . .

They looked in the dark shop windows.

"One thing for sure, Harry," Friday said. "You're never a boring date."

They walked in silence. Their footsteps clicking on the empty sidewalk.

"Hated to miss the movie," Harry said.

More silence.

"Harry—" Friday started.

"I know, I know," Harry said. "Rossiter. Why do I put up with that mutt? Sometimes he burns my ass. We'd have a righteous bust—"

"Harry," Friday said, "you were never a cop."

"—some kid gangsta," Harry continued, ignoring her. "A hooker with so many track marks on her arm it looked like she was wearing long net gloves. Shoplifter with a porterhouse—not a slab of chuck, porterhouse, why not?—under his jacket. . . ."

"You didn't work with Rossiter, you went on ride-arounds."

"We'd have them dead to rights," Harry said. "He'd scare the crap out of them—and let them go. If he ever caught them a second time—no mercy. But first time out, he'd let them go. 'What the hell you doing?' I asked. He said, 'The shoplifter maybe he's got a hungry family, maybe he just hasn't had a real good meal in a while. Hooker—she's somebody's kid. She's a person. Everybody deserves a break. The gangsta—we're talking about a teenager, who wants to feel like a man. I told him, Go sign up for Golden Gloves—get knocked down, knock someone else down. . . .' "

Friday stared at the sidewalk, avoiding looking at Harry.

"Most of the time," Harry said, "the gangsta's a rotten punk, the hooker's a skag, and the guy hugging the Porterhouse is a bum. If they'd all turned out saints, it would've been easy to like Rossiter for his attitude, you know. But they were dregs. And he still saw—wanted to see—something better in them."

"That's why you two are friends," Friday said.

"That's why I put up with him," Harry said. "Plus, we go way back."

"High school," Friday said. "I know. I was there."

They walked some more. Now, in silence again, their footsteps echoing again.

Friday tried once more.

"Harry," she said.

"Yeah, sweetheart?" Harry asked with a Bogart inflection.

Hesitantly, she asked, "Do you ever think about—" She looked away from Harry, up at the clock tower. "Kids?"

"You mean punks?" Harry asked. "Like those jerks? Back there? By the Paramount?"

Friday looked at Harry.

"From that mob?" Harry asked.

"No," she said. "Kids. Babies."

Harry nodded knowingly.

"Left on a doorstep," he said. "They grow up. Orphanage. Foster home. Get in trouble."

"I mean," Friday said, "someone's child."

"But whose?" Harry asked. "That's the question. Turns out kid's real father runs the bank."

Friday sighed.

"Oh, God," she said.

"One night," Harry continued, "the banker's out slumming. Gives the nod to this sexy young thing in a smoky bar. They end up in a seedy hotel. Next day, she shows up at the banker's office. To blackmail him."

"Harry," Friday said, "just once—"

"He hires a private detective," Harry said, "who gets the lowdown on the girl—"

"Please," Friday said.

"—who turns out to be the daughter the banker abandoned years ago."

Friday stopped.

"Harry, I'm not talking make-believe," Friday said. "I'm talking about real babies. The kind men and women make when they're in love. The kind you burp and rock to sleep and diaper and cuddle."

Harry gave Friday a blank look.

"Where's the mystery?" he asked.

Friday gazed at Harry sadly.

"What's the matter?" Harry asked.

"Nothing," Friday said. "Nothing at all."

As they strolled, Harry whistled "Stormy Weather." Friday hummed along, then sang: "*Don't know why there's no sun up in the sky / Stormy weather . . .*" "*Since my gal and I ain't together,*" Harry sang. "*Keeps raining all the time . . .*"

Together they sang, "*Life is bare / Gloom and misery everywhere / Stormy weather . . .*"

Harry took Friday in his arms.

They danced.

"Harry," Friday said.

"Hmm?" Harry said.

"Remember our first date?" Friday asked.

"Tenth grade," Harry said. "Ice-skating on Porter Lake. Until we were the last ones there. It started snowing. I remember you had snowflakes in your eyelashes."

"That wasn't our first date," Friday said. "Sixth grade. One Sunday morning, it must have been early October, you came over before anyone else was awake. I was still in my nightgown. We sat under the arbor in the backyard and ate grapes from the vine. I thought I'd never be happier."

"*Were* you ever?" Harry asked. "Happier?"

"I'm happy now," Friday said.

They danced on the sidewalk from one pool of streetlamp light to another—circling slower and slower until they swayed in place in each other's arms. Their faces closer and closer.

Just as they were about to kiss, Harry saw something over Friday's shoulder.

"Pillette!" Harry said.

He released Friday and headed across the street to the Bay Bank Building.

Friday watched him—and then followed.

CHAPTER 20

The Bay Bank Building was the closest Springdale got to a skyscraper—a modern, glass-and-steel tower. A blue-chip address.

Pillette walked hurriedly up to the front door and entered the lobby. He had a carpenter's folding rule sticking out of his right hip pocket. Through the glass front of the building, Harry saw Pillette press an elevator button and wait.

"The guy who was in Marian Turner's apartment." Harry said. "This time of night? What's a carpenter doing in the Bay Bank Building?"

"Maybe," Friday said, "carpentry."

Through the window, Harry watched the elevator door open.

Pillette entered the elevator. The elevator door slid closed. Harry started into the Bay Bank Building.

"If you follow him," Friday said, "I'm leaving."

"Good thinking," Harry said. "Don't want you in harm's way."

Harry opened the Bay Bank Building door.

"I'll meet you at the office," Harry said without looking back at Friday.

CHAPTER 21

Harry crossed to the elevator bank. He looked up at the digital indicator, which showed the elevator going up from floor to floor:

$5 \ldots 6 \ldots 7 \ldots 8 \ldots 9 \ldots 10 \ldots$

The elevator stopped at eleven.

Harry glanced around, found the door leading to the stairs, which he tried.

Locked.

From his pocket, Harry took two picks—one straight, the other V-shaped.

He put the straight pick into the lock; then, he put in one fork of the V-shaped pick. He twanged the other fork of the V-shaped pick as he jiggled the straight pick. And unlocked the door, which he eased open.

Harry slipped into the stairway.

Carefully, silently, Harry shut the door. He started to climb the eleven flights.

Friday walked toward her car. She looked back at the Bay Bank Building, and retraced her steps.

* * *

Harry reached a landing. A dried, stringy mop leaned upside down in the corner, the stiff yarn strands like uncombed hair. No bucket.

On the door leading out of the stairway was a panel that said *11*. Harry tried the knob. Locked. He took out his picks.

Downstairs, Friday entered the lobby, went to the elevators, and pushed the button. The elevator door slid open.

Upstairs, Harry slipped into the hall and closed the door behind him.

At the end of the hall, underneath a closed door, Harry saw a strip of light. On the door was a brass plaque: *Matthew Cotton, Attorney at Law.*

Harry approached the door and pressed his ear against it. From inside came a low murmur of what sounded like angry voices.

Harry tried the door. Locked. He picked the lock, cracked the door open, and peered in.

Cotton's reception area was dark. Across the room, the door to a private office was half open.

This was the source of the light.

Against the far wall of the inner office were shadows of two men. Harry recognized one as Pillette. The other was a man, about five foot eleven, heavyset. It was Cotton's office; Harry figured it was Matthew Cotton, who had been beefy ever since they'd been in elementary school together.

Harry slipped into the outer office and quietly closed the door behind him.

*　　*　　*

The elevator *dinged.* The elevator door opened. Friday
stepped into the hall. She saw the door to Cotton's office being carefully closed. She crossed to it. Tried the
knob.

Locked.

"Harry," Friday whispered.

Again, she tried the knob. Without success.

"Breaking and entering," Friday said. "Terrific."

She crossed back to the elevator, entered the car,
and pressed the button for the lobby. The elevator
door slid shut.

CHAPTER 22

Harry glanced around Cotton's reception area. The walls on either side of Cotton's door were floor-to-ceiling glass, now covered by heavy beige curtains.

Harry sidled up to the office. To eavesdrop. And to peer through a chink where the curtains didn't quite meet.

Against the far wall of the office, Pillette's shadow loomed over Cotton's. Their voices were muffled, but Harry could make out what they were saying.

"What makes you think I'd pay?" Cotton said angrily.

"You keep acting—" Pillette started.

"Get out of my office," Cotton interrupted.

"—like you got a choice," Pillette finished.

Pillette's shadow advanced. Cotton's shadow raised its hands as if to ward off a blow.

Harry burst through the door.

In the center of the room, Cotton and Pillette both turned toward Harry, who had his unloaded gun out.

"What the hell do you want?" Cotton asked.

Pillette stepped toward Harry, who turned his attention away from Cotton long enough for Cotton to grab a vase and whack Harry over the head.

PART FIVE

Well, there is sorrow in the world, but goodness too.

—Herman Melville
The Confidence-Man

CHAPTER 23

Harry's senses came back.

First, smell: sweet, candy scented. From the rug cleaner—though Harry didn't know it. Then: the acrid taste from the acid reflux that burned Harry's throat.

Sound.

He heard a mumble, which resolved itself into a clear voice. Cotton's voice.

"—don't know how he got in," Cotton was saying.

Touch.

The rough weave of the rug against his cheek.

At last: sight.

The rust-colored rug, the bottom of Cotton's desk, a dust bunny underneath the desk.

Harry's head throbbed.

A vague image emerged from the dark.

"—what he was doing here," Cotton finished.

A face. Cotton's face. Which swam into view. Nose enlarged. Eyes, mouth, cheeks, ears elongated, getting smaller the farther from the center of his face, as if Harry were seeing Cotton through a fish-eye lens.

"God knows what he wanted," Cotton said.

A second face drifted into view. Rossiter's.

Harry smiled. Thought he smiled.

To Rossiter, Harry still looked unconscious. A dead weight. Sightless eyes.

"Did you get the gun?" Rossiter asked Cotton.

A third face—Friday's—hovered over Harry. Pinched with concern. Eyes wide.

Again, Harry thought he smiled. But, to the others, he still looked unconscious.

About the gun, Friday explained, "He never loads it."

Phil—whose face rose from behind the others—scowled. Ruddy with anger. The lines of his forehead bunched together in a V: a dry delta.

"Unregistered gun," Phil said. "Breaking and entering . . ."

Carol—who floated into view next to her husband—also scowled.

"Assault." She spit out the word.

Appealing to Cotton, Friday said, "Harry would never use a gun."

"Something like this," Carol said. "It was bound to happen."

"When some muggers attacked him," Friday said, "Harry *threw down* his gun. It was his code."

Cotton, Pillette, Rossiter, Rossiter's partner, Deborah Sears, Friday, Phil, and Carol all crowded around Harry, who, looking up from the floor, gave them a beatific smile.

CHAPTER 24

Beaming up at everyone, Harry asked, "What happened?"

"You attacked Mr. Cotton," Phil said.

"Are you okay?" Friday asked.

"And his carpenter," Carol said. "Mr. Pillette. You attacked him, too."

Unsteadily, Harry rolled onto one knee, hesitated until the room stopped spinning, took a breath, stood, and looked around. His saliva tasted of copper.

"Where's my hat?" he asked.

Cotton handed it to Harry, who put it on his head and gingerly pulled it low over his right eye.

His head pulsed, a waxing and waning circle of pain, which Harry also felt in his teeth.

"Take it slow, Harry," Rossiter said.

"There was . . . an argument," Harry said.

"Over paying a bill," Phil said. "Mr. Cotton told us."

"For an unfinished bookshelf," Carol said. "What the hell were you doing here?"

"And what's it to you?" Phil said.

"No harm done," Cotton said.

"Wait a minute," Harry said. "Wait a minute. . . . What about Marian Turner?"

"Marian Turner?" Rossiter asked. "That's the one who . . ." Turning to Cotton, he asked, "You know her?"

"New client," Cotton said. "Moved here a few months ago. Sad story. Father dead. Mother scrimped to put her through college. Didn't live to see her graduate. Emphysema. Left Marian a little money. Savings, pension, some life insurance . . . Not enough really to make it worthwhile for me to manage, but she was recommended by an old law school friend."

"She's been missing for over a week," Harry said.

Cotton gazed at Harry, shrugged, picked up a telephone, and punched in a number. Waited.

"Room four seventeen, please," Cotton said into the telephone. "Yes, I'll hold."

"Mr. Cotton," Friday said, "Harry's just a little—"

"Vacation," Cotton said. "In Florida."

"And she emptied her bank account from down there?" Harry asked.

"Harry," Rossiter said, "this is the twenty-first century."

"People don't have to walk into a bank to transact business," Phil said.

"Which is why Pillette had her bank statement?" Harry said. To Pillette, Harry said, "That part of the cabinet job you were doing for her?"

"I don't believe this," Phil said to Carol.

"Marian," Cotton said into the telephone. "It's Matthew. There's just someone here who wants to talk to you."

Cotton handed Rossiter the telephone.

"Ms. Turner," Rossiter said, "this is Officer Brian Rossiter, Springdale PD. We've had a missing person's inquiry."

He listened to the response. Rossiter glared at Harry.

"No, no," he said, "I'm sorry to bother you. Enjoy your stay down there. Good-bye."

Rossiter hung up the telephone.

"What the hell made you think she was missing?" Rossiter asked Harry.

"Mr. Cotton," Carol said, "you know Harry is . . ."

". . . who he's always been," Cotton said. "Still trying to figure it out, huh, Harry?"

"Figure what out?" Pillette asked.

"The mystery," Cotton said.

"What mystery?" Pillette asked.

"*The* mystery," Cotton said.

"Life's a maze," Harry said. "It's easy to get lost."

Cotton went around behind his desk.

"Now," he said, "if you'll excuse me . . ."

"You're sure you don't want to press charges?" Rossiter asked.

Cotton shook his head no.

"You should get your brother-in-law to a doctor," he said to Phil.

"Bender's the shrink we've been talking to," Phil told Rossiter.

"About commitment," Carol added.

"I meant for that bump on his head," Cotton said.

"You mokus son of a bitch," Rossiter said to Harry, "why'd you have to do this?"

Rossiter took Harry by the arm and led him out.

*   *   *

Carol and Phil followed Harry, Friday, and Rossiter to the elevators.

"Okay," Rossiter said, "case closed?"

"The phone call?" Harry said. "It makes me *more* suspicious."

"What?" Friday asked.

"Cotton was a little too eager to prove Marian was all right," Harry said.

"When's the last time you talked to a shrink?" Rossiter asked Harry.

"You're in for it now," Phil said.

Harry winked at his brother-in-law and said, "I've already been hit by the lightning, Junebug. The rest is just waiting on the thunder."

CHAPTER 25

The walls of the hospital examination room were a pale green. Closed venetian blinds dimmed the midday sun.

Another day.

Overhead, fluorescent lights hummed. The floor was the white, Harry thought, of the inside of a refrigerator. And there was a sour whiff of spoiled cabbage—like a smell from the inside of a refrigerator. Which left a stench in his throat.

Harry sat in a straight-back chair, facing a psychiatrist—Harold Bender, a short, bantam rooster of a man, who sat, with his knees almost touching Harry's, his chest puffed out as if he were about to crow.

"Do you know who I am?" Bender asked.

"We're in a hospital," Harry said. "They brought me in to see you. Through the ER. So you're probably staff. But you haven't examined where I got whacked on the head, so you're not an ER doctor. Not a hands-on blood-and-gauze doctor."

Harry studied Bender.

"Your suit?" Harry said. "Expensive. Good tailoring.

I'd say it put you back one K, probably more. You've got to have a rich practice. My guess—you're a shrink."

"So . . . ," Bender said, looking at Harry over the tops of his half-glasses.

When Harry didn't answer, Bender glanced at a clipboard.

"Harry," Bender asked, "what brought you here?"

Harry said, "A police van."

Bender gave a tight smile and asked, "Do you know *why* you're here?"

"I broke up an argument between a banker and a carpenter," Harry said.

"Do you ever hear voices?" Bender asked.

"Yours," Harry said. "Now."

"Do you ever feel people are talking about you?" Bender asked.

"On the way over here," Harry said, "my sister and brother-in-law did a lot of whispering, glancing in my direction."

"Do you have the feeling people are out to get you?"

"They're trying to get me locked up, aren't they?"

Again, Bender looked at his clipboard.

"Anything unusual happen lately?" he asked.

"All the time," Harry said.

"Oh?"

"Don't *you* find life full of unusual things?"

"Like what?"

"The former porter in my building, who used to clean my office . . . Willie Sutcliff. Celebrated his birthday last week. Hundred-and-two years old. Once showed me a dime."

"A dime?"

Harry nodded and said, "That he saved since July 30, 1923."

"A dime . . ."

"Willie came from Northampton," Harry said, "where his father delivered ice. On July 30, 1923, Willie went on the rounds with his father. They stopped at Calvin Coolidge's house."

"The president?" Bender asked. "Do you think Coolidge is president?"

"Why?" Harry asked. "Do you?"

"Of course not," Bender said.

"There you go," Harry said. "Coolidge gave Willie the dime. Four days later, Harding died and Coolidge was sworn in."

"This all has some . . . special significance for you?" Bender asked.

"For *me*?" Harry said. "No. For *Willie*."

Bender studied Harry.

"A dime from a president," Harry said. "That's special. But saving it for all that time . . . Why? *There's* a mystery."

CHAPTER 26

As Rossiter entered the precinct, three-thirty, as usual half an hour before his tour started, Sears was leading a suspect—a bodybuilder with a shaved head, his skull fuzzy—across the room.

"You missed all the fun," Sears said.

"You think so?" Rossiter said. "Aren't you jumping the gun? What time did you go on duty?"

"Johnny Carrot," the suspect introduced himself to Rossiter. "I got myself indicted just to get a little attention."

Carrot wore an Armani shirt, Diesel jeans, *chancletas*, white socks.

"How's your crazy pal?" Sears asked.

Rossiter sank into a desk chair. Sears walked away with her charge.

The precinct was loud with commotion. Rossiter realized he hated the piss-yellow walls.

"You gotta bear with me, Mr. Green," Officer Monroe Lacey was saying to a middle-aged man with skull-like teeth. "I got acid reflux. You ever get that?"

"Couldn't you check for fingerprints?" Mr. Green asked. "Or . . . I don't know . . . some forensics?"

"You watch a lot of cops show on TV?" Lacey asked.

Spotting Rossiter, Lacey asked, "Harry hasn't got you bounced back to the bag yet?"

"I think," Mr. Green was saying, "there gotta be fingerprints all over the car."

"Look, fingerprints, forensics," Lacey said. "You know how much that costs the city?"

Another cop—Kevin Goodyear—led a gangbanger in a bloody shirt back to Booking.

"Hey, big guy," Goodyear said to Rossiter, "heard your ass is in a sling 'cause you keep romancing Dickinson."

"Yo, bitch," the gangbanger called to a hooker, sitting across the room in a bright red rain slicker over her panties and bare breasts.

Goodyear shoved the gangbanger.

"All the acid in my stomach comes up," Lacey was telling Mr. Green, "burns the shit outta my vocal cords."

"I want a doctor!" The gangbanger broke free. Handcuffed, he lurched toward Rossiter. "The fuckin' drunk stabbed me!"

"You mean the civilian you tried to roll?" Goodyear said.

The gangbanger's blood splattered the sleeve of Mr. Green's camel's-hair jacket.

"Jesus Christ!" Lacey said.

He pushed the gangbanger away from him. Two cops grabbed the gangbanger, led him away.

"You might not wanna touch that," Rossiter told Mr. Green, nodding at the blood spatter.

Opening his desk, he pulled out a tissue, which he

offered to Mr. Green, who swiped at the sleeve of his jacket.

"You gotta watch it with the AIDS," Rossiter said.

Mr. Green dabbed at his sleeve and angrily asked Lacey, "Are you going to help me or not?"

"Six A.M.," Lacey said, "we fished a meter maid out of a garbage can floating in the river. Twenty-two pieces of her. Very hard to ID that. So we're a little busy today, but your problem's very important to us."

Rossiter felt the beginning prick of one of his migraines like a flash of distant heat lightning. He rubbed his eyes, swallowed bile, and looked at a young man with a tattoo of his own face covering the left side of his face, who was handcuffed to his chair arm.

The young man glanced at a Ziploc bag on the desk facing Rossiter's.

The bag was filled with dried greenish leaves and twigs.

"Not mine, boss," the young man said.

"You work in a pizza parlor?" Rossiter asked.

"What?" the young man said. "No."

"That rules out oregano," Rossiter said.

A heavyset woman in a white blouse, a tight blue skirt with lateral creases across her belly, and a jacket—Detective Jackie Shoop—sat down at the desk opposite Rossiter, and, without looking at the young man, told him, "Your prints are on their way to Albany."

Rossiter picked up the phone and dialed.

"Linda," he said into the phone, "is Harry out of the examination yet? Yeah? Well, call me as soon as he is."

He hung up and stared at the phone.

"So why don't you tell us your name?" Shoop said to the young man handcuffed to the chair. "Albany matches your prints, we get your name anyway."

"Not if I got no record," the young man said.

"You know a lot about the system for someone who says he's never been in it," Shoop said.

"No convictions," the young man said.

Rossiter sprung out of his chair and put his face so close to the young man's face he could feel the kid breathing.

"Tell the detective your name, you little shit," Rossiter said, "or I'll stick my hand down your throat, grab your lungs, rip them out, and shove them up your ass, got it?"

"Can he do that?" the young man asked Shoop, who shrugged: "I didn't hear anything."

Rossiter's phone rang. He grabbed it.

"Harry skated," Friday said.

Rossiter grinned.

PART SIX

Are we or are we not simians? It is no use for any man to try to think anything else out until he has decided first of all where he stands on that question. . . . If we are fallen angels, we should go this road: if we are superapes, that.

—Clarence Day
This Simian World

Just outside the waiting room, on the sidewalk under the emergency room marquee, Phil stood near the electric doors, smoking a cigarette. He inhaled. The end of the cigarette flared red. He held the smoke in his lungs for a moment, exhaled, a stream of smoke curled in arabesques toward the ceiling.

People entered—bruised, limping, holding bloody towels to face or arm—tentatively, blinking, from the healthy world outside.

Phil, squinting in his cigarette smoke, judged everyone passing: condemning the injured or sick for not being healthy, disdainful of the worried companions, helping the infirm. Wondering if the burning in his chest was indigestion or his heart.

Through the glass doors, he watched Carol approach Friday, who sat on a Popsicle-orange molded plastic chair, staring into a cardboard cup of coffee.

Phil snapped his cigarette butt into the circular driveway and headed inside through the sliding doors.

"Why do you put up with it?" Carol was asking Friday.

"Why do *you*?" Friday asked.

"Aside from genes?" Carol shrugged. "I love him."

"So do I," Friday said.

"You can't marry a madman," Carol said. "Not in this state."

Friday didn't answer.

"What are you going to do?" Carol asked, "play Sam Spade with my brother for the rest of your life, Linda?"

"Linda," Friday said. "I hate that name."

"You prefer what Harry calls you? Friday."

"When *Harry's* calling me that. Yes."

Bender came into the waiting room.

"The nurse told you?" he asked.

Friday nodded.

Phil joined Friday and Carol.

Bender said, "Harry's got what we call partial complex seizure disorder. A limited delusion. He's logical about everything—except who he is."

Neither Carol nor Phil said anything.

Bender shook his head.

"With patients' rights," he said, "it's hard to get a court-ordered commitment."

"He attacked Cotton," Phil said.

"In similar circumstances," Bender said, "you, me . . . Maybe, we'd've done the same."

No one said anything.

"We don't really know the circumstances," Bender explained. "The context."

"We know what Cotton said," Phil objected.

"Legally," Bender said, "it's a gray area."

"My brother-in-law," Phil said, "is a nut!"

"But," Bender asked, "is he a *dangerous* nut?"

Bender shook hands with Carol and Phil. Nodded at Friday.

"Get him to commit himself," Bender said. "Or you'll have to learn to live with it."

CHAPTER 28

In the kitchen, Carol stood at the stove, stirring soup.

"Harry," she called. "Soup's on."

Through the kitchen door, Carol saw Harry in the hall, punching a number into the telephone.

"Customer service?" Harry said into the telephone. "Representative." He waited. Then: "Hey, there . . . Thank God the phone company still employs human beings!"

Sun through the pale green Levolor slats cast stripes across the floor and up the opposite wall.

"It's getting cold, Harry," Carol called.

Turning his back on her, Harry said into the telephone, "Could you tell me my current balance?"

Carol ladled soup into a bowl, which, disappearing from view, she carried to the kitchen table.

"My name is Matthew Cotton," Harry said. He gave Cotton's office telephone number, adding, "My address is Bay Bank Building, 33 Main Street, Springdale, Massachusetts, 01101."

Carol reappeared at the stove, where she scooped soup into another bowl, which she carried out of sight to the table.

"Recent charges?" Harry said into the telephone. "To identify me? Of course. There was a long-distance call I made last night. . . . To Florida."

Carol reappeared and filled a third bowl, which she carried to the table.

"Hang on," Harry said into the telephone. He searched on the telephone table and found a pencil stub. "Okay." Repeating what the operator said, Harry wrote on a pad, "305-555-3720."

Carol stood in the kitchen doorway, saying, "Harry . . ."

Harry nodded and said into the telephone, "You don't know what a help you've been."

Harry hung up the receiver and immediately picked it up again, put it to his ear.

Glancing at the ceiling, Carol called, "Phil. Hot soup!"

Harry punched in the number he'd gotten from the telephone company.

"Well," Carol said, "I'm going to eat before it gets cold."

She retreated into the kitchen.

"The Breakers," Harry repeated what he heard on the telephone. And, after listening to the choices, pressed a 6. After a moment, he asked, "Can I talk to Marian Turner? She's a guest. Turner." Harry spelled it. "I'll wait."

Phil clattered down the stairs and said, "Put on the feedbag, Harry," as he passed through the hall into the kitchen.

"Turner?" Harry again spelled the name. "You're sure?" he asked. "There's no Turner registered. Yesterday? No, no Turner registered in the past week. Thanks."

CHAPTER 29

Harry stuck his head through the kitchen door.

"I'll just wash up," he said, and headed back through the hall to the downstairs bathroom.

Seated at the kitchen table, Phil fished in his inside suit coat pocket for some legal forms, which he handed to Carol.

"Commitment papers?" Carol asked.

"We play along with Harry," Phil explained. "Make up a story. Pretend they're secret documents." He affected what he thought was a spy's voice. *"Slipped to me by a one-legged dwarf . . ."*

"You sound like Boris Badenov," Carol said.

Through the half-open kitchen door, the UPS man, who had just arrived, watched Phil's bizarre behavior.

"In a bordello," Phil said in his cartoon villain's voice as he leaned almost horizontally across the kitchen table, *"staffed exclusively by fourteen-year-old albinos."*

Seeing the UPS man, Phil gave a sickly smile and, taking back the commitment papers, slipped them into his suit coat pocket.

"I tried the front," the UPS man said, "but no one answered. Saw the cars in the driveway, figured somebody must be home, and . . ." He shrugged. "I got another package for Mr. Dickinson."

As Harry entered the kitchen, he grinned at the UPS man.

"Hey, Mr. Dickinson," the UPS man said. "Got another package for you."

Harry took the package. Opened it. Found a paperback book with a lurid cover.

"*The Simple Art of Murder,*" Harry read, "by Raymond Chandler. The twentieth century's greatest work of moral philosophy."

Harry slipped the book into his suit coat pocket.

"Sign here," the UPS man said.

Harry signed.

"'The heroism of everyday life,'" the UPS man said, quoting Harry. "I told my wife that. She said, 'What do you want to be a hero for?' I said, 'For my family.' Remember I told you she didn't want another kid?" The UPS man raised his chin. "Last night, we started working on it. If it's a boy, we'll name it *Harry.*"

Harry handed back the clipboard.

"Good luck," Harry said to the UPS man, who slipped out.

"Harry," Phil said conspiratorially, "this morning . . . At my office . . ."

From his pocket, Phil pulled out the legal papers. He couldn't meet Harry's eyes. Or Carol's.

"I found these secret documents. . . ."

Harry glanced at the papers.

"Look like commitment papers to me," he said, handing them back to Phil. To Carol, Harry said, "Might be home late."

Harry pulled his hat low over his right eye and breezed out.

Carol looked at Phil. who shrugged.

"You got a better idea?" Phil asked.

CHAPTER 30

The argument had reached the point where Stan Billings, a Progressive Policy Institute guy with hooks into the twenty-first century Democratics, took a swing at Roswell Flowers, an unaligned Tea Partier, over whether or not the National Basketball Association's lockout of players violated antitrust laws. Hilly Corrado, a centrist Republican member of the city council, tried to separate them, but he, in turn, was clocked by Jake Golding, a Distributist with anarcho-syndicalist tendencies.

Friday walked in as her father body-checked a Stalinist he'd been arguing with ever since 1956, when they were young and had a falling-out over the Hungarian Revolution.

"Dad," she said, waving at the melee in the living room and heading upstairs. "Guys . . ."

"The union's improper threats of antitrust litigation are having a direct, immediate, and harmful effect upon the ability of the parties to negotiate a new collective bargaining agreement," Billings said between gasps as he struggled to keep a headlock on Flowers.

"Give it up," Barrett Tomlinson, a Red Tory, was saying to Bruce Malcome, an old-fashioned Stalinist. "Sniff me."

"You sniff *me*," Malcome said.

"*This* is what JFK smelled like," Tomlinson said.

"*This* is what JFK smelled like," Malcome said.

"You *know* JFK wore Caswell-Massey Jockey Club," Tomlinson said.

Malcome shook his head and said, "4711 Aftershave."

The timer on the mantel buzzed. The dozen men in the room stopped fighting and started putting tables upright, picking up shards of an overturned vase, cleaning up the mess.

By the time Friday came back downstairs, the men were sitting and standing around the living room with their instruments—Friday's father on his cornet, Flowers on the clarinet, Billings on his drum kit—and had started a rendition of "Mississippi Mud."

Their typical monthly meeting: two hours of hamfisted politics, two hours of jazz.

"That's democracy," Lee explained to a friend Friday had once brought home from college. "We've got everyone here from far right to far left, missing only a neo-fascist and a good bass."

"Hey, kiddo," Billings said to Friday in the break, "I hear your boyfriend had to pony up a bundle for the Detectives' Benevolent, PBA, one of those, to stay out of the nut house."

He grinned, his wrists loose, his sticks pointed at the ceiling.

In two steps, Friday was in front of him. She slapped his face so hard, his right stick went flying across the room, just missing Corrado, who reared back, eyebrows arched.

"Whoa," Flowers said as Friday hauled off to smack Billings again. He grabbed Friday from behind in a bear hug, pinning her arms. "No one meant anyone any dirt."

"You son of a bitch," Friday said to Billings.

"Come on outside, hon," Flowers said. To Lee, who hovered next to him, cornet by his leg, Flowers said, "Give us a minute."

CHAPTER 31

Harry took the half-dozen steps leading to the large sliding glass doors of the Springdale Union two at a time. The light from the lobby spilled into the night. The guard at the door, half-dozing in front of a mini-TV tuned to a rerun of *Frasier,* pushed the sign-in book across the counter toward Harry, who dropped his driver's license on the desk and illegibly scribbled on the appropriate line. On the TV, Niles had just accidently set the couch on fire. Harry was aware of a high-pitched, almost inaudible hum. Some electrical circuit? Tinnitus?

His ears popped.

The elevator bank was in a modernistic cloudy glass wall almost two floors high. Harry hit the "down" button. To his right a bell *binged* and a red arrow lit over an elevator door, which slid open. Harry slipped in and again hit the "down" button.

He faced forward, hat pulled low over his right eye, hands clasped in front of him, staring at his dirty black-and-white spectator shoes. The elevator dropped a floor. Harry leaned out, looked left and right, and exited. The door slid closed behind him. The corridor smelled—like some modern architecture—faintly of burning rubber. To the right, at the end of the hall was a large double door in cherrywood. Over its modern chrome sans serif letters, each letter separately attached to the wall with metal pegs, spelled out *Research*.

Harry entered.

"I need to use the morgue," he said to the kid behind the cherrywood gull-wing counter.

"You can't bring a dead body in here," the kid said.

The kid was tall, maybe six foot four, with sandy hair, watery blue eyes, and pimples. Behind him was a clock almost as big as he was.

"Why would I do that?" Harry asked.

"For the morgue," the kid said.

"You have dead bodies in the morgue?" Harry asked.

"Doesn't everyone?" the kid said.

"I've never heard of that," Harry said.

"Where do *you* keep your dead bodies?" the kid asked.

"What makes you think I have dead bodies?" Harry asked.

"You asked for the morgue," the kid said.

"Old newspaper files," Harry said. "The morgue."

The kid blinked at Harry.

"That's what they call a newspaper's old clips file," Harry said. "In my time. The morgue."

"You mean *Research*," the kid asked.

"Right, kid," Harry said. "Research."

PART SEVEN

"He didn't believe it," Coffin Ed said. "Someone he knew and trusted stuck a pistol against his temple, looked into his eyes and blew out his brains."

Grave Digger nodded. "It figures. He thought they were joking."

"That could be said of half the victims in the world."

—Chester Himes
Blind Man with a Pistol

CHAPTER 32

In Lee's backyard, Friday sat on one of the seats of her old swing set, red paint flaking and rusted. Flowers sat on the other. Overhead, stars seemed to move in and out of focus, as if someone were adjusting a range finder. Somewhere down the block, someone was mowing a lawn. The small motor rose and dropped in pitch as the mower moved back and forth. The air smelled of cut grass. Friday felt the chill on her sides under her arms. The swing seat was cold. She shivered.

"How much do you trust me?" Flowers asked.

"I never thought about it," Friday said.

She dug her toes into the ground and pushed her swing back.

"What's your first memory of me?" Flowers asked.

As the swing approached the earth, Friday braced her feet and gave herself another push.

"You were always dropping by for dinner," Friday said.

She swung toward and past Flowers. The breeze made by her swinging blew hair around her face.

"Uh-huh," Flowers said.

"I remember you standing on the back porch with Lee, while I was on the swings," Friday said. "Like this."

She pumped.

Flowers watched her go up and come down, go up and come down.

"You were always coming and going," Friday said.

"Do you know where I was?" Flowers said. "When I was coming and going?"

As Friday swung past him, she turned her head to keep him in view.

"Everywhere," she said.

"You know why I was in New Delhi?" Flowers asked. "Accra?"

"You mean your job?" Friday asked. "Advertising. J. Walter Thompson."

"Once upon a time," Flowers said.

When the swing hit its lowest point, Friday stuck out her feet. Braked. Came to a stop.

"You were a spy," Friday said, surprising herself.

"USIA," Flowers said. "United States Information Agency. I wanted to be part of Kennedy's team."

"I thought spies retired to Antibes or Kingston," Friday said.

She looked sideways at him, resting her cheek on a fist that held the swing chain.

"You *are* retired," Friday said.

"Black Leaf 40, MK-Ultra, dirty tricks," Flowers said. "I wasn't involved in anything like that. Not directly."

"Not directly?" Friday asked.

"What do you think the most useful skills were?" Flowers asked. "In my line of work."

"How about that," Friday said. "A spy. In Springdale. Does Nancy know?"

"I met Nancy at the Farm," Flowers said. "When I was training. She was an accountant."

"What about Jessie?" Friday asked.

"She didn't need to know," Flowers said.

"Childhood's rough enough, huh?" Friday said.

He waited.

"Most useful skills?" Friday asked. "Your tradecraft?"

"You read too many thrillers," Flowers said.

"You were deep cover?" Friday said. "Are you blushing?"

"You make me feel like Harry," Flowers said.

"A romantic?" Friday asked.

"There nothing romantic in what I was doing," Flowers said. "Not mostly."

Friday pushed herself on the swing again.

"But I don't know that there's so much difference between me and Harry," Flowers said.

"You deal with reality," Friday said.

"Whose reality?" Flowers said. "Let me tell you a story."

CHAPTER 33

"Whose reality"

This is the story Flowers told Friday, as Friday later remembered it.

———

Palgham looked like a town out of the American Wild West, Flowers said, his swing making a small arc to and fro. Asiatic cowboys on mustangs galloped up the dusty main street. Hard-looking men lounged in front of stores that sold clay pots, tarpaulins, bolts of cloth, camping supplies. Unlike in other parts of India, the children did not crowd around begging. Instead, they looked suspiciously at us. One boy, about six years old, was herding goats. When he passed us, he spit right in front of my shoes, and insultingly grinned. His teeth were black, rimmed at the gums with lines of red that could have been betel stains—although so far I had not seen anyone chewing betel in Kashmir.

We had arrived in Srinagar a few days before. From our houseboat roof, I looked down into one of the largest estates on the shore of Nageen Lake. A lawn, mowed by a bullock dragging a rotary blade, sloped up from the water's edge to plots of blue, red, and yellow flowers. Beyond the garden was a terrace with white wicker furniture. Beyond the terrace was a brick house.

A man sat in the garden in a lawn chair, reading a book that lay open on his lap. He was immaculate in white *kurta* pajamas. On the ground next to him was what I at first thought was a large Irish setter and what, moments later, revealed itself to be a human being—apparently a servant.

The man in white tapped the arm of his chair, and the servant turned the page of the book.

"Did you see that?" I asked Nancy and Jessie.

But the man in white seemed to have stopped reading. Nancy and Jessie went downstairs, Nancy to change into something cooler and Jessie to paddle in the small *shikara* that came with the houseboat.

Our bearer cleared the breakfast dishes. Above my head, the breeze ruffled the canopy, which made a sound like fingers snapping.

The scent of lotus blossoms, which were as large as cabbages, hung over the lake.

I picked up the book I had been reading, an odd volume of Prescott's *History of the Conquest of Peru*, which someone had left in the houseboat library and which, exhausted by the flight from Delhi but too excited by the exotic surroundings to sleep, I had picked up the night before.

I opened the book to the chapter on Francisco de Orellana, who in 1540 sailed down the Amazon and returned to Spain with tales of El Dorado.

"His audience listened with willing ears to the tales of the traveler; and in an age of wonders, when the mysteries of the East and West were hourly coming to light, they might be excused for not discerning the true line between romance and reality. . . ."

I remember the passage.

It seemed like it described my life. As it was then.

It could describe Harry's life. As it is now.

The grocery *shikara* pulled up to the catwalk connecting the houseboat to the dock. Displayed in the boat were cartons of Colgate toothpaste; flat blue tins of Nivea; bottles of Dettol; bags of barley, corn, and oats; baskets of apricots, apples, miniature peaches, pears, watermelons, perfect striped spheres that looked like soccer balls, and artichokes that looked like monstrous metal-leafed eggs.

When I climbed back to the roof, the man in white had returned to his reading. I saw him tap his chair arm, saw the servant reach out and turn the page.

We later met him on one of the three swimming rafts in the lake. He introduced himself— Laksman Roa. He asked if this was our first trip to India.

"I heard Kashmir was paradise," Nancy said.

"Oh, yes," Laksman said. "It would be if the

Kashmiris did not remind you of it every five minutes."

That night, Nancy, Jessie, and I reclined on the mattress of a taxi *shikara*. I had left the front curtains open so that we could look at the full moon, orange as a mango, which hung above the mountains surrounding the valley. As we passed the estate next to our houseboat, we heard, coming from its open windows, an Italian opera. The house was dark except for one room on the second floor. Loud enough to rise above the music was what I assumed to be Laksman's voice, singing along with the recording.

The following morning, when Laksman saw us breakfasting on our houseboat roof, he waved at us and helloed. Moments later, his bearer trotted up our dock and handed our bearer an envelope, which I opened as Laksman, on his lawn, made encouraging gestures.

Laksman's stationery was thick as cardboard and had a red crest on top. In purple ink, Laksman had written, "I would be honored if you would walk in my garden."

His gardens were extensive and elaborate with streams that ran along man-made channels from terrace to terrace and fountains that cast miniature rainbows in the sun. Flowers as complex and angular as quartz crystals gave off a bittersweet smell. Unlike anything else I've ever come across. Kingfishers, the turquoise of the nylon of Jessie's backpack, flickered from branch to branch.

Remember this is the land of the Nishat Bagh

Gardens and not that far from the Shalimar Gardens.

Laksman's bearer followed us, carrying a tray with tall glasses of Campa Cola, Limca, and Gold Spot.

"Now," Laksman said, "the only Americans who come here are hippies. They rent the poorest houseboats in the poorest part of the lake. No cook. No boy to clean. No one to heat the water. They stay for a month or two or three and go away—to Goa, to Katmandu, to Yunnan Province in China."

"We wanted to go on a pony trek in the mountains," Nancy said.

"Indeed," Laksman said. "Will you allow me to be your guide?"

We left Srinagar at dawn and drove four hours into the mountains, stopping at the ruins of an ancient Hindu fort. I climbed the worn steps and stood on a huge stone platform. Nancy was below, following a narrow passage. Across a gulf where part of the fort had collapsed into what must have been an underground hall, Jessie stood on another stone platform.

Shielding her eyes with a salute, she squinted up at a wall as Laksman pointed out some detail.

I worked my way down and up the heap of stone blocks and examined the wall Laksman had shown Jessie. Among other, more commonplace images, not quite erased by erosion, was a bas-relief of a man being beheaded.

We arrived in Palgham in the mid-morning. For two hours, Laksman went in and out of shops, getting supplies, renting equipment, hiring people for the trek. The cook, a thin man with one milky white eye and long, claw-like fingers, swaddled three squawking chickens in a dirty cloth to be bundled on the back of a pack pony.

"That's cruel," Jessie said.

"It's their custom," I said.

"Jessie's right," Nancy said. "It is cruel."

By twelve we had set off, a train of six ponies: Nancy, Jessie, Laksman, and me, followed by two pack ponies that carried huge swaying loads. The cook and the four pony handlers walked alongside, clicking, whistling, and chucking at the animals. I wore a Red Sox cap. Nancy wore a wide-brimmed straw hat with a red ribbon around the brim. Jessie, bareheaded, carried a blue parasol that Laksman had insisted she take for protection against the sun.

Jessie was outraged, but afraid to disobey Laksman.

She did look a little silly.

I never got a picture of that.

Because of the altitude, the air was thin. In town, the breeze had smelled of coriander, cardamom, and burning dung. When we started the long climb into the mountains, it smelled of sweet grass. The road was wide enough for a car to pass, although in the three hours we were on that stretch, clopping along, we saw only one car, a government sedan that racketed by in a cloud of dust and blue exhaust, which choked us.

We stopped for lunch on the side of a hill. A few hundred yards down the slope was a low mud hut. Three children, girls with gold nose studs and with faded brown shawls draped over their heads, edged toward the ground cloth on which we sat.

Jessie hid the parasol, which was closed, under the cloth. After that, she refused to carry it.

She handed the girls squares of chocolate, which they examined. One girl, about eight years old, licked the candy, made a sour face, and threw it away. The other two children threw away their chocolate without tasting it.

The cook served us Western-style fried chicken and cucumber-and-butter sandwiches that had the crust cut off. The pony handlers sat apart, passing a hookah. On the road above them, a horseman, silhouetted against the dark blue sky, charged past. He leaned over his animal's stretched-out neck, his silver ornaments flashing in the sun.

The path narrowed. In places, it climbed at what seemed a forty-five-degree angle. Loose rocks and snake-like roots made the ponies' footing unsure. To the right, a cliff face rose above us. To the left, the land dropped sharply hundreds of feet. Laksman insisted that the handlers hold the bridles of Nancy's and Jessie's ponies and lead them along the more treacherous parts. When Nancy objected, I said, "I don't think Laksman's heard of women's lib."

Nancy wasn't amused.

Jessie snorted. She didn't want any help either.

Half an hour later, rain hit suddenly and violently. The path turned into running mud through which the ponies churned. We had to shout to be heard above the roar of the wind.

At one of the narrowest points in the path, the front legs of my pony gave out. The animal knelt, pitching me over its head. As I fell, I twisted to keep from sailing over the steep path and plummeting down the sheer drop. After that, Laksman insisted that a handler lead my pony, too.

"Let's wait for the rain to stop," I shouted through the rain and wind to Laksman.

Laksman turned in his saddle and shouted back at me, "Not possible."

Laksman dismounted and gave his reins to the handler who had a grip on the bridle of my pony. I leaned down so Laksman could shout confidentially into my ear, "If we are not at the government ranger station by nightfall, the dacoits will come."

"Dacoits?" I shouted back.

Laksman glanced at Nancy and Jessie, who sat on their ponies, waiting for the procession to start again. Nancy had draped a waterproof cloth over her head. Jessie was using the parasol again, trying without a lot of luck to keep off the rain.

"Hill pirates," Laksman said. "They will steal the horses, rape your good wife, take the child, and kill you and me."

"What about them?" I pointed at the pony handlers.

"They are probably dacoits, too," Laksman said. "But I told them you had left all your valuables in Srinagar."

The storm lasted for an hour and a half and stopped as abruptly as it started. The sun came out. The path widened into an upland meadow. The few trees were elongated. You know Giocometti? The trees looked like Giocometti figures. In the distance was a glacier. Dark blue. Like the sky.

"One more hour," Laksman said. He added for my benefit, "We shall not be late."

By the time we reached the government station, an empty one-room shack in a field of sparse grass and rocks the size of big chairs, easy chairs, our clothes had dried. The pony handlers pitched our tent and Laksman's tent, modern ones with zippered mosquito netting in the doors. Then, they pitched their own tent, an animal-skin lean-to. The cook pitched his tent, an Indian army surplus pup tent.

Nancy, Jessie, and I washed in the stream, which was so cold it numbed my hands and made them feel severed at the wrists. Laksman stood on the bank above, looking not at us but keeping watch on the thin woods on the other side of the stream. When we climbed back to the camp, Laksman handed us a pile of clean folded clothes: long shirts and loose pants, white for me and Jessie, maroon-and-purple-patterned for Nancy.

We crawled into our tent and, contorting ourselves, changed. Crablike, I raised my bottom and supported myself with one hand while with the other I dragged off my dirty clothes and pulled on the clean outfit.

One by one, we emerged from the tent into the twilight.

The sky was streaked with red and gold. I mean: real gold. That deep, almost bloody color gold can have. The reflection on the glacier made it look like a glass door of a furnace.

"Tibet is called the Roof of the World," Laksman said. "This is called the Roof Garden of the World."

He was washed and dressed in an immaculate, flowing white *kurta* and pajamas. On his feet were purple-and-gold sandals.

The cook brought us a proper British tea: a tray with a pot, cups and saucers, freshly made scones, jam, and honey. He, too, was washed and in a clean change of clothes, a snowy-white waiter's jacket over white pants. But his hands were bloody from just having slaughtered one of the chickens for dinner.

"Wait," Nancy said.

She ducked into the tent and came out with our camera. This was before digital cameras. It was a 35-millimeter Nikon, I think. I've had so many cameras since then. And before. When I was a kid, I had my grandfather's handheld bellows camera with a little cube on top, which you used as an eyepiece.

After arranging Jessie and me, Laksman and

the cook, into a row, Nancy adjusted the focus and beckoned to the youngest of the pony handlers. She pantomimed taking a picture, stood the young man where she had been, and handed him the camera. He looked suspiciously at it, the way, at lunch, the hill children had looked at the squares of chocolate.

Today, who knows, maybe they all would have laptops and wifi and cell phones and would be singing the latest hit of whoever is today's top pop star.

But then . . .

"Probably, he has never held a camera before," Laksman said.

Nancy took the young man's hands and raised the camera to his eye. He winced at her touch but let her move his index finger to the shutter button. After some more pantomime, Nancy hurried back to the group and fit herself in between me and Jessie.

"Now," she said.

Laksman said something sharply to the young man, who did not push down the shutter button.

Apologetically, Laksman told Nancy, "It's no good. I will take a picture of you. Then, you can take a picture of me."

At night, Laksman took me aside and said in a low voice, "My tent is on one side of your tent. The cook's tent is on the other. You will, I think, be safe."

The cook had built a campfire in front of our tent. In front of his tent was the cooking fire, which had died down to embers. In front of the pony handlers' tent was another small fire, not much more than embers, around which the handlers passed the hookah. The whole camp seemed a cozy room hollowed out of the darkness.

"You are where few Americans have been," Laksman said. "This is another world even from Srinagar. I will make you feel at home."

He stood. One hand on his chest, the other reaching into the dark toward the Himalayas, he sang "*La donna è mobile.*"

In the middle of the night, a delicate sound like a zipper being pulled woke me. I sat up in my sleeping bag. Nancy lay with her sleeping bag tucked under her chin and her legs curled. Jessie lay half out of her sleeping bag, which was bunched around her waist.

A red leaf—like a sumac leaf—seemed to be growing out of the side of the tent.

It was a knife blade, catching a reflection from the dying fire in front of the mosquito netting of our tent door. The zipper sound was the blade cutting the tent fabric.

The knife blade vanished. Through the slit appeared a head, which looked like a trophy mounted on a wall. Below the chin, an arm snaked in as though it were a tentacle protruding from the man's neck. The hand reached for the camera case, which lay next to Nancy.

The man, whom I recognized as the young pony handler who had not taken our photograph, must have surveyed the interior of the tent from the tent door before cutting through the wall.

"Stop!" I shouted.

The young man looked at me.

"Stop!" I shouted again. Louder.

The head vanished.

I scrambled out of the tent.

Laksman was hugging the pony handler, pinning the man's arms to his sides. The cook appeared, banging a knife handle against a pot. The three other pony handlers huddled together near their fire.

Nancy and Jessie crawled from our tent. Nancy wrapped a large woolen shawl around her body. Jessie wore ribbed thermal underwear.

To no one in particular, I said about the young pony handler, "He tried to steal the camera."

"He is bad," Laksman agreed.

Loudly, he said something first to the young pony handler and then to the other pony handlers, who glared at the young man.

Two of the pony handlers grabbed the young man from Laksman's embrace. The fourth pony handler, the oldest and fiercest-looking, yelled something at the young man.

Laksman interpreted: "The boy is his son. He is saying his son shamed him. No one will ever again hire his family for treks unless the boy is punished."

Laksman said something to the fierce-looking pony handler, who spit on the ground.

"You were wronged," Laksman told me. "You must mete out justice."

The cook gave Laksman the knife he had been banging against the pot. Laksman gave the knife to the fierce-looking pony handler. The fierce-looking pony handler gave the knife to me.

The two pony handlers who held the young man pushed him facedown onto the ground. The fierce-looking pony handler yanked his son's arm out straight and knelt on his hand.

"Please," Laksman said to me. "Proceed."

"What am I supposed to do?" I asked.

"You must cut off his hand," Laksman said. When I hesitated, Laksman added, "This is not your country. This is not Delhi. This is not Srinagar."

"No," I said.

"These are hill people," Laksman said. "You must follow their customs."

"Tell the father I will not report the boy," I said. "They will still be able to get work on treks."

I dropped the knife and, waving Nancy and Jessie ahead of me, climbed back into our tent.

I did not sleep. I did not know it then, but Laksman also stayed awake, keeping guard on our tent from his tent's doorway. I expected the pony handlers to sneak away in the night, but in the morning, when I came out of my tent, they were loading the packhorses. On the trip down the mountain, the pony handlers—especially the young man—were sullen. In Palgham, I paid the cook and the pony handlers, who did not look me in the eye.

Trying to show that I had no hard feelings, I

gave the fierce-looking pony handler a large tip. The man jerked as though he had gotten an electric shock, but he took the money.

"Did I insult him?" I asked Laksman during the drive back to Srinagar.

"You surprised him," Laksman said.

"He thinks I'm a fool?" I asked.

"The foolish one is his son," Laksman said. "And you did not allow him to atone for his foolishness."

"He thinks I am weak?" I asked.

"By not doing justice, you gave the boy a terrible punishment," Laksman said. "They think you are cruel."

———

Sitting on his swing, Flowers again asked Friday, "Whose reality?"

PART EIGHT

Don't come bothering me with your miracle! I don't want it—at any price. I don't want it. . . . Because it would force me to believe in God—who doesn't exist.

—Andre Gidé
Lafcadio's Adventures

CHAPTER 34

In the morgue, Harry did not find any references to Marian Turner; but he found a dozen references to Matthew Cotton, most of them about his work with the symphony orchestra or other charitable organizations or his involvement in real estate investments in the area, turning their old Classical High School into condominiums, tearing down the Bing Theater at the "X" and replacing it with a mini-mall.

One reference was to a lawsuit against him by the children of a man whose estate he executed. They had challenged his fees.

Harry took some notes in his pocket notebook, turned off the computer, and left.

"What do you think the most useful skills were," Flowers asked again, "in my line of work?"

He pumped until his swing was sailing up and back in a wide arc.

"Paying attention to details," Flowers answered his own question. "To what makes the moment the moment. Like right now. If you had to choose details to conjure up this moment, what would they be? The light spilling through the kitchen window onto the porch steps? The smell of the cut grass?"

"The cold swing on my thighs," Friday said.

"Then," Flowers said, "you use the details to make up a story about what's happening. That's all Harry does. That's not nuts. That's human. Humans are pattern-making animals."

"Who laugh," Friday said. "*That's* what makes us human."

"When someone like Billings talks like that about Harry," Flowers said, "he's showing how afraid he is of Harry's reality. Of how Harry connects the details. Which I guarantee is more interesting than how Billings does it."

Flowers pumped. He rose backward high into the night until he was backlit by stars.

"What's the point of getting upset?" Flowers asked as he sailed down toward, past, and up in front of Friday, high, again backlit by stars.

"You know the score," he said, his voice shredded by his movement.

Friday pumped, trying to keep up with him. To swing as high as he was.

"I didn't even know," Friday said, "we were keeping score."

She pumped harder.

"I didn't know it was a game," she said.

Flowers sailed past her again. Up behind her. Down toward her.

"Sure, you did," he said.

As the swing started up another arc in front of her, Flowers jumped off.

Friday stopped pumping. Let herself slow down, her arcs getting shorter and shorter.

Friday watched Flowers climb the two steps to the kitchen door, through the light spilling from the kitchen window, which moved along his body as if he were being scanned.

He leaned over and tugged at his right sock.

Friday's swing slowed until she was almost, not quite, still.

CHAPTER 35

Harry sat at the desk of a bank officer—Taylor Rand, Harry's age, in a baggy off-the-rack blue pinstriped suit, blue shirt with white collar, red-and-blue-striped tie, saggy black socks, and highly polished wing-tipped shoes. The overhead lighting reflected off his bald head, which had mottled spots and a pinhead-sized scab. His complexion was as lumpy as oatmeal. His eyes were dead.

"Am I boring you?" Harry asked him.

"No," Rand said, "not at all, Mr. Dickinson. I trust you're not unhappy with how we're handling your mother's trusts? Your accounts?"

Harry flattened Marian Turner's bank statement between them.

"So you see," Harry explained, "part of my credit check involves confirming all extraordinary financial activity in the three months preceding any mortgage application."

"Harry," Rand said, "Mr. Dickinson—when we were in school . . . Then, when your mother left you her estate . . . We have to be professional, but I still think of you as . . ."

"You can call me Harry."

"Not while we're doing business," Rand said. He tapped his right forefinger on his green blotter. "How long have you been thinking of selling your place?"

"It's big for me," Harry said.

"Have you told your sister?" Rand asked. "Your brother-in-law?"

"Phil makes a good living," Harry said. "They'll find a place."

"It's just," Rand said, "ever since your great-grandfather built the house . . ."

"You think," Harry asked, "I'm crazy—"

"Eccentric, maybe."

"—to sell?"

"Oh, yes. To sell. It's eccentric. I'd say it might be seen as eccentric to sell."

"It's a bad market."

"Terrible market."

"I could wait."

"Maybe if I talked to Carol or Phil."

"My mother didn't leave the place to them."

"Of course, but—"

"You think they have a better head for business than I do."

"I think," Rand said, "they should be consulted."

Harry rubbed the indentation on his upper lip.

"I don't want you to be uncomfortable," he said.

"I'm glad you understand," Rand said.

"This is how we can take you out of the middle," Harry said. "I can move my trust to another bank, have them handle the sale, and you don't have to feel any pangs of conscience."

"No, no, Harry—Mr. Dickinson—I'm not saying I won't do as you wish," Rand said. "It's just . . ."

Harry cocked his head and looked at Rand.

"Well," Rand said, "I don't see why Miss Turner didn't come to *us* for a mortgage."

"Maybe the economy."

Rand nodded. "The economy."

"And I'm happy to hold the paper."

"Your exposure . . ."

"As long as I know Miss Turner is good for the mortgage."

"Which is why you came to me, I understand."

"I'm sure," Harry said, "it has nothing to do with the rumors."

"Rumors?" Rand asked.

"You and I both know the damage that can be done by irresponsible talk."

"What rumors?"

"If you could just confirm her withdrawal," Harry said. "If I'm going to hold the paper, I want to make sure she's good for it. And a withdrawal of such a large sum . . ."

"This bank, Harry, Mr. Dickinson, is the oldest in the valley."

"The signature on the slip . . ."

"*And* the most secure."

Harry glanced at his watch.

"I have three other appointments this afternoon," he said.

"You understand," Rand said, "there's no way I can show you the actual slip."

Rand's left eye twitched. He typed on his terminal.

"All I can do is check the computer," Rand said. "If

that's not good enough . . . Here we are. The withdrawal was made on—"

"I *have* the date," Harry said.

"—by Mr. Cotton," Rand said.

"Matthew Cotton," Harry said.

Rand nodded.

"He was two grades below us at Classical," Rand
said.

"A sophomore," Harry said, "when we were
seniors."

"I remember him from the all-high-school band,"
Rand said.

"You played the clarinet."

"Oboe," Rand said. "I still play."

"With Cotton?" Harry asked.

"I don't see much of him," Rand said.

"As Miss Turner's trustee," Harry asked, "he has
her power of attorney?"

Rand hesitated.

"Otherwise," Harry said, "he couldn't have made
the withdrawal."

Harry stood.

"See how simple it was," Harry said. "You didn't
have to violate any confidence, really. And don't
worry. I'll tell people I trust the bank whatever the
rumors about defaults."

"Defaults!" Rand stood—but Harry was out his
door. To himself Rand said, "If I didn't know the son
of a bitch was so simple, I would have said he just
played me."

On the street, Rand's office behind him, Harry
grinned.

CHAPTER 36

Lee plucked an *e* from the typecase and slipped it into the text in his composing stick: *The principle of government in capitalist socie . . .*

"Did you know Flowers was a spy?" Friday asked.

She was sitting halfway down the stairs to the basement, watching her father set type. The shop smelled of sawdust and the benzene used to clean the type, which tickled Friday's nose and made her eyeballs itch.

"Everyone knew that," Lee said, finding a *t, y . . .*

"Some cover," Friday said.

"Eventually knew it," Lee said, opening his composing stick and moving the text into a galley. "The way he hopscotched around the world, it became pretty obvious."

"Make any difference you were a Trotskyite?"

Lee shot her a glance.

"Sorry," she said. "Trotskyist."

Lee adjusted the composing stick, put in a lead, and started setting type.

"He had Q clearance," Lee said. "On loan to some department, DOE, maybe, something to do with nuclear something or other."

"No one talked about it?" Friday asked. "His being a spy?"

Lee glanced over the top of his glasses at his handwritten copy, clipped above the type case, and found letters without glancing down.

"As much as people talk about Harry," Lee said.

"People do talk about Harry," Friday said.

"Not as much as you think," Lee said.

He finished the sentence:. . . *political machinery in the hands of the ruling class*.

"They always talk to me," Friday said.

"People talk to fill empty lives," Lee said. "Anything unusual—"

"Unusual?" Friday repeated.

"—is enough," Lee said. "Eighteen-eighties New York society was buzzing about hashish hors d'oeuvres. Nineteen ninety-seven, everyone was giddy over *The Full Monty*."

"Always the historian," Friday said.

"Nineteen ninety-seven isn't history," Lee said. "It's my life. Eighteen eighty-six. All London was talking about a giant, eight foot tall, from China, Chang Woo Gow—"

"Harry's no freak," Friday said.

"Neither was this guy," Lee said. "Married a woman from Liverpool, had two kids, apparently, opened a tea room in Bournemouth. Just tall. That was enough. After the novelty wears off, everyone settles down. People accept Harry for what he is."

"And what is he?" Friday said. "A madman? An eccentric? A pain in the ass?"

"A charmer," Lee said. "Who gets into trouble. You know that."

CHAPTER 37

The only light in Harry's office filtered through the dirty plate glass window behind Harry's desk. Harry sat, his feet up, shoes propped on the green blotting paper, his hat pushed back on his head, *The Simple Art of Murder* open in his hand.

"'Down these mean streets a man must go who is himself not'" Harry read, "'who is neither tarnished nor afraid.'"

The doorbell rang.

Harry continued reading: "'The detective in this kind of story must be such a man. . . .'"

From the outer office, Friday entered in a hurry.

"Harry . . . ," Friday said.

Harry continued reading: "'He must be a man of honor. . . .'"

Friday stopped to listen.

"'If there were enough like him,'" Harry read, "'the world would be a very safe place to live in, without becoming too dull to be worth living in. . . .'"

"'If there were enough like him,'" Friday repeated softly, "'the world would be a very safe place to live in, without becoming too dull to be worth living in.' "

"Chandler wrote that in 1950," Harry said. "It's still true."

Friday kissed Harry.

"What'd I do to deserve *that*?" Harry asked.

"You wouldn't understand," Friday said.

She opened the door to the outer office and said, "Rossiter to see you."

Rossiter entered, face redder than usual, accentuating his pockmarked cheeks, eyelids drooping, a conscious effort to look less angry than he was.

Friday paused in the doorway

"Did you go to the bank today," Rossiter said, "asking about Marian Turner's account?"

"She's missing," Harry said.

"She's in Florida," Rossiter said.

"Not at the hotel Cotton called," Harry said.

"So she checked in under a different name," Rossiter said. "People who want to make sure they're not disturbed on vacation do that."

"And Cotton emptied her account," Harry said.

"He's her *lawyer,* for crying out loud!"

"You got a line on that carpenter? Pillette?"

"One more stunt like this bank business, Harry, and they're going to lock you up."

"I did a UCC check," Harry said.

"Harry . . . ," Rossiter began.

"Came up empty," Harry said. "I did a Skip Trace. Nothing."

Rossiter raised his voice: "*Listen to me, Harry.* You ever been to a psychiatric hospital? Guys in bathrobes shuffling around the day room, working on their saliva control. Harry, trust me. It ain't Club Med."

Friday—alarmed—glanced at Harry, who frowned, oblivious to Rossiter's warning.

"Maybe we could pick up Pillette on an out-of-state credit check," Harry said.

Rossiter turned to Friday.

"What do we do?" he asked.

"Harry," Friday said, *"leave the woman alone!"*

CHAPTER 38

Alone in the basement print shop, Lee bent to pick up the bleached skull of a rodent—a rat, a mouse, a shrew—which he held out at arm's length. Like Hamlet contemplating Yorick's skull.

When he was eight, Lee thought, Harry started coming down here to work . . . no, play, in the shop. And to hang out with Linda. While he distributed the pied type, he'd keep glancing at her as she set one of the revolutionary leaflets she used to slip through neighbors' doors: *What is to be done?* Hmm, *The Little Lenin Library: Since there can be no talk of an independent ideology formulated by the working masses themselves in the process of their movement, the only choice is—either bourgeois or socialist ideology. . . .* The leaflet that got her in trouble with the cops, who figured it was the work of a subversive cell—which in a way it was. A cell of one. She was ready to go to prison. Was fascinated by Dahlgren's stories of going before HUAC dressed as Ben Franklin. Made him tell her over and over (loved the fur hat) about the hearing with Abbie Hoffman and Jerry Rubin. About Danbury. Imagined herself a teeny-bopper on the cell block. *The division of labor converts the product of labor into a commodity, and thereby makes necessary its conversion into money. . . .* She knew her Marx. *Malthus' theory, which incidentally was not his invention, but whose fame he appropriated through the clerical fanaticism with which he propounded it . . .* I wish she hadn't taken the copy I'd framed down from over the toilet. She was a good Red. Until Harry distracted her with his stories of gumshoes and dames. Late capitalist fantasies of rough justice, carried out by a surrogate of the state when the state can no longer guarantee justice because the game is rigged by malefactors of great wealth. *Behind every great American fortune is a great American crime.* She'd quote that when she was six and get a pat on the head. At home. Not at school. At school, they corrected her: Andrew Carnegie was a great philanthropist. A great man. Built all those libraries, I told her, where the working class could educate themselves to challenge the state. Doesn't matter. Carnegie, Frick had blood on their hands. The Homestead Strike. Amalgamated Iron and Steel Workers. The most hated men in America. Not the only ones. They should get in line. *Behind every great American fortune is a great American crime.* Did she understand what it meant? Does she understand what it means now? For Harry, a great American crime is a chance to redeem human agency. A counter-utopian diversion. Until the whole system is swept away, there can be no redemption. Only individual grandstanding. Not that that's what Harry thinks he doing. He doesn't have that kind of ego. Not *that* kind . . . but ego. That's all Harry is. Infantile ego. Remaking the world in his image. How can I blame him for that? Without scientific analysis, political, economic, dialectic things can seem hopeless. Money, power, flows upward. The proletariat—um, the proletariat vanished long ago. The consumeriate. Adidas, iPads, flat-screen TVs; lottery tickets; a fortunate accident with its attendant corporate lawsuit, the *real* lottery, getting hit by a Staples truck . . . No chance for a revolution there. I guess my dream of a more compassionate society is as wacky as Harry's fantasy of a noir world. I'm as delusional as he is.

Lee placed the rodent skull on a shelf.

Linda and Harry, he thought. I want grandchildren.

CHAPTER 39

Harry crouched outside Marian Turner's apartment. He jimmied the door, snapped on latex gloves, and, holding a penlight in his mouth to free both hands, started searching, lifting cushions, feeling along the underside of easy chairs, opening drawers, shaking books, palpating throw pillows. . . .

In the kitchen, Harry checked inside the refrigerator, in the bread box, inside coffee cans, cereal boxes—

The front door opened and closed.

Harry froze, his hand in a box of Cheerios. The oaty cereal smell made him hungry.

Cotton and a woman appeared in the kitchen doorway.

The woman was dressed in a beige suit, a white blouse with a Peter Pan collar. The sheen on her panty hose reflected the beam from Harry's penlight.

"Who are you," the woman asked, "and what are you doing in my apartment?"

Taking the penlight from his mouth, Harry glanced down at the Cheerios.

"Checking to see if you have enough for breakfast?" Harry said.

CHAPTER 40

In the police station, Harry sat at a young patrolman's desk, the officer who had brought him in: moon-faced, blue eyes with odd black circles outlining his irises, and a rash on his left cheek.

Razor burn? Harry wondered.

The patrolman smelled of baby powder. His name was—Harry had discovered—Aeneas Touvalis.

Around them cops were bringing in and taking out suspects, a few in handcuffs. A female cop was squatting next to Harry, thumbing through a bottom file drawer. Harry could peer down her cleavage. Her breasts were the cream of old ivory. Freckled.

Harry crossed his legs.

"So," Touvalis said, "you were checking up on someone you don't know but think is missing, except the people she *does* know aren't worried about her, and this missing woman comes home to find you've broken into her apartment. That about it, sport?"

Officer Ruth Wyler led an old woman into the precinct by the hand.

"Sergeant," Wyler said to Edgar Vallet, "this is Connie Beverly."

Harry glanced at the old woman, who was hunched over almost parallel to the ground with osteoporosis.

"Mrs. Beverly . . . ," Vallet said, casting a questioning look at Wyler.

To Touvalis, Wyler asked, "The coffee hot?"

"It was two hours ago," Touvalis said.

"How do you take your coffee, Mrs. Beverly?" Wyler asked.

"It's ever so kind of you, but I'm not sure I need a cup of coffee, Ms.—"

"Officer."

"—Wyler."

"You were shivering outside."

"It's a long walk from my apartment," Beverly said. "Fourteen blocks."

Harry said, "I'm happy to get you a cup of coffee, Mrs. Beverly."

"Sit tight, sport," Touvalis said to Harry.

"When I saw you outside the House, the precinct," Wyler said to Mrs. Beverly, "I thought you got off the bus."

"Oh, no," Beverly said. "I never use the bus. Not since they raised the fare."

Maxine Eyer, an undercover cop dressed like a stripper, spangled bodysuit, cut high on the thighs, under her tan belted trench coat, color-of-the-day silk scarf around her throat, was standing by the coffee machine with Jimmy Ozu, the patrol supervisor, who wore a MCKINLEY FOR PRESIDENT button.

To Ozu, Eyer said, "Wyler pulled in another of her strays."

"Walking is so much more healthful," Mrs. Beverley said to Wyler, "don't you think?"

"When you're in the House," Harry said, "the department supplies the coffee."

Touvalis and Wyler glared at Harry, who stood up and crossed to Mrs. Beverly.

"Sit Mr. Sunshine down," Vallet said to Touvalis.

"Why, thank you, then," Beverly said to Harry. "Milk and sweetener, if you please."

Touvalis stood, but Harry was already at the coffee machine, nodding affably at Wyler and Ozu, slipping in coins, pressing a button, and whacking the side of the machine when the cup didn't immediately drop.

"Nice outfit," Harry said to Eyer, who screwed up the right side of her mouth.

"I'm undercover at Lace," Eyer said.

"You think Lace an easy place to strip?" a hooker called out from the holding cage, where she sat on a bench bolted into the wall. "Place is a pigsty. Filled with cops."

Touvalis walked to Harry, who said, "Be right with you."

Wyler told Vallet, "Mrs. Beverly wants to report a Peeping Tom."

"Oh, more than one, Sergeant," Mrs. Beverly said. To Harry, she said, "Many more than one. They all come. Up my fire escape. Every night. To watch me. The Peeping Toms. It's almost like having an audience."

Harry folded the paper cup of coffee into Mrs. Beverly's bony hand. Kept his hand around hers for a moment longer than necessary.

Staring at Touvalis, Vallet pointed at Harry and pointed at the chair Harry had been sitting in.

"These Peeping Toms," Harry asked Mrs. Beverly, "you say they come every night?"

"Oh, yes," Beverly said.

Touvalis touched Harry's elbow to lead him away, but Harry was concentrating on Mrs. Beverly.

"How long has this been going on?" Harry asked.

Touvalis shrugged at Vallet.

"Let me see," Beverly said. "Benny—that was my husband, my . . . one, two—yes, *fourth* husband—"

"*Fourth* husband!" Eyer whispered to Ozu.

"Benny died last August," Beverly said. "August third. Two-thirty-three in the morning. I remember, because we just got a digital clock. We'd always had a regular clock—a round clock with the hands, minute hand, second hand . . . and I was thinking you can only be precise—*that* precise—with a digital."

"Which means," Harry said, "you suddenly become aware of how fast the minutes are passing. Like life is a taxi, and the meter keeps ticking as your fare gets higher and higher until you know you can't afford the ride anymore."

"Your husband just died?" Vallet said, trying to take control of the situation back from Harry.

"Six months ago," Beverly told him. "That's right."

"How long were you married?" Harry asked.

"To Benny?" Beverly turned back to Harry. "Fourteen years."

"Fourteen years," Vallet said, trying to edge between Harry and the woman.

"Isn't that funny." Mrs. Beverly turned her body to keep facing Harry. "Harry, Larry, Harry Two, and Benny—"

"I'm also a Harry," Harry said, turning with Mrs. Beverly, unconsciously excluding Vallet.

"How nice," Mrs. Beverly said.

"My name's Vallet," Vallet said. "Edgar Vallet."

"I was married to each of them for fourteen years," Mrs. Beverly told Harry. "I got married—the first time, I was very young."

"What happened to the other three?" Harry asked.

"Died," Beverly said. "All my husbands—all my marriages, we were very happy. Never considered divorce, oh, no. I've been lucky. All happy marriages."

"All your husbands died?" Vallet asked.

"Heart attack. Heart attack. Cancer. Heart attack."

"And the Peepers?" Harry asked.

"Six weeks after Benny died, they started showing up."

"We're going to look into those Peeping Toms, Mrs. Beverly," Vallet said. "We'll get some blue-and-whites to cruise the neighborhood. Some foot patrols. That should do it."

Ignoring Vallet, Harry said, "I wouldn't worry about the Peepers anymore."

"That's so good to know," Beverly said. "And so kind of you."

"That's what they're here for," Harry said, gesturing at Vallet and the other cops, who stood around them in a ragged circle.

Harry took out one of his cards.

"You ever get concerned," Harry said, "any time, day or night—you call me, you hear."

He scribbled on the back of the card.

"This," Harry said, "is my private number."

"Don't hesitate to call us," Vallet said, also handing Mrs. Beverly a card. "Especially some night when you're all alone."

"Those nights can get long," Harry said.

Mrs. Beverly nodded at Harry.

"You hear those noises on the fire escape," Harry said, "you just call my friend Rossiter. He's in this precinct."

"Or me," Vallet said. "Sergeant Edgar Vallet."

"He'll be right over," Harry said about Rossiter.

"And if he's not available," Vallet said, "I'll be right over."

"Why don't I escort you home, Mrs. Beverly," Harry said.

"That would be lovely," Mrs. Beverly said. She nodded to Vallet. "Thank you, dear." To the room in general, as if taking a curtain call, she said, "Thank you all."

"I'm afraid," Vallet said, sounding almost like Harry, "Harry has some pressing business here. Allow me."

Vallet took Mrs. Beverly's arm. Together, they headed for the exit.

"She's got her own reality," Touvalis said.

"Ours is better?" Wyler asked.

As Vallet and Mrs. Beverly left, a mook, Johnny Carrot, handcuffed to a bench, said to no one in particular, "I break one store window. A shoe store. Then another—a stationery store. Then a Papaya King. I got to break three windows before anyone calls the cops. What they always say—never a cop around when you need one."

"Let's go, sport," Touvalis said to Harry, leading him back to his desk, adding, an afterthought, "That was nice, what you did, with the old broad. This chair okay? You comfortable? This shouldn't take long."

Rossiter came into the room with some forms, which he tossed onto Touvalis's desk.

"Okay," Rossiter told Touvalis, "Miss Turner isn't going to file a complaint." To Harry, he said, "Let's go."

Rossiter and Harry walked down the hallway toward the exit.

"What the hell were you looking for?" Rossiter asked.

"Clues," Harry said.

"To what?" Rossiter asked.

"Marian Turner's murder," Harry said.

"She's pretty pissed off for a corpse," Rossiter said.

"What if Turner found out Cotton was fiddling with her money?" Harry asked.

"Harry," Rossiter said, "she doesn't have enough to make it worthwhile. Not for a big shot like Cotton, who probably keeps money that would make you and me rich in his sock drawer."

"Never steal from the big dogs," Harry said. "They bite. Steal from the tykes. Chances are they won't even bark."

"A little kibble here?" Rossiter said. "A little kibble there?"

"It makes a meal," Harry said. "And, if he's stealing from her, she's not the only one. But Turner barks. Threatens to blow the whistle. Which would ruin Cotton."

"You've got it all figured out, huh?" Rossiter said.

"He's got to shut her up," Harry said. "She's new in town, no relatives, no friends."

"Harry . . ."

"A perfect victim."

"Harry . . ."

"Cotton kills her. With some help."

"He bribes Pillette?" Rossiter asks.

"Or leans on him," Harry said. "Maybe Pillette's in hock to the bank. Who knows."

"And Turner?"

"The woman *claiming* she's Turner, you mean? Cotton's girlfriend? Pillette's? Okay, I start investigating."

"Harry!"

"Cotton thinks fast. Turner was blond? His girlfriend's blond. No one knows Turner well enough to make a good ID. Even her next door neighbor hardly ever saw her."

"*Harry!*"

"We check Turner's college yearbook," Harry said. "Her picture's got to be in that."

Rossiter stopped and yelled, "Harry!" so loud two passing patrolmen glanced at him.

"You got to watch that blood pressure, Rossiter," Harry said. "Your face is all red."

"If you so much as make a phone call to her," Rossiter said, "I'll bust you myself.

PART NINE

A man with bad feet . . . shouldn't be a bartender.

—Daniel Fuchs
The Apathetic Bookie Joint

CHAPTER 41

Route 91 was almost empty. A sixteen-wheeler, a blue Camry, a van with a painting of a smiling pizza with arms and legs trucking Crumb-like toward a hungry crowd—and Harry, who turned off at the exit for the University of Massachusetts.

In the library, students went in and out carrying books. A couple sat on the bottom step. The girl wore two blond braided pigtails—she should be in a dirndl, Harry thought as he passed them.

At the information desk, Harry asked, "Where do you keep yearbooks?"

CHAPTER 42

Vallet bawled out to two officers, Liam Connor and Bryce Reubens, who were leading a young man with a shaved head, bristly like a Chia Pet. "A Pedicab driver? You're out six hours and all you come back with is a Pedicab driver you *think* was pimping for some hooker you never saw?"

"He ran," Reubens said.

"Look who's here," Rossiter said. "Stewie Griffin and the House Mouse."

"Why the hell they put you on the street?" Vallet asked Connor and Reubens. "We're not that desperate." To the Pedicab driver, Vallet said, "What were you thinking? Nobody can pedal faster than a cop car." To Rossiter, Vallet said, "Is Harry your bright light in the dark? And you have to turn him on to see your way?"

"Who complained?" Rossiter asked.

"Someone did," Vallet said.

Rossiter shrugged and said, "Harry screwed up."

"Anything anyone can tag *you* with?" Vallet asked. Again, Rossiter shrugged.

"CO wants to see you," Vallet told Rossiter.

As Rossiter entered Commanding Officer Deputy Inspector Frances Harding's office, the man said, "You got to be dumber than your nut-bird friend."

"Turner got a rabbi downtown?" Rossiter asked. "Or was it Cotton?"

"From what I gather," Harding said, "by the time Miss Turner's door hit your ass on the way out, she was on the pipe."

"How high is her contact?" Rossiter asked.

"High enough to hang you in a sling," Harding said. "You should've arrested the nut-bird. Harassment, B-and-E, something, anything."

Rossiter took his shield and gun and put them on Harding's desk.

"Is it worth it?" Harding asked.

"I had a ball," Rossiter said.

"Did it get you what you wanted?"

"I guess not."

"What the fuck did you want?" Harding asked. "It's not your party."

"Harry's a good guy," Rossiter said. "Not right, a guy like that gets the shaft."

"Hunter goes into the woods," Harding said, "clocks a bear, aims, shoots, misses."

"I heard it," Rossiter said.

Harding ignored Rossiter and continued:

"Enraged, the bear throws the man on the ground and brutally sodomizes him. Next Saturday, hunter goes back to the woods, clocks the bear, aims, shoots, misses. Enraged, the bear throws the man on the ground and brutally sodomizes him. Third Saturday, hunter, back in the woods, clocks the bear, aims, shoots, misses. The bear strolls over to him and says, *'This isn't about hunting, is it?'* This isn't about Harry, is it?"

"We've been friends since we were kids," Rossiter said.

"Not about loyalty, either," Harding said.

Rossiter started out.

"What's bugging you, Rossiter?" Harding asked.

"It's not about me," Rossiter said. "My life is good."

"You know the old song?" Harding asked.

"Fuck you," Rossiter said.

"A knight in shining armor, that it?" Harding asked. "Like your nutcase pal."

Rossiter opened the door.

"Aren't you forgetting something?" Harding asked.

The right corner of Rossiter's mouth crimped up: almost a smile. He went back and picked up his shield and gun.

"You were ready to quit over this?" Harding asked. "Really?"

CHAPTER 43

In the Dickinson living room, Carol arranged some daylilies in a vase on a side table. Phil sat in a leather easy chair across from Jack O'Neill, a fat, fiftyish lawyer with cheeks so pink and grainy they looked made of marzipan. His eyes—hidden in pouches of flesh—were crescents, as thin as fingernail clippings. He smelled of bay rum and cat pee.

O'Neill was going over some notes he'd made on a yellow legal pad:

"Subject: Removal of . . . name . . . That's Harry Dickinson . . . To . . . hospital . . . That's Indian Orchard Psychiatric Clinic . . . Pursuant to section 9.45 of the State Mental Hygiene Law . . . Hum-ah, hum-ah . . . This here is just legal jargon. Hum-ah, hum-ah . . . Here we are. This directive is based on information provided in conversation with . . . family members . . . That's *you,* Phil. You don't mind if I call you *Phil,* do you, Mr. Dickinson?"

"Not Dickinson," Phil said. "LeGrange. Yeah, sure, you can call me Phil."

"And you, Carol."

"*I* mind," Carol said.

"That I call him Phil?" O'Neill asked.

"That you call me Carol."

O'Neill gave the grin of a shark that's been threatened with a swizzle stick.

"Look, Mrs.—"

"*Miz.*"

"—LeGrange. Or do you use your maiden name? I know it must be hard framing your brother Harry like this—"

"It's not a frame," Carol said.

"Harry *is* crazy," Phil said.

"Sure he is," O'Neill said. "*That's* why you're trying to find a legal way to get around the law."

"We only called you because we don't want to wait," Carol said.

"Don't bullshit a bullshitter," O'Neill said.

"I don't think I like you, Mr. O'Neill," Carol said.

"Isn't the legal system a bitch?" O'Neill said. "It makes you *wait*. Tell me, Phil, what is it? You get conservatorship of your brother-in-law's money when he gets locked up?"

"That's irrelevant," Carol said. "And impertinent."

"We're doing it for *him*," Phil said.

O'Neill studied Carol and Phil.

"Ten years, I been in the business of railroading relatives—crazies, grandparents, minors, once even a pet Siamese that inherited," O'Neill said, "and I never once met anyone who said they were doing it for *themselves*."

O'Neill flicked the pad.

"With this affidavit," he said, "I got almost enough to put Harry in the loony bin till he climbs into his grave and pulls the turf up to his chin. Just one more time, let him kick the dog in the balls."

O'Neill slipped the pad in his briefcase.

"Don't worry," O'Neill said. "We'll get him. Even if he is as hard to nail as your average EDP."

"EDP?" Carol asked.

"Emotionally Disturbed Person," O'Neill explained. "Fruitcake."

"I'd rather you didn't call my brother a fruitcake," Carol said.

"You don't want me to call him Phil," O'Neill said. "You don't want me to call *you* Carol. And you don't want me to call the cuckoo *fruitcake*. I'll call you all the Mormon Tabernacle Choir, as long as your check clears the bank."

O'Neill stood.

Phil got up to escort O'Neill to the door. Carol put out a restraining hand to stop him—and she made no effort of her own to be polite.

"Don't bother, Carol," O'Neill gave his shark's grin again, "I'll let myself out."

When the door closed behind O'Neill, Carol said, "He makes me feel like washing."

"You want a pal or a lawyer?" Phil asked.

"Poor Harry," Carol said.

"You want to wait until Harry does something to get himself thrown into jail?" Phil asked.

"A mental hospital," Carol said. "Jail. Is there that much difference?"

"Yes," Phil said, "there is. A lot. And if we *don't* get

Harry help, he may be *lucky* to end up in jail. Harry keeps playing detective, someday he's going to run up against someone who's not playing. You rather visit him in a hospital or a morgue?"

CHAPTER 44

In the stacks of the library, Harry ran his finger along the spines of the college yearbooks. He really didn't have to. He knew the book would be at the right end of the shelf, but he liked the feeling, like running a stick along a picket fence. Harry had never run a stick along a picket fence, but he had read about boys doing that in books when he was a kid and he had seen boys do it in movies and it struck him as an innocent and old-fashioned thing to do. He didn't think about why he wanted to do something innocent and old-fashioned.

Harry came to the 2010 annual, which he took down from the shelf.

He flipped through the pages until he came to the T's, where he found a photograph of Marian Turner, blond, pretty, similar to the woman who caught him in Marian Turner's apartment.

But *not* her.

Harry ripped out the page.

CHAPTER 45

Harry parked up the street from Marian Turner's apartment. Behind the steering wheel of his car, he was alternately sipping coffee from a paper container and eating an apple turnover, which flaked onto his shirt front, when the woman claiming to be Marian came out the front door.

Harry put down the coffee and pastry and snapped a Polaroid picture of her.

He was one of the few people in the city who still used a Polaroid. Polaroids were not used in classic hard-boiled detective novels, but it seemed more appropriate than a digital camera. And it was handy, though Harry had to search for film through mail-order firms.

The woman pretending to be Marian Turner got into a car and drove off.

Harry followed.

At the Forest Park branch of the post office—a yellow-brick building that had been constructed in the 1930s, a WPA-style eagle in bas relief over the door—the woman pretending to be Marian Turner parked and entered.

Harry parked and looked through the revolving glass doors.

She went up to the *Postal Money Orders* window and transacted some business.

Harry couldn't tell what.

She went out through the revolving door, hurrying past Harry down the steps.

Harry went into the building. As he emerged from the revolving door, he looked behind him, as if calling out to the woman.

"Okay, sweetheart," Harry said, "I'll take care of it."

The post office was nearly empty.

Harry approached the *Postal Money Order* window. He reached into his pocket, pulled out some slips of paper, and purposely tripped, spilling the paper, which he scrambled around retrieving.

At the window, Harry sorted through the dropped pieces of paper. The clerk waited.

"I had it right here," Harry said. "Damn . . . Must have lost it when I tripped. I thought I picked up everything."

"Look, chief," the clerk said, "either tell me what you want or come back when you figure it out."

"My wife . . . She was just at the window here."

"The one bought the money order, yeah, yeah?"

From his wallet, Harry took out some bills.

"She's worse than I am," he said. "Made it out twenty dollars short. Could we just add that to the money order she got?"

"Got to make out a new one," the clerk said.

"You sure?" Harry asked.

The clerk gave Harry a sour look.

Harry handed the clerk the bills.

"Same as the other," Harry said.

The clerk sighed, got the copy of the previous money order he just made out, and started writing the new one.

Reading the old money order, he recited, "'*Twenty dollars. Margaret Resnick. 16 Beechwood . . .*' What is it—street, avenue? Your wife didn't say."

Guessing, Harry said, "Street."

CHAPTER 46

Rossiter soaked in the tub, steaming water up to his chin—which, given his size, meant his legs had to be propped against the wall over the faucets. Where his thighs left the water, the difference in temperature made his legs feel cold. Even though the room was warm.

Everything's relative, he thought without knowing he thought it.

The pine salts he'd poured into the tub as he ran the water made him think of Christmas, cheeks tingling from sleet, sledding in Forest Park down Dead Man's Gulch, named sometime in the distant nineteenth century. How many generations thrilled to the name of the modest slope a hundred yards from the bandstand, leading to, in winter, a frozen rill?

"How's Linda?" Maggie asked. "And that knucklehead boyfriend of hers?"

Rossiter shrugged. Water sloshed over the side of the tub onto the tessellated floor.

"You want to eat after your bath or after you sleep?" Maggie asked. "I hate this tour."

She sat on the closed toilet seat, her elbows on her

knees, knees together, feet pigeon-toed, hair falling forward, her blouse hanging loose in front.

"How long we been married, buttercup?" Maggie asked. "You're looking down my top?"

"It's the nipple-to-breast ratio that matters," Rossiter said. "Not the size of the breasts."

"So you've said," Maggie said, leaning farther.

Rossiter flicked water down her cleavage.

She reared back and said, "Prick."

But laughed.

"Where's Chloe?" Rossiter asked.

"At piano," Maggie said. "Looking for a nooner? We have time. She won't be home till late."

Maggie studied her husband.

"You in the mood?" she asked.

"In the mood to be in the mood," he said.

Maggie nodded.

"Your periscope's down," she said. "And here I figured you were on a rekki."

"Reconnaissance," Rossiter said, "is the easy part."

"But no torpedoes loaded?" Maggie said.

Rossiter slid down until his hips were out of the water by the faucets and his head was submerged.

"We got to get a bigger tub," Maggie said out loud to herself. When Rossiter breached, water pouring from his head like dreadlocks, Maggie repeated, "We got to get a bigger tub."

"Chloe seem okay to you?" Rossiter asked, rubbing both eyes, blinking. "No outbursts? Bad temper?"

"Are you serious?" Maggie asked. "She's thirteen. Army wants to kick ass, they should send thirteen-year-old girls to Iraq, Afghanistan, wherever. Scare the holy shit out of the enemy."

"She's keeping up at school?" Rossiter asked. "Getting enough sleep?"

"Doing drugs, you mean?" Maggie asked.

"You notice anything?" Rossiter asked.

"She's high on life, your daughter," Maggie said. "Like her father."

"Do you think we could tell?" Rossiter asked. "Her world . . . What do we know? Your world . . . What do I know? You may see things different from me. I'd never know your red isn't my red."

"You're not worried about Chloe," Maggie said. "You're worried about Harry."

At last, Rossiter, water just below his chin, said, "He's got his cock in a meat grinder, and someone's going to turn on the switch." Rossiter flicked his eyes sideways at her for a second. "And I can't protect him anymore."

Maggie still waited.

"You know that guy who survived Hiroshima and escaped to Nagasaki just in time to be A-bombed twice? I feel like him. Sometimes," Rossiter said, "you have to squint at the world to see it plain."

CHAPTER 47

Harry stopped his car at a crossroad in the outskirts of Springdale. He held a city map up to catch the fading light. The creases created shadows on the map. Harry popped open the glove compartment and fished out a yellow plastic camp flashlight, which he shined first onto the map, then onto a street sign that said *Beechwood Avenue.*

"Sue me," Harry said. "I was wrong."

In the glare of the Indian Orchard Mall, Friday stopped at a store window, displaying erotic lingerie.

She entered the store.

Beechwood Avenue was in a rural area. Few houses, far apart. Harry's headlights picked out a mailbox: Number 16. A ramshackle trailer, half hidden in the weeds. Through the filthy, cracked windows, Harry saw lights. And from inside the trailer, he heard a woman singing "Blue Skies."

Harry got out of his car, walked to the door.

Across a quarter-acre of brush, half hidden behind the neighboring trailer, a strip of yellow bug-light across his feral eyes, crouched a half-naked boy, dirty white jockey shorts, so skinny even in shadow his rib cage looked like a vulture-picked carcass.

"A wild child," Harry decided, "like Mowgli. Wonder where Akela is? The wolf pack? Baloo? Bagheera? Kaa?"

Harry knocked on Number 16.

The door opened, revealing a woman—sixty-six, maybe, a beautiful face despite, maybe because of, the wrinkles. Her eyes were violet. Her mouth was full and sexy.

She was wearing a garish, multicolored Mexican skirt, a Celtics T-shirt, and a man's torn wool overcoat. She looked—and smelled—as if she hadn't bathed in months. And she was clearly drunk.

Harry asked, "Margaret Resnick?"

Inside Victoria's Secret, Friday went from rack to rack, picking out an outfit—a lacy red bustier, silk stockings, black spike heels.

Margaret Resnick sat in her trailer at the built-in table, pouring herself a shot of peppermint schnapps. Harry held up the Polaroid photograph.

"You think I don't know my own daughter?" Margaret asked.

"She says her name's Marian Turner," Harry said.

"You been busted as many times as she has," Margaret said, "you collect a lot of names." She sighed. Under her T-shirt, her bosom heaved. Absently, she straightened the cloth. "Brenda developed early. Eleven years old, she looked like a woman. Charged the boys a dollar a feel. By junior high, she was working the streets. Dropped out of high school when she got into an escort service. Two years later she was running the place."

"She ever mention a Marian Turner?" Harry asked.

"My daughter sends money every month," Margaret said, "but she doesn't come here. She's too classy. An ex-hooker. Too classy, huh."

She poured and drank another shot of schnapps. And stared into the empty glass.

"I heard you singing," Harry said.

Margaret gave him a suspicious look.

"You have a lovely voice," Harry said.

Margaret still looked at him, suspiciously.

Harry sang, *"Blue skies smiling at me / Nothing but blue skies do I see . . .* I love that song."

"That and 'There's a Small Hotel.' "

"The first time my brother-in-law heard the song, he thought it was 'There's A Small Cartel.' "

"When I was younger," Margaret said, "a lot younger, I sang in clubs. I was pretty good. Then . . ." She shrugged. "Rock and roll. No one wanted to hear 'Blue Skies.' "

"Would you sing it?" Harry asked.

Margaret studied Harry, decided he was not teasing her, and started to sing. She tilted her face to one side. Closed her eyes. Her shoulders relaxed. She glowed.

* * *

In the Victoria's Secret dressing room, Friday tried on the sexy outfit she had picked out. She vamped in front of the mirror.

CHAPTER 48

Inside Harry's office building, the elevator doors opened on his floor. Harry stepped out and saw light under his door. He eased his key into the lock, carefully turned the door knob, and burst into the room, his outer office, Friday's office—where he saw, standing awkwardly in the middle of the room, Friday wearing the outfit she bought at Victoria's Secret: lace bustier, stockings, spike heels.

"Working late?" Harry asked.

He tossed his hat onto the coatrack and showed Friday the picture of Marian Turner from the year-book and the photograph of Brenda Resnick.

"Marian Turner—Cotton's Marian Turner—is Brenda Resnick," Harry said. "I followed her, took a picture, got to her mother. . . ."

Friday didn't look at the pictures.

"Harry?"

Harry turned around.

"Look at me," Friday said.

Harry looked at her.

"You got a haircut?"

Harry picked up the telephone and dialed a number. It was an old black rotary table phone.

"Rossiter?" Harry said into the phone. "It's Harry—"

Harry's expression changed.

Slowly, he put the phone handset back in its cradle.

"He hung up on me," Harry said.

"I can understand the impulse!" Friday said.

Friday pulled on her dress. So angry that she messed her hair and smeared her makeup—and didn't even adjust the dress, which hung on her awry.

"What happened?" Harry asked. "You have to dry out your dress? You spill something?"

Harry gazed at Friday, who, still angry, kicked off her spike heels and put on flats.

"You are so beautiful," Harry said.

"What?"

Harry took Friday, now fully dressed and a mess, in his arms.

"Sometimes," he said, "it's like I'm seeing you for the first time."

Harry kissed Friday, who came out of the embrace almost awestruck at Harry's eccentricity. He's the only man who would be more turned on by her ordinary outfit than by her sexy lingerie—who, in fact, would not even notice the lingerie.

"Harry," she said, "you're amazing."

"I know," Harry said.

Again, they kissed.

"The detective," Harry said, "usually falls for the client."

"You don't have a client," Friday said.

They kissed.

"He never notices his assistant," Harry said.

"Until she takes off her glasses," Friday said.

"You don't wear glasses," Harry said.

"That saves time," Friday said.

CHAPTER 49

Friday sat on the edge of her desk, fixing her hair. Harry was tying his tie.

"After the detective notices his assistant," Friday asked, "what happens then? Happily ever after?"

"First," Harry said, "the detective solves the mystery."

"And if there *is* no mystery?"

"There's *always* a mystery."

Harry kissed Friday and headed out of the office.

"Where are you going?" Friday asked.

"Got to see a man about a hearse," Harry said.

The door closed. Then, after a moment, reopened. Harry reached in, grabbed his hat from the clothes tree, fit it on his head, pulling it low over his right eye, and closed the door behind him.

Friday hesitated. Then, she grabbed her hat and coat, turned off the light, and hurried out of the office.

CHAPTER 50

Harry came out of his building into Court Square and headed up the street. People he passed greeted him: *Hey, Harry . . . How you doin'? What's new?*

Keeping out of sight, Friday followed.

Men and women were leaving the bank building after work. Bucking the tide, Harry entered. Waiting at the elevator bank, Harry whistled a bit of Gershwin's "Treat Me Rough." When he got to the bridge, he improvised a little tap: a time step—

A passing car momentarily blocked Harry. Friday leaned to the right to keep him in view.

—a shuffle. Flap, flap, flap. Ball charge. Step kick left. Step kick right. A traveling Irish with a ball change. Big finish.

The elevator door slid open.

Harry stepped onto the elevator.

Friday entered the lobby and pressed the elevator button.

On the eleventh floor, Cotton's door was ajar. Inside the office, a dim light glowed. Harry eased the door open and slipped in.

As before, the outer office was dark. The door to the private office was open.

Inside the room, the desk light was on. Against the far wall was the shadow of someone holding what looked like a sap raised over his head.

"*Drop it!*" Harry shouted as he burst in—on a janitor who dropped his pint bottle of rye—the man and the sap in the shadow.

"Just wetting the whistle, chief," the janitor said.

Friday entered.

"What the hell are you doing?" she said.

CHAPTER 51

Outside the bank building, Harry and Friday stood on the sidewalk.

"Are you out of your mind?" Friday asked. "What am I saying? Of course you are."

"Pillette got here before us," Harry said. Confidently.

"He probably did," Friday said. "For all we know so did Cotton's electrician, plumber, and landscaper. . . . Harry, you're out of control."

"Don't worry, Friday," Harry said, chucking her on the chin with a knuckle.

"That's all I do," Friday said. "What are you looking for?"

"Evidence," Harry said.

"Of what?" Friday asked.

"Of man's inhumanity to man," Harry said.

"Oh, Harry," Friday said.

Harry got into his Packard and drove away, as Friday watched.

PART TEN

Out in the world the ugly sound continued and would be a long time dying.

—Allen Drury
The Promise of Joy

CHAPTER 52

"Lee!" Friday called as she let herself into the kitchen, juggling two brown paper grocery bags. "I got some nice tilapia at the Price Chopper."

Lee didn't answer.

Friday left the groceries on the kitchen table and called down into the basement, "Lee. Do you want your fish pan-fried?"

Friday heard Lee, upstairs, cough.

Climbing the stairs, she said, "You want bread crumbs or panko? I know, I know. Bread crumbs. You hate change. That's a hell of a note for a revolutionist."

In his bedroom, Lee grunted.

Friday found him struggling to sit up in bed. He was in his blue striped pajamas under the covers, three pillows crumpled behind him.

"In the middle of the afternoon," Friday said. "How long have you been asleep?" And then more seriously, "You look like hell."

Lee coughed into the back of his right hand, writhed out from under the covers until he was sitting up against the pillows.

"Jack Kennedy used to nap in pajamas every day after lunch," he said.

Lee threw back the covers, swung his legs around so they hung over the side of the bed, and started to stand.

"I figured I'll fry it up in some beer batter," Friday said. "I got a six-pack of Theakston."

But Lee had dropped to the floor as if he'd been sapped.

CHAPTER 53

Harry's big purple Packard sailed up Main Street, anachronistic among the small, contemporary cars. A dinosaur among ducks. From a tape player on the front seat next to Harry came Ella Fitzgerald and Chick Webb's "Sing Me a Swing Song."

In Longmeadow, Springdale's rich suburb—big Tudor houses set back on two-acre plots—Harry parked the Packard and got out.

Leaves covering the front lawn swirled up and, turning into small birds, took flight. The breeze held a taint of manure from someone's garden.

CHAPTER 54

"Your father has a bleeding ulcer," the emergency room doctor told Friday. "He's losing a lot of blood."

Hand on Friday's elbow, the doctor steered Friday through the curtains around Lee's bed.

"He needs a transfusion," the doctor said.

"I heard that," Lee called out. "You think the curtain's made of cinder blocks?"

Friday twitched back the curtain. Lee thrashed, dislodging the oxygen clip in his nose.

"I don't want scab blood!" Lee shouted. "You get me a union donor. And I want to see his card. Or you let me die!"

CHAPTER 55

Lights were on in one wing of Cotton's house. Harry edged along the terrace to the French doors. Cast on the white curtains covering the doors were two shadows, like the ones Harry saw on the wall of Cotton's office.

Harry put his ear to the glass. From inside, he heard Cotton's and Pillette's voices.

"—lucky last night," Pillette was saying.

"This is the last payment," Cotton said. "You've bled me enough, Pillette."

"I haven't begun," Pillette said.

Pillette's shadow advanced on Cotton, as Harry kicked in the French doors.

Startled, Pillette turned toward Harry, as Cotton pulled a gun from an open wall safe. Brenda stood by, wrapping a strand of hair around her right forefinger.

Harry stopped.

Cotton aimed, not at him, but at Pillette.

"You're an embezzler, Cotton," Pillette said. "Not a killer."

"I'm a Renaissance man," Cotton said.

Cotton pulled the trigger.

Pillette—shot in the chest—fell backward over a chair. Cotton turned his gun on Harry and approached. With his free hand, he frisked Harry.

"Last night," Harry said, "the cops took my gun."

"Well, I've got mine," Cotton said. "And—unlike you, Harry—I'll use it. Even if you *are* unarmed."

"Boy, Cotton, did you ever botch this thing up," Brenda said.

"It was a good plan," Cotton said. "You'd have to be crazy to be suspicious."

"I guess we lucked out," Brenda said.

"Brenda, I saw your mom today," Harry said. "She's got a wonderful voice."

"Shit, Cotton," Brenda said, "he knows who I am. We've got to kill him."

"You think he's just a john you can roll," Cotton asked.

"You prick," Brenda said.

"That's uncalled for, Cotton," Harry said. "Brenda's mom told me how Brenda pulled herself out of the streets, ended up running a service, and look at her now . . . Well dressed, elegant. Out of the low life, involved with a prominent lawyer. I think she's done pretty well for herself."

"He's right," Brenda said. "I'm not some whore you can insult."

"Pillette," Cotton said, "we can get rid of him, because no one cares. Turner, no one knew. This one . . . He's got relatives, friends. . . . Anyway, we don't have to kill him. Who's going to believe him?" To Harry, Cotton said, "Turn around."

Hands raised, Harry turned his back to Cotton.

"You're going to ruin your pitching arm," Harry

said. "Why don't we sit down and discuss this. Like gentlemen. Over a meal. A good meal."

"You can stall as much as you want, Harry," Cotton said.

"A spectacular meal," Harry said.

"The cavalry's asleep at the fort," Cotton said.

"Mushrooms à la grecque. Jellied eggs, jellied beef, jellied pigeon, jellied pheasant, jellied partridge, jellied duck, little lobsters in lettuce, shrimp in aspic, whelks in wine, limpets in brine, oysters, mussels, crab and asparagus, crayfish in butter, salade niçoise, salade à la d'Argenson, tongue and tomato, ratatouille, pickled prawns, turnips Lyonnaise, à la reine, à la russe, creamed Brussels sprouts, shallots à la suisse, *endive en sauce dure, chou-fleur en verdure,* artichokes au gratin with parsley, Egyptian peas sprinkled with chives, Algerian beans, Sudanese greens, eel pâté, lamprey pâté, salmon pâté, turbot pâté, blackbird pâté with truffles, lark pâté, hare pâté, quail pâté with fois gras, woodcock pâté, thrush pâté, sweetbread pâté with mushrooms and Velouté sauce, glazed suckling pigs, a whole lamb, huge lobsters, veal Prince Orloff, six geese, braised duck, tiny white potatoes, coquilles Saint-Jacques and escargot maison, cheeses colored like cornflowers, orchids, dandelions, goldenrod, jonquils, violets, Bries runny as phlegm, Vimoutiers, Camembert, Corsican Asco, *Oude Kaas*, Edam, Gouda Etuve, Munster Gerome, with aniseed, fennel, caraway, goat cheese in bay leaves, in grape leaves, in lemon leaves, bloodred Livarot and black Pra-Perron, Pont-l'Eveque, Port-Salut, rum-flavored Brunet, late Cachat, early Amou, magenta Gros Perre, Bavarian creams, carmel custards, apple charlotte, tartes aux peche, tartes aux

pommes, kumquats, loquats, mangos, melons, lion's-
foot grapes, grapes from Badau, Medici, Frankenthal,
long Black Spanish, Chasselas, Black Alicante, sultanas,
figs, dates, apricots, candied orange rinds, candied
lemon rinds, candied lime rinds, candied plums, gua-
vas, papayas, pineapples, pomegranates, gooseberries
in sherry, quince in white wine, black currants, and
Rire de Mort."

Cotton whacked Harry on the side of the head
with his gun.

CHAPTER 56

When Friday clicked off her cell phone, Lee, stabilized with union blood, sitting up in bed, in a double room with no roommate, reading—and with a stubby pencil furiously annotating—a Christopher Hitchens book, asked, "Harry?"

"He broke into the banker's house," Friday said.

"Banker, huh?" Lee said. "I hope he did a lot of damage."

"Harry's the one who was damaged," Friday said.

"I'll be okay," Lee said. "Sounds like the guy needs you."

CHAPTER 57

It felt as if a pane of glass had shattered on Harry's face.

But glass wasn't cold.

Glass wasn't wet.

Harry jumped up, water streaming over his face, down his shirt, which stuck to his chest.

He plucked away the soaked cloth. Shook his head, blinked water out of his eyes.

Rossiter stood in the middle of the living room holding an empty, dripping saucepan.

Harry fished in his right hip pocket and pulled out his handkerchief, which he used to scrub his face and wipe the top of his head. Harry stuffed the handkerchief, damp, back into his hip pocket.

Friday and Carol helped Harry stretch out on the couch in Cotton's library. Rossiter, Cotton, Phil, Bender, and two uniformed cops stood in a semicircle around them.

The room was neat. Everything—from the shiv-shaped letter opener to the crystal paperweight—was where it should be. The room smelled of some kind of air freshener. Or disinfectant cleaner.

There was no sign of Pillette's murder.

Where the wall safe had been was an oil painting—an imitation of Constable—of cows nose-to-tail heading back to a barn.

"Harry," Rossiter said, "you got to find another hobby."

"So does Cotton," Harry said.

When he sat up, he winced.

"The gang's all here," he said.

"Breaking-and-entering," Rossiter said. "Second time in twenty-four hours."

"This time, Detective," Cotton said, "I'm afraid I'm going to have to press charges."

Harry surveyed the room.

"Where's Brenda?" he asked.

"Who?" Rossiter asked.

"Where's Pillette?" Harry asked. "The body?"

"There's no body, Harry," Friday said.

"Where's the gun?" Harry asked.

"Can you manage it out to the car?" Rossiter asked.

"Try the wall safe," Harry said. "Maybe the gun's in there. Behind the painting."

"Detective, please," Cotton said. "It's late. I have an early morning appointment."

"Indulge me," Rossiter said.

Cotton swung the painting away from the wall, opened the safe, and stood back.

Rossiter approached the safe.

"May I?" he asked Cotton, who waved his hand in a be-my-guest gesture.

Rossiter went through the safe's contents.

"Bonds, a will, an envelope"—he waved it at Cotton—"filled with cash?"

"I'll open it," Cotton said. "Count it in front of you. If you want."

"Harry," Rossiter said. "There's no body. There's no gun."

"He hid it, got rid of it while I was out," Harry said.

"Is there any other way I can assist you?" Cotton asked Rossiter.

"Brenda's mom," Harry said. "The trailer."

CHAPTER 58

Outside Cotton's house, a row of cars started up and slowly drove along the street: two squad cars, Carol and Phil's Subaru, Friday's Tercel, and Rossiter's Impala.

"You ever hear the story about the boy who cried 'wolf,' Harry?" Rossiter asked. He didn't look at Harry, who sat next to him. In handcuffs. Loosely attached.

"Sure, Rossiter," Harry said. "In the end, there really was a wolf."

CHAPTER 59

Harry led the two uniformed cops, Rossiter, Friday, Carol, and Phil to Margaret Resnick's trailer. Harry caught sight of Mowgli—in a red and blue Hilfiger T-shirt and baggy khakis—disappearing into the neighboring trailer. One of the cops knocked on Resnick's door. No answer. He knocked again. Inside, a light went on. After a while, the door was opened by an old man, clearly in his late eighties, who looked as if he'd been asleep in his overalls.

"We're looking for Margaret Resnick," Rossiter said.

The old man mumbled something incomprehensible, then made a wait-a-minute gesture, searched in his pockets and found his false teeth, which he put in.

"It's the middle of the night," the old man said.

"Margaret Resnick?" Rossiter repeated.

"No one by that name here," the old man said.

"She lives here," Harry said.

"Nope," the old man said.

"I was here this afternoon," Harry said.

The old man looked Harry up and down.

"Nope," he said.

Harry started into the house, but was restrained by Rossiter, who asked the old man, "You mind if we look around?"

The old man shrugged.

Rossiter and the others entered the single room—the room in which Harry had visited Resnick.

Except Resnick was not there.

And there was no sign of any female presence.

"I've lived here twenty years," the old man said. "Never heard of no Margaret Resnick."

Harry looked at Rossiter, shrugged, and said, "*Wolf.*"

Rossiter told one of the cops, "Get Bender on the radio. Tell him we'll meet him at the hospital."

CHAPTER 60

Springdale Municipal Court. Part A.

Judge Harry Loomis presiding. A youngish-looking man, graying blond with a cowlick, and indigo eyes, dark like a computer's Blue Screen of Death.

"Docket ending 638," the bridgeman was saying. "The People versus Truman Anton on a 195.00—official misconduct—and 195.05—obstructing governmental administration."

"Counsel," Loomis said, "for the record, state your name."

Harry surveyed the room.

The court had been built during the Depression and above the bench had a mural of a Pilgrim and an Indian lounging on either side of the Massachusetts State Seal. Around their feet, spilling from a curdled-cream-colored cornucopia were pumpkins, squash, corn, apples, and grapes. To the right of the Indian, railroads branched out across plains and farms to distant mountains. Muscular farmers steered plows pulled by blocky oxen. To the left of the Pilgrim, factories and dynamos and blast furnaces, rank upon rank, led to distant cities with towering skyscrapers.

Muscular factory workers hammered red-hot steel plates. Airplanes crowded the skies.

Harry noted the absence of muscular bankers.

"I'm informed the defendant has a hundred twenty thousand equity in his house," Loomis was saying. He pronounced *defendant* with the accent on the last syllable. "I'm setting bail at one hundred thousand dollars."

The room had high ceilings and, below the ceilings, walnut paneling. The bottom two-thirds of the wall had been renovated in the 1970s with an institutional, nondescript substance that looked—to Harry—like pine-patterned plastic.

Loomis sighed. "Next?"

Harry stood before the bench. To one side was O'Neill. A little behind them were Rossiter and Bender.

Friday, Carol, and Phil sat on molded orange plastic chairs, watching the proceedings.

Harry could smell O'Neill's lilac aftershave.

"Pinaud Clubman Vegetal," Harry said to O'Neill. "You got that from the barbershop on the corner of Webster and Hollins, I'll bet."

"Mr. Dickinson has a clean sheet," Loomis said.

"Only place I know still uses the stuff," Harry said to O'Neill.

"Roots in the community," Loomis said.

"I like that," Harry told O'Neill.

"Mr. Dickinson," Loomis said.

"Mom-and-pop business," Harry explained to Loomis.

"I know the shop," Loomis said.

"Needs all the custom it can get," Harry said.

"Farley's," Loomis said.

"Corner of Webster—"

"And Hollins."

"Jimmy Farley's what?" Harry said. "Must be eighty-five."

"Eighty-seven," Loomis said. "He's been cutting my hair since I was a kid."

"Me, too," Harry said. "Used to get a crew cut."

Loomis smiled at his own memories.

"My brother used a wax stick to make the front hairs stick up. No Mohawks. No pink tints, dye . . . Another world."

"Dodgers still in Brooklyn," Harry said.

"You got me there, Mr. Dickinson," Loomis said. "I don't go back that far."

"Neither do I," Harry said. "But it's nice to think of back then."

Loomis sighed again and said, "Yeah. Back then . . ."

"Jock Whitney invented the crew cut," Harry said. "Or named it."

"He from Classical?" Loomis asked about the high school.

"Out of town," Harry said.

"Your Honor," O'Neill interrupted.

"Is this the man who . . . ?" Loomis glanced at the bridgeman. "Is this the 5150?"

"I'm the 5150," Harry said. "The consensus is: I may be a danger to myself or others."

"Are you?" Loomis asked.

"A danger to malefactors, punks, miscreants, yeggs?" Harry said. "Absolutely!"

"Yeggs?" Loomis asked.

"Burglars," Friday said.

Loomis looked at her. Sharply.

She met his gaze.

"Yeggs, huh?" Loomis said. And studied Harry.

"Normally," Loomis said, resuming his official tone, "I'd be inclined to let Mr. Dickinson go under his own recognizance. But . . ." Loomis picked up a sheet of paper. He looked over his half-glasses at Carol and Phil's lawyer, Jack O'Neill, and said, "Mr. O'Neill, this affidavit?"

"A history lesson," O'Neill said.

"I can see that," Loomis said.

"Tonight," O'Neill said, "the cuckoo did a banana job. Par for the course."

Loomis picked up another document—commitment papers—and, scanning the courtroom, said, "Dr. Bender?"

Bender stood up.

"We have the clinic van outside," he said.

Loomis sighed.

"My opinion," O'Neill said under his breath, half-turning to Phil, "no one wants it, but your brother-in-law's on his face, and the count is nine."

"Given the circumstances," Loomis said, "I'm going to remand Mr. Dickinson over to an appropriate psychiatric facility for observation."

Loomis banged his gavel.

"They can only hold you initially, Mr. Dickinson," Loomis told Harry, "for seventy-two hours."

"You look like you could use a trim," Harry said to Loomis, who touched his hair. "Give my best to Jimmy."

"Will do," Loomis said. "And, Mr. Dickinson . . ."

Harry smiled.

"Good luck," Loomis said. Then: "Next case."

PART ELEVEN

There is a Smile of Love
And there is a Smile of Deceit
And there is a Smile of Smiles
In which these two Smiles meet.

—William Blake
"The Smile"

CHAPTER ELEVEN

CHAPTER 61

Sun sparkled on the mica in the stone steps of the courthouse. Friday squinted in the glare. Plante hurried across the street toward her.

"Not now, Sonny," Friday said.

"When?" Plante asked.

"Never," Friday said.

Friday started to move around Plante, who blocked her.

"Linda," Plante said, "I know I must look like an ambulance-chaser at the accident. But it's over. Harry's never going to be there for you. Not in the way you want him to be."

"Don't," Friday said.

"And I know," Plante said, "even if I *do* convince you, I'm *still* running a distant second."

"Please," Friday said, trying to get around him.

"If a miracle happened and you agreed to marry me—" Plante started.

"Sonny." Friday stopped and faced Plante.

"—every day, every minute of every day," Plante continued, "I'll know you'd be wishing it was Harry. How do you think that would make me feel? But

I love you so much I'm willing to put up with that, to *be* second choice. Doesn't that count for anything?"

"Yes, Sonny, yes, it does," Friday said. "I wish I could just accept. Accept that I can never have Harry, not the way I want. Accept it—and be sensible and marry you. I wish I could. For *both* our sakes. But I can't."

Friday walked off.

"I hope," Plante called after her, "the hospital has long visiting hours."

CHAPTER 62

Carol, Phil, and Bender walked diagonally down the courthouse steps, angling toward the parking garage.

Friday intercepted Bender.

"Will he ever be better?" she asked.

"Valproate," Bender said. "It's an anti-convulsive. We dose Harry up. Within a day, maybe two, the delusions begin to vanish."

"It's that easy?" Carol asked.

"Or Clozaril," Bender said. "Just as effective. Just as quick. Or Phenolal. Similar. But even more effective. Schizophrenics who've taken it have been out there for years. Twenty-four hours, completely changed."

"Changed?" Friday asked.

"The advantage is you don't have to keep giving it," Bender said. "One dose and—" He snapped his fingers. "Symptoms abate. A miracle."

"This miracle," Friday asked, "one dose and . . . Is it irreversible?"

"In many cases," Bender said, "yes."

"Many cases?" Friday said.

"It's for the best," Carol said to Friday. "For him. For you. They'll straighten him out. You'll finally be able to get on with your life."

"He has to cooperate, doesn't he?" Phil asked.

"Have you ever known Harry to be difficult?" Friday said.

"He's always difficult!" Phil said.

"He's a people-pleaser," Carol said.

"I suppose that's one way to describe it," Friday said. To Bender, she said, "He'll cooperate."

"There's more than one way to skin a cat," Bender said.

"I wonder what the cat thinks about that," Friday said.

Harry came down the courthouse steps with Rossiter and two cops. Rossiter saw Friday and gestured to the uniformed cops to leave Harry and Friday alone for a moment.

"Seventy-two hours," Harry said, "and I'll be out, get back to work."

"They have a drug," Friday said. "If you take it, you could . . ."

Friday hesitated.

"Could what?" Harry asked.

Friday, near tears, couldn't answer.

"Friday, I'm a good detective," Harry said. "From the evidence, I'd say you want me to take this drug."

Without meeting Harry's eyes, Friday nodded her head.

"Happy to oblige," Harry said.

"Pack a suitcase for him," Bender told Carol. "Comfortable clothes. A bathrobe. Pajamas."

Two burly psychiatric orderlies led Harry away. The first orderly stumbled as he lost the heel of his left shoe.

Harry picked up the broken heel, which he handed to the first orderly, who said, "Into the van, sport."

"Give me a minute," Harry said.

He shook hands with Rossiter.

"Come visit," he said.

"Sure, Harry," Rossiter said.

Harry turned to Carol.

"Sis," he said.

"If there was any other way . . . ," Carol said.

Harry gave her a kiss, turned to Phil and said, "I'll even miss you, you son of a bitch."

They shook hands.

"Get better, Harry," Phil said.

Harry turned to Friday—who broke down.

"Oh, Harry," she sobbed.

They embraced.

"Hey," Harry said, "I've been in tougher jams than this."

Harry adjusted his hat, which he pulled low over his right eye, and climbed into the van. One of the orderlies slammed and locked the door. He joined the other in the front of the van.

Bender waved them on. The van drove off.

"If he takes the drug tonight," he said, "by tomorrow morning, Harry could be normal. Just like everyone else."

"Yeah," Friday said, wiping her eyes and nose with a handkerchief. "Just like everyone else."

CHAPTER 63

Harry sat on one of the two facing built-in benches that ran along the van's side, singing, *"Don't know why there's no sun up in the sky / Stormy weather / Since my gal and I ain't together / Keeps raining all the time . . ."*

Friday watched the van drive away, its brake lights blinking once before the van turned the corner at the end of the block.

Her tears made it hard for her to fit the key in her car door. Rossiter came up beside her, took the key, unlocked the door, and handed the key back.

"Let me buy you a drink," Rossiter said.

Twenty minutes later, Friday sat in a booth across from Rossiter. A candle flickered in a red-tinted dimpled-glass hurricane lamp.

"Harry will be just like everyone else," Friday said. "That's what Bender said. Do *you* want Harry to be just like everyone else?"

"The world is crappy," Rossiter said.

"But Harry turns the crap into adventure," Friday said. "Romance."

Friday finished her drink, scotch, Glenmorangie. Gestured to the waitress for a refill.

"Crazy," Friday said. She shrugged. "Maybe he is."

The waitress brought Friday's refill.

Rossiter repeated, "The world is crappy."

Friday took a thoughtful sip of her drink.

"But Harry's in shape," Friday said. "How the hell could Cotton knock him out?"

"Don't start," Rossiter said.

"Unless—" Friday began.

"What?" Rossiter said. "There *was* a body? A gun in the wall safe? Cotton's a killer? Nothing is what it seems? *This* is what happens when you hang out too much with Harry."

"It does," Friday agreed. "*If* you're lucky."

CHAPTER 64

Phil parked his three-year-old Subaru in the driveway of their house. Carol looked through the passenger-side window at the big wedding-cake Victorian. The low sun reflecting off the glass made all the windows blind.

"Well," she said, "it's done."

"Should have been done years ago," Phil said.

They got out of the car and walked to the kitchen door, which Phil unlocked.

"It's going to be lonely," she said.

"Harry's a big boy," Phil said. "He can handle it."

"I was talking about me," Carol said.

CHAPTER 65

The van stopped in the circular drive in front of a low, modern building, vaguely collegiate. Like the administration offices of a well-endowed state university.

The Indian Orchard Wellness Center. Recently renamed. For the previous hundred years, it had been called the Indian Orchard Clinic for Psychopathology.

The orderlies jumped out and opened the van's back doors.

"Let's go, sport," the first orderly said to Harry, who emerged from the back of the van and jumped down to the ground with a flourish.

"Your broken shoe," Harry said.

The orderlies walked Harry toward the clinic's front entrance.

"A friend of mine—" Harry said.

"Get a move on," the first orderly said.

"Nunez," Harry said. "Diogenes Nunez. He could fix that shoe right up. What's your name?"

"Beausejour," the first orderly said. "Pete Beausejour."

"Nunez could make that shoe just like new, Pete,"

Harry said. "Court Square Shoe Shine. Tell him I sent you."

"This guy's going into the nuthouse, and he's worried about *me*!" the first orderly said to the second orderly. To Harry, he said, "Dickinson, you're really something!"

"So are you, Pete," Harry said. To the second orderly, Harry said, "So are you. Fact is, I never met someone who wasn't."

The first orderly shook his head in amusement and incredulity at Harry's good humor, as he tapped a code on a metal keypad and opened the door to the clinic.

CHAPTER 66

Outside the bar at Court Square, Rossiter steadied Friday, who took a deep breath and a wobbly step toward her car.

"Let me drive you home," Rossiter said.

"I'll be fine," Friday said.

Friday lurched toward her car, unlocked the door. She had trouble climbing behind the driver's wheel. Rossiter looked on, gnawing his lower lip. Finally, Friday gave up getting into the car. She slammed the door.

"I'll get a cab," she said.

Rossiter hesitated.

"Six years old," Friday said with great dignity.

Rossiter gave her a puzzled look.

"Last time I had a babysitter," Friday explained.

Rossiter raised his hands shoulder high in an *okay-okay* gesture and tilted his head.

"Call if—"

"If what?" Friday asked. "If I run across any mysteries? The only mystery is why Harry's locked up and someone like that lawyer, O'Neill, isn't."

"O'Neill's not dangerous," Rossiter said.

"He was," Friday said, "to Harry."

Rossiter headed up the street, stopped, and turned. Friday waved. Rossiter continued up the street. Out of sight.

CHAPTER 67

In the living room, Phil sat in his chair, reading the newspaper. Carol wandered about the room—adjusting a knickknack on the mantel, straightening a picture frame, picking up and putting down a throw pillow.

"It's out of our hands," Phil finally said.

"*You* didn't want him locked up?" Carol asked.

Phil shrugged.

"The courts did it," he said.

"We *let* them do it," Carol said.

The doorbell rang. Carol crossed the room into the hall and opened the front door. Outside was the UPS man and a young red-haired woman.

"My wife, Joy," he said to Carol.

Joy carried a child in her arms. Another child stood beside her, holding out a foil-wrapped package.

"It's still warm," the kid said.

"My wife and kids," the UPS man said. "She baked the bread from scratch."

The child handed the package to Carol, who, bewildered, took it.

"Bread," she said.

"Is this a bad time?" Joy asked.

Joy glanced at her husband for help.

"We just wanted to give this to Mr. Dickinson," the UPS man said. "To Harry."

"To thank him," Joy said, "for . . ."

Again, Joy glanced at her husband for help.

"He'll know," the UPS man said. To his wife, he said, "We better hurry or we'll miss the movie."

They started to leave. But Joy paused, turned back to Carol.

"Your brother must be a remarkable man," she said.

Joy hurried down the porch steps after her husband and child. Clutching the bread, Carol gazed after her.

"Yes," Carol said. "He must be."

CHAPTER 68

Rossiter's hangout, Chip's, smelled of sour beer and old grease. The knotty pine walls were covered with fading photographs, yellowed, curling newspaper headlines, fly-specked business cards stuck randomly to the wood with rusty flat-head tacks.

At the far end of the bar, two men sat with beers, talking sports. Halfway down the bar sat Ruby, a busty twenty-two-year-old blond hooker in high heels, a miniskirt, a tea-colored rayon blouse, and a waist-length fur jacket. She had a hacking cough.

Rossiter smiled: Harry would dress her up, he thought to himself. Turn the cough into TB and the hooker into Camille, a tragic heroine he'd try to save.

He sat a few stools down from Ruby.

He *would* save, Rossiter added to himself. Yeah, he thought, he'd dream up all sorts of fantasies for her, but he'd try to do something for her, too.

He nodded.

"That's more than most people would do," he said out loud without realizing it.

"What's that?" the bartender asked.

"Johnny Walker Black," Rossiter said.

The bartender poured the drink and clapped it in front of Rossiter, who took a sip.

He glanced at Ruby, who gave him a tentative smile.

"You ready for a refill?" he asked her.

"Stinger," she said.

The right side of her mouth pulled down as if she were a stroke survivor.

To the bartender, Rossiter repeated, "Stinger."

"I heard," said the bartender, who made the drink and put it in front of Ruby.

"Ruby," she said. "What's yours?"

"Brian," Rossiter said.

"You a cop?" Ruby asked.

"Off duty," Rossiter replied.

"Nowhere to go?"

Rossiter nodded.

"You live in the neighborhood?"

Rossiter nodded.

Ruby shrugged and said, "We're both local. That makes us neighbors."

CHAPTER 69

Harry sat on a ladder-back chair in the clinic intake office. Across a desk from him sat an officious woman with luxurious dark hair, done with a 1940s curl—Anne Thurber—who was filling out a form on her computer.

"Social Security Number?" Thurber asked.

Harry recited the numbers.

"Insurance carrier?"

Harry didn't answer. Thurber glanced up from her monitor to find Harry scrutinizing her.

"Mr. Dickinson?" she said.

Still, Harry didn't answer. He studied her.

"Are you all right?" she asked.

"I've been trying to figure out who you remind me of," Harry said.

"Mr. Dickinson," Thurber said. She cleared her throat meaningfully.

"It's the hairstyle," Harry said.

Thurber returned to the form.

"Insurance carrier?" she asked.

Harry snapped his fingers.

"Laraine Day," Harry said. "In *Mr. Lucky.*"

"Laraine Who?" Thurber said. "Mr. What?"

"In the beginning of the movie," Harry said. "When she's keeping watch on the docks. Waiting for Cary Grant. Everyone else thinks he's gone for good. But she believes in him. Believes he'll come back." Harry cocked his head to the side. "I'll bet *you* have something . . . In your past. An intrigue. Some secret love . . ."

"No," Thurber said.

But she blushed.

"Someone everyone else has given up on—" Harry said.

"No," Thurber said.

"—but not you," Harry said.

Thurber dropped her eyes. She folded her hands on her lap.

"My fiancé," she said. "Five years ago, he disappeared in Afghanistan. MIA. Everyone says he's dead."

"I *knew* it," Harry said. "You *are* a mystery woman."

When Thurber looked up at Harry, her eyes glistened.

CHAPTER 70

Friday sat on the marble steps leading up to Symphony Hall. Behind and above her were a dozen columns, ridged like celery stalks; the carved leafy acanthus of each column's capital also looking celery-like in the fading light. The clock in the campanile rang six. The breeze carried a peppery scent, which made Friday sneeze.

When Friday was a child, her parents took her regularly to the monthly Thursday night concerts. They sat in their regular box, stage right. Last year, not having been to the symphony for years, decades, she called to arrange a subscription for the monthly Thursday performances, but they'd been discontinued. Not enough demand.

The cold of the stone steps seeped through her skirt into her skin.

The kiosk that sold hot chocolate when Porter Lake froze went out of business in the eighties. The heat from the cardboard cup had penetrated her wool mittens. The cocoa had burned her lips and the tip of her tongue and made a ball of fire in her throat— deliciously contrasted with her numb cheeks and freezing eyelids. Skating was discontinued a few years after.

Around the same time, the city stopped paying to keep up the maze of rose arbors in Forest Park, where she and Harry used to stroll in the summer, drenched in the perfume of roses, the vines and blossoms making complicated shadows on their faces. What was left now was a tumble-down row of rotting wood and thick, pulpy, overgrown rose stalks.

From half-a-dozen blocks away, cars whined past on the interstate: A constant bagpipe drone that, since the highway had been built in the fifties, had become the downtown's sound track. Because of the highway, passing traffic now avoided the town. Hotels and restaurants closed. Every third or fourth bulb was burned out in the lights along Main Street—turn-of-the-century Bishop's Crook lamps, which hung over like the Indian pipes growing in the marshes on the edge of Friday's property, down by Snake Creek.

The cold air touched her inner thighs.

Friday squeezed her legs together.

More than half of the branch libraries had shut. The museums were opened only three days a week.

What happened?

During their last high school reunion, 90 percent of the class came in from out of town. Harry, Friday, and Rossiter were among a handful who didn't leave after graduation.

Almost everyone else had left. To New York City. Boston. Washington. Chicago. Seattle. Austin. San Francisco.

Of course, the city would begin to die.

For Harry, none of this mattered. The main library

still felt like home. The museums may have reduced their hours, but when they were open, they still were a refuge. At Symphony Hall, the few, occasional remaining concerts were a treat. In the winter, Harry enjoyed carrying a thermos of hot chocolate. He'd find half-hidden ponds, which he'd shovel clear; they'd skate in secret, private spots.

Harry would stroll through the broken-down rose arbors, thrilled by what he described as the Gothic neglect: all the park needed was a hermit in his hermitage.

The rerouted traffic on Route 91, Harry figured, protected the town from becoming part of the East Coast Megalopolis. Libraries and museum hours became, in their scarcity, more valuable. He, Friday, and Rossiter shared a bond by staying in Springdale.

Friday shivered, crossed her arms, and scrunched up her shoulders for warmth.

Harry made no effort to turn the grim into gold. The grim—the real—was magical enough. It was just how he saw things. A gift—Friday thought—he shared with those around him.

Being committed to the mental hospital—how would Harry transform that into romance?

Not hard, Friday told herself: mysteries often had a detective locked away and doped up in a sanitarium.

Friday smiled.

Yeah, she thought, even this could be part of Harry's fantasy.

Until the drug kicked in.

PART TWELVE

Who put the sodium amytal in the Hill & Hill?

—Nelson Algren
"The Captain Has Bad Dreams"

CHAPTER 71

Rossiter came out of the bar with Ruby, who shivered even though it wasn't that cold.

"At your place?" she asked. "You have anything to drink?"

"My place is too far," Rossiter said.

"Mine's not," she said. "I got a bottle of Jack."

She coughed.

"Some cold you got?" Rossiter said.

Ruby shrugged.

"You okay with a hundred?" she asked. She pronounced it *hunner-ed*. "And ten for carfare."

"You live in the neighborhood," Rossiter said.

"Sure," she said, "but not this neighborhood."

"Don't hustle me, Ruby," Rossiter said.

"Then," she said, "don't go all cop on me."

Rossiter started to say something. But Ruby stopped, leaned over, and gave in to a spasm of coughs.

"This cold," Rossiter asked. "How long have you had it?"

"My roommate says it's maybe bronchitis," Ruby said.

"You ought to go to a doctor," he said.

"I got so many's I *ought* to do," she said.

She coughed again, gasping for breath.

Rossiter stepped into the street to hail a cab.

"Let's get you to a hospital," he said.

"What about the session?" she said. "Don't beat me for the money, mister."

"Brian," Rossiter reminded her.

"Sure," Ruby said. "Mine's—"

"Ruby," Rossiter said.

"That," she said, "is a first."

Up the block, a cab with a vacant light on turned the corner.

"Mostly," she said, "guys don't remember. I mean, why should they? Look, I appreciate the thought, but I only booked one session tonight. I got rent, you know. I got to put in my time."

"The visit to the doctor," Rossiter said. "We'll put it on the clock."

"The emergency room?" Ruby asked. "The whole *nine*?"

Rossiter checked his wallet.

"I've got enough for three hours," he said, handing her the money. "After that, the doctor hasn't examined you yet, you're on your own."

The cab stopped next to them.

"I like you," Ruby said.

Rossiter held the cab door open for her and said, "I'm a regular Prince Charming."

CHAPTER 72

Two male nurses led Harry down an antiseptic, pale green hallway that smelled of pine disinfectant.

"You got one of the rooms with cable," one of the male nurses said.

"What's your name?" Harry asked.

"Why?" the nurse asked. "You unhappy about something?"

"Mine's Harry," Harry said.

He stuck out his hand, which the nurse looked at, pulling back his chin.

"Dickinson," Harry added.

Harry kept his hand out.

"Leon," the nurse said at last, quickly taking and quickly releasing Harry's hand.

"Glad to make your acquaintance, Leon," Harry said. Turning to the other nurse, Harry held out his hand.

"Lex Luthor," the other nurse said.

"You an evil genius, Lex?" Harry asked.

"You bet, Superman," the other nurse said. "What the fuck you want my name for?"

"You get a lot of lawsuits here?" Harry asked.

"Only from the patients who start out nice," Lex said. "After a few days, they get that I'm not their new best friend, I'm a nurse, and they get bent out of shape."

"It must be hard on you," Harry said, "handling all that hope."

They stopped at a door, which Leon opened.

The bedroom was about fifteen by eighteen feet. Plain. A bureau, a chair, a desk, a bed. Functional furniture. What you might find in a medium-range motel.

When Harry twitched back the yellow curtain, he found bars over the glass.

"Okay, Dickinson," Leon said. "You're home."

CHAPTER 73

Lee was sleeping when Friday slipped back into his hospital room.

"Give it a day or so," the nurse had said. "See how he's doing. Then, you can take him home."

Her breath was minty. Inadequately covering up cigarettes.

"All my men are in hospitals," Friday said.

"Umm," the nurse, half-listening, said.

When Friday sank into the tan Haitian-cotton-covered chair, Lee mumbled something indistinct in his sleep. Friday used the handkerchief she took from her pocketbook to dab drool at the corner of her father's mouth. She kissed his bristly cheek. He smelled of printer's ink and benzene, coffee, Old Spice, sweat. He smelled like Father.

CHAPTER 74

Rossiter stood at a vending machine, getting a cup of coffee. Without having to fight with the machine.

Behind him was a tall man, mid-thirties, in a warm-up suit. Unshaved. Unbathed. Homeless? Rossiter wondered.

"You waiting long?" the man asked.

"A little over an hour," Rossiter said.

"I've been waiting an hour and a half," the man said.

"What are you here for?" Rossiter asked.

"Heart attack," the man said.

"Relative?" Rossiter asked. "Friend?"

"Shit, no," he said. "Me."

Rossiter took his coffee. The man fed coins into the machine.

"You're here for your heart," Rossiter said. "You think coffee's a good idea?"

"Way I figure it," the man said, "caffeine gives me another attack, I finally get into the doctor."

Rossiter walked back to a bench as Ruby came out from her examination.

"Thanks for staying," she said.

Rossiter shrugged.

"They give you a prescription?" he asked.

Ruby showed Rossiter the slip of paper.

"I went to an ATM," Rossiter said, giving her another handful of bills. "Get yourself some break-fast; by the time you finish, the drugstore'll be open, you can fill the prescription."

He started to walk away.

"Can I buy you, like, a cup of coffee, something?" Ruby asked.

Rossiter shook his head no.

"Can I ask you something?" Ruby said. "Helping me . . . Why'd you do that?"

"You coughing like that," Rossiter said, "if I went home with you, I was afraid you'd buck me off."

"No," she said, "really."

Rossiter thought a minute, tugging on an earlobe.

"Because of a friend," Rossiter said.

"I don't understand," she said.

"I'm not sure I do, either," he said.

CHAPTER 75

Pressure in her bladder woke Carol. That, and the black tomcat, Milton, who stood on her chest and sniffed her face, which he did when he was hungry.

She lay there, too comfortable to get up, knowing she'd have to use the toilet eventually, not wanting to dislodge Milton, whose whiskers tickled her face. She felt the cat's breath on the left corner of her mouth.

Outside, an owl gave a ghostly call. Or a ghost called like an owl.

Odd notion.

Carol smiled.

Well, she was Harry's sister.

As kids, she had helped Harry when he'd built rambling earthworks in the backyard, roads and towers, populated by tiny olive-colored soldiers. She watched as Harry draped sheets over the dining room table and backs of chairs to make tents under which they huddled in the filtered light. Harry spun tales of bad guys, pirates, brigands, desperados, smugglers, elegant second-story men in top hats and tails. Harry wore his father's oversized vests and wide ties, which

Carol tied for him in Windsor knots. And his father's fedora.

She glanced at the bedside clock.

She'd been sleeping only for twenty minutes, but it felt like hours.

She lifted her head slightly from the pillow, which was damp with sweat. With a knuckle, she wiped away the drool from the corner of her mouth.

In her bra and panties, which she'd slept in, she shuffled into the bathroom. After peeing, the toilet seat cold under her, she shrugged on her quilted flowered bathrobe, fumbled her feet into her backless cloth slippers, and searched the upstairs. No Phil. At the top of the back stairs, the service stairs when she and Harry were little and their parents had staff, she listened. Silence. She descended the steps and searched the downstairs, turning on and off lights, as she moved through the rooms. No Phil. She went up the front steps and was going back into her room when, passing Harry's room, she saw what she had previously missed: Phil sitting in the dark in Harry's wing chair.

"Indigestion," Phil said from the dark.

Because his face was shadowed, she couldn't see his mouth move. An uncanny effect.

"Indigestion," Carol repeated.

Phil didn't respond.

Carol shifted her weight from one foot to the other.

Phil was silent.

Carol shifted her weight again.

"I'm going back to bed," she said.

Phil was silent.

After hesitating, Carol walked along the hallway to their bedroom. Before entering, she stopped and looked back toward Harry's room, where Phil sat in the dark.

CHAPTER 76

Harry lay on his back, staring at the cream-colored ceiling. From other rooms he heard snores, coughs, snorts, the usual early morning sounds.

Harry's thoughts skidded from this to that: the surprised expression on Pillette's face when Cotton shot him, Margaret Resnick's singing, Friday's eyes as they said good-bye.

This was the first time in years Harry had not slept in his own bed.

CHAPTER 77

Carol sat across the kitchen table from Phil, who stared at the green, blue, and red Price Chopper sticker on a brown-speckled banana. She almost gagged on the smell of the overripe fruit.

Neither could sleep.

A car's passing headlights raked the kitchen wall.

Phil raised his cup and gazed across the top of his coffee. As he sipped, he narrowed his eyes against the steam.

"... unseasonably mild ...," the radio weatherman was saying.

Carol lowered her eyes, unable to meet her husband's gaze.

CHAPTER 78

Waking in an uncomfortable hospital chair, Friday heard her father singing.

"'The copper bosses killed you, Joe. They shot you, Joe, says I.'"

Friday's mouth was stale. Her eyes were sticky. She rubbed the lids with her knuckles.

Lee was sitting up in bed, his unshaved cheeks grizzled, his uncombed hair standing straight up, beaming at her.

CHAPTER 79

Harry was dressed, hat brim shading his eyes, when an orderly brought a breakfast tray.

"Egg white omelet," the orderly said, "whole wheat toast with Smart Balance."

"I didn't have a heart attack," Harry said. "I'm here because you think I'm crazy."

"I got no opinion," the orderly said.

Harry went into the bathroom, ran the cold water, scrubbed his face, stood over the toilet, peed. His urine smelled rank. He came back out and sat on a chair, which he scuffed up to the table holding the tray.

"Did you wash your hands?" the orderly asked.

"Every morning, I shower," Harry said. "Wash my whole body. Pull on my shorts, slacks, you get the drift. . . . My hands, hey, I don't wear gloves. My hands get dirty. My cock's been covered by my boxers. It's the cleanest part of me. I wash my hands *before* not *after* I piss."

"Like I said," the orderly shrugged, "I got no opinion."

CHAPTER 80

Friday entered the lobby of Harry's office building. It was so early no other business was open. She hardly noticed the familiar smell of dusty carpet and mouse droppings or the Switzerland-shaped stain on the wall next to the staircase going up to Harry's office. She unlocked the door and went in.

On the floor, just below the letter slot, was some mail that had been delivered the previous day. Friday scooped up the letters and shoved them into her overcoat pocket.

She snapped on the overhead light, three sixty-watt bulbs in a bronze-painted circular fixture decorated with an ivy pattern. At her desk, she picked up the ammo box in which her birthday present had come.

Jerry, the day janitor, stuck his head into the room. Jerry had a bald head, flattened on both sides, and overgrown, tangled eyebrows.

"Everything okay, Ms. Chapin?" he asked.

Friday nodded.

"You're in early," Jerry said.

Friday put down the ammo box.

"Thought I'd better check up," Jerry said.

"Thanks, Jerry," Friday said. She didn't look at him.

Jerry started to go.

"Jerry . . ."

Jerry stopped.

"Tomorrow," Friday asked, "could you get me some empty cartons?"

Jerry nodded.

"I better start packing," Friday said.

"Mr. Dickinson moving to a fancier office?" Jerry asked.

"He'll be closing down the business," Friday said, still not looking at him.

"Sorry to hear that," Jerry said.

"Me, too."

Friday went into Harry's office. She stood in the middle of the room in the dark, looking around. She sat at the desk, turned on the green-shaded lamp.

"Oh, Harry," she said.

Aimlessly, she flipped through the mail. The return address on one envelope caught her attention.

"'New England Correction Information Services,'" she read aloud.

She opened the envelope, took out the letter, and read: *Dear Mr. Dickinson: As per your request and the criteria you supplied regarding a Mr. Benjamin Pillette, we did a county by county search of Rhode Island and Connecticut. In 2006, in Providence County, Mr. Pillette was charged with extortion. The disposition in this matter was a disorderly persons offense via plea bargain. Three days and $25 fine.*

Friday looked over one shoulder, then over the other—reality check—and said, "Extortion."

Rushing into the hallway, Friday called, "Jerry!"

Jerry was pushing a bucket on wheels as he mopped the floor.

"Forget about those boxes," she said. "We may not be closing up shop after all."

CHAPTER 81

Friday parked her Tercel near Cotton's house. All the lights were off. In the low, slanting early morning sun, the clipped hedge cast rectangular shadows. From the lawn, fifty or so small blackbirds swirled into the sky like a cloud of mosquitoes. The air smelled of gasoline.

Friday slipped out of the car and sneaked up to the French doors leading to Cotton's library. The broken panes of glass had been covered with plywood squares.

Friday tried to pull off one of the plywood squares. Too hard. She glanced around, found a gardener's trowel on the terrace, and used it to pry off the plywood.

The sound the plywood made falling to the terrace froze Friday—but there was no response from the house. So—carefully—Friday reached through the empty pane and opened the door. She replaced the plywood, using the heel of one of her shoes to tack it back on.

Then she entered the dim library.

CHAPTER 82

Harry got out of bed and wandered around the room. He opened a desk drawer.

One of the attendants, Sal, looked in and asked, "Hey, Mr. Dickinson, what're you looking for?"

"Evidence," Harry said.

"Evidence of some crime?" Sal asked.

"Evidence," Harry said, "of human habitation."

Sal plumped the pillow on the bed, checked his wristwatch, and said, "Doc'll be here in a few minutes to take your vitals and give you another cocktail."

Carol stood on the back porch, right elbow in her left hand, right hand holding a Marlboro to her mouth, right eye squinting against the smoke, when she heard, behind her, the kitchen door open, screen door open, kitchen door close, screen door slam.

She stiffened.

"There are ants in the kitchen," she said. "We've got no toilet paper. The porch light's been out for two weeks."

Phil put his arms around her, below her arms.

"You never make the bed," she said.

He pressed himself against her bottom.

"Great timing," she said around her cigarette.

But she didn't pull away.

Phil slid his hands under her arm, cupping her breasts.

"What if the neighbors see?" Carol asked.

"The hell with the neighbors," Phil said.

Carol flicked away the cigarette and leaned forward, elbows on the porch railing.

CHAPTER 83

Friday crossed Cotton's study to the painting. She ran her hands along the sides of the frame, which swung easily on hinges. Revealing the wall safe.

From her pocket Friday took an emery board and filed the tips of her fingers, as Harry had taught her. From her other pocket, she took a stethoscope, fitted in the earplugs and held the diaphragm next to the combination lock, as Harry had taught her.

She spun the dial to the right three times to clear the mechanism, then slowly turned the dial—as she had when she cracked the lock on her birthday present—waiting for the feeling and the sound of the tumblers falling into place.

Friday felt and heard the first tumbler.

She turned the dial to the left.

Click.

Friday grinned.

She turned the dial to the right.

Click.

Friday turned the handle. The door swung open.

Inside was a gun. Cotton must have put it back.

Harry was right about that, too.

She heard a car—Cotton's Lincoln—pulling into the driveway. Friday closed the safe and swung the painting back into place.

The car stopped.

Friday hid beside a large bookcase. Cotton and Brenda entered through the French doors.

"For a small guy," Brenda was saying, "Pillette weighed a ton."

"Bodies do, Brenda," Cotton said.

"What if they find him?" Brenda asked.

"What?" Cotton asked. "You don't think we buried him deep enough?"

"We should have gotten rid of him like we did with Marian," Brenda said.

"The trash compactor?" Cotton said. "A nice solid brick of human remains. Which we still have to dispose of. That may be more romantic, but it comes down to the same thing: six feet under in the middle of a swamp."

"What about my mother?" Brenda asked.

"We gave her and her boyfriend enough to keep them in schnappes for the next twenty years," Cotton said.

"And when the cops find them in Hartford?" Brenda asked.

"*If* they find them," Cotton said. "What are they going to do? Take the word of two old drunks?"

"What about us?" Brenda asked.

"By the time they check up, we'll be in Costa Rica," Cotton said. "Out of reach."

Cotton kissed Brenda.

"Don't worry so much," Cotton said.

Cotton and Brenda went upstairs. Swiftly and silently, Friday crossed the room and slipped out through the French doors.

PART THIRTEEN

Two steps sufficed to bring them within sight of its source, which was repellant. It was there by the roadside, seething in the sun, with blowflies covering it and flying all around it—a little mound of excrement.

—Thomas Mann
The Black Swan

CHAPTER 84

In his room in the clinic, Harry sat in the chair, his feet propped up on the desk, his hat pulled low over his right eye, singing, *"Don't know why there's no sun up in the sky / Stormy weather / Since my gal and I ain't together / Keeps raining all the time . . ."*

Bender entered with a mouse-haired nurse, who carried a tray with a pitcher of water, a glass, and a small paper cup like a diner's coleslaw cup.

Harry pushed his hat up.

"Hey, Doc," he said.

Bender looked closely at Harry, his eyes—Harry noticed—slightly bulging.

"How are you feeling?" he asked.

"Normal," Harry said.

"Normal, hmm?" Bender made a note in a leather-bound pocket diary.

"Letts?" Harry asked, referring to the diary brand.

"Let's?" Bender asked. "Do what?"

"What?" Harry asked.

"You said *Let's,*" Bender said.

Harry confirmed, *"Letts."*

"Yes?" Bender asked.

Harry nodded: "Letts."

"Yes," Bender said. "Let's. . . ."

He waited for Harry to finish his thought.

"Letts," Harry repeated.

Bender nodded—a signal to the nurse.

"I'll get the orderlies," the nurse said.

She put the tray on the bed and hurried out of the room.

"Just relax, Harry," Bender said.

"Relax?" Harry said. "The windows are barred."

"Does that make you angry?" Bender asked.

"Sure doesn't make me giggle," Harry said.

"Make you want to . . . I don't know, lash out?"

"You think that would get rid of the bars?"

"Do you?"

"Of course not."

The nurse returned with two large men in white smocks and white pants.

Harry held out his right hand.

"Harry," he introduced himself.

The two large men looked at each other and then looked at Bender, who handed Harry the paper cup.

"Got another bit of your new life here, Harry," he said.

From the paper cup, Harry took a blue-and-white pill.

"This is my new life, huh?" he asked.

Bender nodded.

"It's awfully small," Harry said.

Bender poured water from the pitcher into the glass and held the glass out to Harry.

"What're these pills going to do?" Harry asked.

"Make you happy," Bender said.

"I am happy," Harry said.

"Your brother-in-law and sister aren't," Bender said. "Your girlfriend isn't."

"So this pill," Harry said, "it'll make *them* happy."

Bender nodded.

"By tomorrow—maybe sooner—you'll be a new man," Bender said.

Harry popped the pill into his mouth, took a swig of water, and swallowed the pill.

CHAPTER 85

Friday let Rossiter's phone ring until the answering machine clicked on.

She hung up, sat in the car, holding her cell phone.

Rossiter wasn't at the precinct. He was on a late shift. He slept during the day. Maybe he was still asleep. Maybe he was out. Errands? He didn't have hobbies.

Clouds dimmed the sun.

Was his cell out of juice?

Friday started her car engine.

CHAPTER 86

Harry left his room and wandered down the clinic hallway, peering into open doorways.

After four empty rooms, Harry found a man about sixty-five, sitting in a chair in his bathrobe, staring vacantly into space.

In the next bedroom was a woman in her mid-forties propped up in bed. She was staring at the television. A man galloped away from the camera in black and white. The sound was off.

Two more empty rooms.

Then: a seventeen-year-old boy standing at a window, gazing out. He was not looking at the file of prehistoric wild turkeys crossing the dark lawn.

In the common room, a man about Harry's age sat on a couch: lank blond hair, mottled forehead, slack mouth, dewlaps along his chin, arched eyebrows and mad eyes.

When Harry came in, he looked up.

"You got the time?" he asked Harry. *Sang* to Harry.

"You had a stroke?" Harry asked.

The guy nodded, twisted up his face, trying to talk, stuttering, finally sang, "It helps to sing."

"I don't have the time," Harry said.
"Neither do I," the man sang.
The man returned to his thoughts.
So did Harry.

CHAPTER 87

Deborah Sears was working out on a heavy bag in the precinct gym when Friday entered. The room smelled stale. Like the bottom of an unventilated hamper.

"You know where your boyfriend is," Sears said, "so you got to be looking for Rossiter."

"Your tour's not over," Friday said. "What're you doing haunting the House?"

Sears hit the bag and grunted.

"Your boyfriend's dangerous," she said.

"So am I," Friday said.

"Yeah?" Sears said.

Friday went around the bag and hit it from the other side.

"You think you're doing your boyfriend a favor," Sears asked, hitting the bag, "trying to get him out of the loony bin?"

"Is that what I'm doing?" Friday asked, hitting the bag.

"Why else would you be creeping round here?" Sears asked.

Friday hit the bag. Hard.

"Your boyfriend teach you that?" Sears asked.

"Yeah," Friday said.

They both hit the bag.

"If it was me in the crapper," Sears said, "Rossiter wouldn't bail me out."

"Harry's an old friend," Friday said.

"I'm his partner," Sears said. "Old friendship doesn't trump that."

"You think so?" Friday said. "Then tell me where he is."

"Which gets me . . . what?" Sears said. She stopped hitting the bag. "A gold star in heaven."

Friday continued working the bag.

"You think I'm a bonehead?" Sears asked.

"I think you'd do what I'd do if the situation was reversed," Friday said.

"I would never be in love with a cuckoo bird," Sears said.

Friday stopped hitting the bag. She was out of breath. Her blouse stuck to her sweaty sides.

"No way," Sears said. "I'm not a bonehead."

Friday started to leave the room.

"Fuck!" Sears said, and punched the bag. "You know Elvira's? The massage parlor under the Arch? On the South Side? That's where he's cooping. Most of the guys on the job flop there when they got to take a break."

"Why not you?" Friday asked.

Sears appraised Friday's nipples, stuck to her damp shirt.

"Same reason I don't go to Schmulley's Roumanian when I'm on a diet," Sears said.

CHAPTER 88

Afternoon light streamed through the solarium windows scintillated on the far wall, making the room seem underwater. Harry entered and stood uncertainly. To his left two women sat talking across an old, unshaved man in gray sweatpants, a blue striped pajama top, and a tattered maroon bathrobe.

One of the women—skinny, with a helmet haircut—pawed through a large tan canvas bag between her thighs. Digging out one scrap of paper after another, glancing at them, tossing them onto the blond wood table in front of them.

The breeze through the screen and barred windows smelled of citronella. And—Harry thought—wet newspaper.

"Where's my colorist?" Skinny Woman said, her head close to the bag as she looked. "Where's Dennis, my colorist? At Oscar Blandel."

On the other side of the Old Man, the second woman—whose face-lift gave her narrow eyes like a Tartar—exhaled a scarf of smoke.

"No smoking," the Old Man said without moving.

The Smoker—Skinny Woman's visiting sister, Harry

concluded—stubbed her cigarette onto the tabletop, scattering shreds of tobacco.

"Right!" the Smoker said to Skinny Woman. "Your colorist should know if my husband's screwing a gymnast."

"Physical therapist," her sister said.

The Smoker tapped another cigarette from a pack, plugged it between her lips, and, snapping open a red enameled Cartier lighter, lit it.

"He dates the desk clerk," Skinny Woman said, "or I dunno, the concierge. Somebody at the Marriott."

"No smoking," the Old Man said, not moving.

"Here . . ." Skinny Woman found her colorist's business card and slipped it across the table.

On the other side of the solarium, in the rippling light, a man in a green Navy Patrol cap with a gold senior chief anchor-shaped hat badge, blue work pants, and an orange Carhartt shirt coiled invisible rope.

Harry stood, uncertainly.

"I told you," the Smoker said, "Richard wouldn't cat around with anyone poorer than he is."

Skinny Woman flicked her long red nails at the business card.

"Fine," she said. "You know what? Take the card. You can't sleep, give him a call. Mention my name."

"I trust my husband," the Smoker said, as Harry crossed to the window next to the guy coiling invisible rope. "No, I don't. . . ."

"And," Skinny Woman said, eyeing Harry, "if you ever need a good colorist, you have his card."

Outside, a seagull dive-bombed, snatched a bit of

something from the crushed-shell path leading to the Connecticut River oxbow, and shot back into the sky.

Harry shifted position so he could continue eavesdropping on Skinny Woman, who was asking her sister, "You have your party all planned?"

The Smoker said, "He's still resisting the Beluga."

"Sevruga's just as good," Skinny Woman said. "At a quarter of the cost."

"Come on," the Smoker said. "Fifteen years together, I deserve Beluga."

"Fifteen years, you deserve a purple heart," Skinny Woman said. "But you'll end up getting farmed American."

A tall man in Marc Jacobs with gelled hair standing up in spikes came into the solarium, trailed by a pale woman—his young wife? Harry wondered—in a crazy mix of polka-dotted skirt, raw silk smock, the blue of skim milk, no bra, plastic flip-flops, a fuchsia scarf unsuccessfully trying to hold her matted hair in place.

Gelled Hair was ignoring the woman—maybe a daughter?

Harry studied their body language, how careful they were not to touch, even brush against each other as they sat on a couch, side by side, gazing at anything but each other.

"Well," Gelled Hair was saying into his iPhone, "frankly, Eric, I don't really give a shit. Pay the guy overtime. . . . ."

"He should pull into your driveway in a Porsche," Skinny Woman said, "with a big, red bow around it."

"He doesn't like his new office!" Gelled Hair was saying into his cell phone. "People are killing each other for that spot."

"The band's a problem," the Smoker said, exhaling a cloud of smoke.

"No smoking," the Old Man between them repeated. Tonelessly.

"The bass player has one eye," the Smoker said. "Like Popeye. It's"—she closed one eye—"like he's winking, but he can't wink. It's a little disturbing. I think he really needs the work."

"He'd suck my dick," Gelled Hair said into his phone, "if I got him onto the third floor."

"Creole menu," the Smoker said. "Beans and rice. Crab and cornbread. . . ."

"Anyone who brags about eating dog in Hanoi is not above this kind of thing," Skinny Woman said. "Trust me."

Through the window, Harry watched another seagull shoot out of the sky, pluck something from the shells, and sail up.

The guy coiling invisible rope looked back over his shoulder at Harry and said, "It's hidden by the crab-apple trees."

Harry nodded at the scene out the window.

"Down by the oxbow?" he asked.

The guy nodded.

"What is?" Harry asked.

"My twenty-four-foot 2007 Bayliner 245 Bow-rider," he said. "Waiting for me to go over the wall."

"You breaking out of this joint?" Harry asked.

"After I've paid my dues," the guy said.

Holding the invisible rope in his left hand, the guy held out his right in greeting.

"James Vincent Forrestal."

Harry shook his hand.

"Harry Dickinson."

"Secretary of Defense," Forrestal said.

"I would've thought you'd be older," Harry said.

"Never should have changed it from Secretary of War," Forrestal said. "*Secretary of War*. Hell, I bombed Hiroshima and Nagasaki. *Secretary of War*. Yeah. Truman never should have fired me. You know how many people I killed? I mean overall. Not just with the Bomb."

"Pussy," said another man, who came up to them. "Fucking desk jockey."

The new guy was—Harry figured—mid-thirties. Stringy hair, beard, eyes trying too hard.

"You sent your witches to do your killing," Forrestal said to the new guy.

"*Stick a fork in them, see if they're done,*" the guy said. "I didn't mean it literally."

"Anyone who died on my watch," Forrestal said, "it was in the interest of national defense."

"I thought it was cool when they did, though," the new guy said.

"You think you're Charlie Manson," Harry said, getting it.

"He's a homicidal psychopath," Forrestal whispered in Harry's ear.

"My kills?" Manson whispered in Harry's other ear. "I'm a piker compared to Mr. Secretary of War over there."

"I've never had any luck with roses," Forrestal said across Harry to Manson.

"I always figured you for a green thumb," Manson said.

"You don't want to know about *his* thumbs," Forrestal told Harry about Manson.

"They die to spite me," Manson said. "Flowers. People . . ."

Harry moved off.

"He's going to call you, my soon-to-be ex," Skinny Woman was saying as Harry headed out of the solarium. "Soon-to-be ex, God willing."

"God doesn't take sides in divorces," the Smoker said.

"God was never married to Richard," Skinny Woman said.

"No smoking," the Old Man said. No effect.

"Pop," Skinny Woman said to the Old Man, "this is not the best day for you to go ballistic."

Harry left the solarium.

CHAPTER 89

Friday drove into and out of the shadow of the Arch. Two blocks up on the right, she parked across from the white Victorian with peeling paint and ancient green-gray asphalt shingles.

She crossed the dark street, across the dead grass lawn and onto the Victorian's porch. A loose board popped under her. She rang the bell. Rang again.

Inside the house, a flickering black-and-white desk monitor showed a high-angle shot of Friday, looking at her feet. The receptionist, a white blond named Duffy, held a telephone handset to her chest, tapped a finger with a long curved black-lacquered nail on an intercom button, and into the intercom said, "Who?"

On the porch, Friday said, "Skip the small talk, Duffy, and buzz me in."

"Geez, Linda," Duffy said over the intercom, "I haven't seen Harry since you guys helped us out when Cee-Cee couldn't get an order of protection against her old man. You know he don't play here."

"I'm looking for Rossiter," Friday said.

The door buzzed.

Friday pushed it open and entered the Victorian.

"The Big Guy's in back," Duffy said, telephone handset still pressed to her chest. "We had a problem."

"You always have a problem," Friday said.

"It's the line of work," Duffy said. "Like being in the mouse shift at a cheese factory."

The room was stuffy with sandalwood incense. The compact fluorescent bulbs in the lamps, spiraled like soft-serve ice cream, gave a flat white light, which made Duffy look even paler, not quite as if she were in clown makeup but a little skull-like. She held up a finger and talked into her telephone handset.

"I need the name you checked in under at the hotel," Duffy said.

Behind Duffy, on a high shelf over the parlor door, a TV was tuned to Chris Matthews, who leaned forward into the camera, brows furrowed.

The sound was off.

A brown corduroy-covered sofa and two easy chairs, one upholstered in cream-and-red flowers, the other broad blue-and-wine-colored stripes, surrounded a coffee table.

Two hookers, naked except for G-strings—Marty, a skinny brunet with a cat's face, and Tif, short-haired, hennaed, with too many piercings—played cribbage.

"Seven," Tif said.

"Eleven," Marty said.

Marty sat on the couch, leaning forward, left elbow on left knee, breasts swaying.

Tif slouched in a chair, legs over an overstuffed arm, twisting to play her card. "Fifteen," Tif said. "Two points. Peg it for me, will you, hon."

"Hey, Linda," Marty said. "Long time . . ."

"No, we call you back at the hotel," Duffy said into the telephone, "for security."

"Rossiter?" Friday asked.

"Do animals have a sense of humor?" Tif asked no one in particular.

"*Our* security," Duffy said. "Not yours."

"Twenty-five," Marty said.

"Go," Tif said.

"His nibs," said Rossiter, coming in from the back and pointing at the top card on the stack.

"I'm only letting you kibbitz because you got a gun," Marty said.

"What the hell you doing here?" Rossiter asked Friday.

The dim hallway led back to half-a-dozen small rooms. Only two of the doors were closed.

"You mean: What's a nice girl like me doing in a place like this?" Friday deadpanned.

Tif barked a single laugh.

"They're having a slow night," Rossiter told Friday.

"I need to talk to you," Friday said.

"We're a leading economic indicator," Marty said.

"My date in Room Three," Marty asked. "Still alive?"

"Bozo passsed out," Tif told Friday. "Finished the better part of a bottle of Ketel One. Which," she said, with a doubtful glance at Rossiter, "he brought himself."

"Yeah, yeah," Rossiter said. "You don't serve liquor. You don't sell dope."

"It's about Harry," Friday said.

"Now," Rossiter said, "why did I know that?"

"Rossiter's okay," Tif told Friday. "Just he don't come by so often."

"Sleeping Beauty will survive," Rossiter told Marty.

"Room Seven's free if you want to bunk, Big Guy," Duffy called from her desk.

Rossiter sat on the couch next to Marty. The springs sagged under his weight.

"I mean it, Rossiter," Friday said. "This time it's serious."

"With Harry," Rossiter said, "it's always serious."

"How come we don't see you more?" Tif asked.

"I've got no sale's resistance," Rossiter said.

"I think Harry's right about Pillette," Friday said. "Cotton, too."

"Do I got to go back and entertain my public?" Marty asked Rossiter, who shook his head *no* and said: "He's sleeping like a baby."

"Long as I don't have to change his diaper," Marty said.

"Sure, he's right," Rossiter told Friday, "just like he was right last time about the fifteen-year-old who was kidnapped who turned out to be thirty-two on a bender with some Ashley Madison man. And the time before that when—"

Tif shuffled the cards and leered at Rossiter. "Next time, we'll play Hearts, and I'll let you shoot the moon."

"I hate this tour," Rossiter said, heaving himself up and starting toward a room where he could nap.

Friday followed.

"I'm not crazy," she said.

"And neither is Harry," Rossiter said. "The world is full of mysteries, right?"

Friday stopped.

"You won't help?" Friday asked.

"Friday," Rossiter said, "Harry's safe, where he'll get some help. In two minutes, when I sack out in back, I'll be safe, too. If I'm lucky, I'll even sleep off this migraine."

Friday stood, legs apart, fists on her hips.

"Harry's right," she said. "The world *is* full of mysteries."

"You think I'm going to suddenly get sentimental?" Rossiter asked. "Like Harry?"

"Harry's not sentimental," Friday said.

"What is he?" Rossiter asked.

"A good man," Friday said. "And I thought you were, too."

"You know, Friday," Rossiter said, "you're a real hard-ass."

"You're wrong, Rossiter," Friday said. "My ass is nice and soft."

She turned and headed out.

CHAPTER 90

Standing, back against the wall, was an old man—eighties, Harry guessed—who stared blankly into space.

"You okay, chief?" Harry asked.

"He doesn't talk," another inmate—a heavyset man, pink as a piglet—said. "He was a member of the *Judenrat*. Austria, I think. A kid. Inherited the job from his grandfather, the rabbi, I think. Cooperated with the Nazis—loading his neighbors onto the cattle cars until he had to ship a bunch of kids. Refused. Got a gun. Held it on some big Nazi. Couldn't kill the Nazi. Because the Nazis would kill so many in retaliation. Couldn't load the kids. Couldn't kill himself. He's *still* stuck. His file was out in the shrink's office. The week I arrived. The shrink went to the can. I read the file. Why not?"

"You don't seem crazy," Harry said.

"Neither do you," Piglet said.

And wandered away.

Harry looked kindly into the old man's eyes.

For a long time.

But the old man never looked back.

PART FOURTEEN

You wanted an explanation, I'll give you an explanation. You wanted I/Thou, I'll give you I/Thou.

—Stanley Elkin
The Living End

"You want to pick up breakfast?" Sears asked when she met Rossiter leaving Elvira's.

"Breakfast," Rossiter said, gesturing at the moon, low in the sky and huge. "Quarter to eight P.M."

"Chinese?" Sears asked.

"What'll we have for *dinner*?" Rossiter asked. "Scrambled eggs?"

They were passing through the Meatpacking District on the route back to the precinct to clock out. Rossiter stopped across the street from Jackie's, where a girl was struggling with the doorman as her embarrassed boyfriend looked on.

"But Tate said he'd put us on the list," the girl was complaining. "Lisa Alpert. . . ."

The doorman moved her away from the wine-colored velvet rope.

"End of the line, sunshine," he said.

"Don't touch me, creep," Alpert said.

The crowd was getting restless.

"It's a bitch waiting your turn, huh, princess," someone behind her in the crowd said.

Arc lights gave the scene a sulfurous, sepia, old-fashioned look.

"She look underage to you?" Sears asked.

"To me," Rossiter said, "they all look underage."

"Too much money," Sears said about the kids. "Too much time."

"Tate promised I'd be on the list," Alpert said to the doorman.

The doorman pointed to three leggy model types and their older male escort.

"You," the doorman said, "ladies—bring your friend."

He unhooked the velvet rope. Alpert dodged past the rope. The doorman grabbed her and said into his Nextel, "Anthony, we got a problem."

Rossiter hit the siren and nosed the car through the crowd.

"She left her pretty boy outside the rope," Sears said.

The embarrassed boyfriend, hands deep in his pockets, headed down the block away from the club.

"He's hitting the bricks," Rossiter said. "I don't get the feeling this was a long-term relationship."

When the bouncer—Anthony, the doorman had called him—came out of the club, Rossiter, who glanced at him in the rearview mirror, said, "Isn't that what's-his-name? Scocci. Your pal."

Sears twisted around to look through the back window.

"What the hell is Scocci doing here?" she asked.

"This why he wanted a transfer to the day shift?" Rossiter said.

"Lots of cops moonlight," Sears said.

"Lots of cops lose their jobs for moonlighting," Rossiter said.

He'd stopped the car and through the rearview was watching Scocci trying to handle the crowd.

"Let's get out of here," Sears said.

"We cut your boyfriend some slack?" Rossiter said.

"I don't do guys," Sears said. "You know that."

"And when someone finds out we knew?"

"You're a real prick, Rossiter," Sears said.

Rossiter shrugged.

"Just a practical guy," Rossiter said, "who doesn't want to get his tit in a wringer."

But he put the car in gear and slowly moved up the block away from Scocci.

"Give him a head's-up," Rossiter told Sears. "I see him here moonlighting tomorrow night, I feed him to the wolves."

CHAPTER 92

Friday pulled into the clinic parking lot a little before nine. In the dark, she waited, listening to an oldies station. "Gallows Pole." Randy Newman's "Short People." Dylan. Paul Simon.

The shift changed. People came. People left.

Friday got out of the car and headed across the lawn. Circling the building, she came to the kitchen door, which was open. Two cooks were standing a few feet away, smoking cigarettes and taking nips from a pint of Wild Irish Rose.

Cautiously, Friday started toward the open door. But one of the cooks, a guy in his late twenties with acne-scarred cheeks, spotted her and called out, "Hey!"

Friday glanced at the guy's plastic ID, which hung from a beaded metal chain around his neck—Fred Barrett—and went into a role.

"Melody Jarrell," she said, taking Fred's hand and holding it seductively between her two hands. "Platinum Escorts. I'm here to visit one of the patients."

She winked.

"A lonely gentleman," she said. "I've never worked

a hospital before. Tell me . . . they're not deadbeats, are they? The patients? I mean, I came all the way from Winchester Square. I'm already in for twenty dollars, taxi ride . . ."

As she talked, Friday sidled toward the open door.

"Look, miss—" Fred started.

"I won't be but a half-hour," Friday said. "That's what the call was for." She smiled at Fred. "You going to be here when I get out?"

Fred glanced at his companion, an older man, all sinew, with bristling gray hair. His ID said: Allard Breck.

"Some poor dope on the wards wants a little fun," Fred said.

Allard shrugged. Couldn't care less.

"Keeping her out," Fred said. "It's not our job."

Allard lit a new cigarette.

"Half an hour?" Fred said to Friday.

Friday nodded.

"These guys are quick off the mark," she said.

"And then you come back here?" Fred asked.

Friday fluttered her eyelids.

"I'll be looking for you," she said and took a step through the door.

"You get caught," Fred said, "I don't know anything about it."

"You're so romantic," Friday cooed.

She entered the building.

CHAPTER 93

From a laundry cart, Friday grabbed a doctor's white smock, crisp from starch, which she shrugged on. She found a stairwell, smelling of pine cleaner, and climbed to the second floor. She walked along the hallway, whispering at each door, "Harry . . ."

A nurse came out of a room ahead of her. She looked suspiciously at Friday, who introduced herself, "Driscoll . . . Elizabeth Driscoll. Call me Betty . . . or Bet. Whatever . . ."

Friday walked beside the nurse—a little closer than necessary. The nurse uneasily squared her shoulders.

"It's my first night on the job," Friday said. "Say, maybe you could explain how they work vacation time."

"Look," the nurse said, "I've got to—"

"It'll just take a couple, three minutes," Friday said. "I mean, not that I should worry about vacation time, since I just started. But I like to plan ahead."

The nurse edged toward a staircase.

"I've got to see a patient on Two-East," the nurse explained.

"Right," Friday said. "Look—"

Friday took a piece of paper from a pocket and pretended to read something on it.

"I'm trying to find this new patient Dickinson," she said. "Harry Dickinson. Just brought in."

The nurse checked her clipboard.

"One-zero-three-West," she said.

The nurse started up the stairs.

"Thanks," Friday said. "Hey, when's your break? Maybe we could have a cup of coffee?"

The nurse hurried to the landing above.

"I'm going to be busy all night," she said.

"How about tomorrow?" Friday called after her.

From the top of the stairs, the nurse said, "It's a busy week."

The nurse disappeared around the corner of the landing.

Friday smiled.

CHAPTER 94

The bar was crowded with on-duty cops, taking a break, and off-duty cops from the earlier tour, who didn't want to go home. The walls were covered with yellowing newspapers—cop headlines—behind cracked and discolored plastic. A foot and a half below the ceiling was a shelf which ran around the room, displaying softball trophies, sports caps, chipped beer steins, some with hinged caps, old plastic models of 1950s airplanes, and various ratty record books— sports, Guinness, World Almanac—to settle bar bets, never consulted. A urine-and-sweat-tinged fug slowly circulated, stirred by a stuttering fan. A CD system played the Doors' "People Are Strange."

Rossiter and Sears sat across a scarred wooden polyurethaned table, drinking coffee and eating their middle-of-the-night breakfast. A waiter put pie in front of Sears and shortcake in front of Rossiter. Rossiter shifted his bulk on the wooden bench, his thighs almost upsetting the table.

"One strawberry?" he asked.

"It's called straw*berry* shortcake," the waiter said. "Not straw*berries* shortcake."

"You won't give Scocci a pass, one of your own," Sears said, "but for this guy Dickinson you put your dick on the chopping block."

"Harry and I used to make mud pies together," Rossiter said.

"You going to eat that?" Sears asked.

"Every night after supper, played Horse in my driveway."

"Back when Horse was a game not a drug."

"Joined the Scouts together."

"You know how many calories that is?" Sears asked and forked a piece of shortcake and whipped cream.

"'The Cub Scout follows Akela,'" Rossiter said. "'The Cub Scout helps the pack go. . . .'"

"Goodie-goodies, the two of you," Sears said.

"'The pack helps the Cub Scout grow,'" Rossiter said.

"'The Cub Scout gives goodwill,'" they said in unison.

"My brother's troupe," Sears said, "the Cub Scout gave good head."

"I'll bet you were one hell of a Brownie," Rossiter said. "Harry, me . . . we went to the Jamboree together."

"What did you get patches for?" Sears asked.

"Merit badges?" Rossiter said. "Indian lore, safety, insect study . . ."

"I played the clarinet," Sears said.

"For the Brownies?" Rossiter asked.

"Fuck the Brownies," Sears said. "Who had time for the Brownies?"

"What'd you play?" Rossiter asked.

"'When I'm Sixty-Four'?" Sears said.

"Clarinet's not a big rock instrument," Rossiter said.

"Sly and the Family Stone, 'Dance to the Music,'" Sears said.

"On the clarinet?" Rossiter asked.

"'*Tsiganeshti*,'" Sears said. "'*Ba dem Zeiden's Tish*.'"

Rossiter narrowed his eyes: a question.

"'At Grandfather's Table,'" Sears said. "Klezmer. Yiddish. Whatever."

"You're Jewish?" Rossiter asked.

"Methodist," Sears said. "My grandparents were. Me? My God's vanilla. Not much taste. But pure."

"So why *Ba dem yackety-yak*?" Rossiter asked.

"My clarinet teacher was a big Jew," Sears said.

"Big as me?" Rossiter asked.

"Big in the neighborhood," Sears said. "Important. Symphony orchestra. Dances. Ninth grade, we still had sock hops in the church basement."

"The Big Jew would play a church basement?" Rossiter asked.

"Every other kid's playing 'Peter and the Wolf,'" Sears said. "*Bad um dum, dum dad um* . . . The Cat!"

"I wanted to be the Wolf," Rossiter said.

"You played French horn?" Sears asked.

"I played the radio," Rossiter said, "the record player."

"I had a recording," Sears said. "Narrated by Arthur Godfrey."

"Every year, the school did 'Peter and the Wolf,'" Rossiter said. "They never had a French horn."

"Who was that guy?" Sears asked. "The singer Arthur Godfrey fired?"

"So they let some lucky kid play it on a kazoo," Rossiter said.

"Thirty years after," Sears said, "my mom and dad still talked about it."

"Never got the chance to play it," Rossiter said. "Not even on the kazoo."

"Talked about it more than the Kennedy assassination," Sears said.

"Then," Rossiter said, "I graduated from junior high."

"Julius LaRosa," Sears said. "That was the singer's name."

"And that was it," Rossiter said. "Never got to play the kazoo."

"I think he—Arthur Godfrey—was such a big deal because he had this integrated singing group," Sears said.

"No more 'Peter and the Wolf,' " Rossiter said.

"My father thought that was cool," Sears said. "Nineteen sixties—it still got my mother's goat."

"Arthur who?" Rossiter asked.

A cop in a two-for-one gray three-button JoS A. Bank suit and an off-white shirt with a red tie sat down next to Sears, who shifted away from him. Hugging the wall.

"Wearing your TV shirt, McChesney," Rossiter said. "You working some eleven-o'clock-newsbreak-stay-in-tune-for-the-sports-and-weather case?"

McChesney was rail thin, sallow, his skin the shiny brown of the polyurethaned table.

"How's IAB?" Sears said, staring into the middle distance.

"Don't start, Sears," McChesney said.

"Hey, Connie," Sears said, "I'm not the one who re-upped in Internal Affairs. Twice."

"Last time I saw you," Rossiter said, "when you were still on the street going after bad guys, I remember you nailed Public Enemy Number One."

"A dangerous—what?" Sears grinned. "Long-meadow drunk?"

"He was trying to buy drugs right off the West Springdale Bridge," McChesney said.

"That's worth a commendation," Sears said to Rossiter.

"You think this makes me pop a chubby," McChesney said, "busting the balls of a good cop."

"You got that right," Sears said. "My partner, here, is a good cop."

"You talk to the CO?" Rossiter asked.

"I wanted to reach out to you first," McChesney said. "You being Harry's friend and all." McChesney half-turned toward Sears, who still did not look at him. "This guy—Dickinson—when he commits one of his cute felonies, your partner—the good cop over here—ever give him a pass?"

"You ever bend the rules?" Sears asked her partner.

"I'm an Eagle Scout," Rossiter said.

"We can do this in my office?" McChesney still addressed Sears. "On video. If you want."

"Let me know when," Sears said. "I'll wear my Clinique."

McChesney got up.

"You change your mind," he said, "give me a jingle."

Two steps away from them, McChesney hesitated.

He licked his thin lips, made a *tk-tk* sound with his tongue.

"You going to ask me for a date," Sears said, "come right out—say it."

"Me?" McChesney said. "Why would I want to step in that swamp."

Sears waited.

Under the table, Rossiter shifted his feet. The table heaved.

To Rossiter, McChesney said, "Your pal's getting a rough break."

Rossiter stared him down.

"I'm just saying," McChesney said.

McChesney left.

Outside, Rossiter and Sears headed to their car.

"I'm drunk," Sears said.

She fished in her left pants pocket.

"I got my keys," Rossiter said. "Leave your car."

"My paycheck," Sears said. "I keep forgetting to go to the bank."

"Use the ATM like the rest of us," Rossiter said.

"Put my check in a machine?" Sears said. "You trust them? You know what, Rossiter, this shift, night shift, it don't matter, we're freaking vampires . . ."

As she opened the passenger door of Rossiter's car, she said, "Your pal Harry's got a gun, right?"

"He's in the hospital," Rossiter said. "Anyway, the gun's a prop. Harry hates it when he spills his coffee. He's not going to leave a mess."

CHAPTER 95

Friday found Harry lying, fully dressed, in bed in the dark. His hat beside him.

"Harry," Friday whispered.

Harry sat up.

Friday slipped into the room and closed the door behind her.

"How'd you get in here?" Harry asked.

"I was taught by the best," Friday said.

She kissed Harry.

"You were right," she said.

"Right?" Harry asked.

"Marian," Friday said. "Cotton's safe. The gun. We got to get you out of here."

"Why?" Harry asked.

Harry was listless.

"Did they already give you a shot or something?" Friday asked.

"Pills," Harry said.

Friday searched Harry's face.

"You okay?" she asked.

"It's been a long day," Harry said.

Harry started to lie back down. Friday stopped him.

"Harry," she said, "it's like *The Big Sleep*. When they gave Marlowe the drug."

Harry shrugged.

"You've got to fight it," Friday said.

Friday took Harry's arm, got him out of bed and to the door.

"Your hat!" she said.

Friday turned back to the bed and Harry's hat.

Harry said, "Yeah . . ."

"You're leaving without your hat," Friday said.

Harry shrugged.

"You never go anywhere without your hat," Friday said.

Harry shrugged.

"The pill works," Friday said.

"I guess," Harry said.

Friday grabbed the hat and put it on Harry's head.

CHAPTER 96

Harry and Friday hurried down the clinic hall.

"You saw Cotton's gun," Harry said.

"We go back," Friday said, "get it, and—"

"We call the police," Harry said, "let *them* handle it."

Friday shot Harry a disappointed look.

"Before you took the pill," Friday said, "you wouldn't have said that."

"Look, Linda—" Harry said.

"*Linda?*" Friday said. "You call me Linda?"

A night watchman came around the corner ahead of them.

"So, Mr. Dickinson . . . ," Friday said, going into a role.

"It's not going to work," Harry muttered.

Friday tried harder.

"You were explaining the difference between alligators and crocodiles," she said.

The night watchman stopped and studied them.

"Now," Friday said, "*which* one has the narrow snout?"

As they passed the night watchman, Friday smiled at him.

"Ma'am," the night watchman said, "where're you taking that patient?"

Friday hurried Harry along.

"Insomniac," Friday explained. "Late-night panic attack. We're walking it off."

The night watchman started after them.

"Can I see your staff ID?" the night watchman asked.

Friday ran, half-dragging the reluctant Harry after her.

Outside, Harry and Friday headed across the lawn toward the parking lot. Behind them, in the clinic, lights went on. An alarm bell started ringing.

As she ran, Friday said, "You called me *Linda*!"

Harry said, "It's your name."

They reached the Tercel. Friday started the motor even before Harry had his door closed.

"What have they done to you?" she asked.

"Not *half* what they'll do if they catch us," Harry said. "*Let's go!*"

Friday put the car in gear and, scattering gravel, peeled out of the clinic grounds.

PART FIFTEEN

People were funny. They got a big thrill out of
hunting a live man who was free in the streets.

—Ben Hecht
1001 Afternoons in Chicago

"Friday called," Rossiter's wife, Maggie said, the moment Rossiter came through the mudroom door.

"Telling you I'm a hard-hearted bastard," Rossiter said. "Where's Chloe?"

"You think I need her to tell me that?" Maggie said, throwing over her shoulder the red-checked dish towel she'd been holding. "Doing homework."

"How long ago did Friday call?"

"Two, three hours. Maybe less."

"Old news," Rossiter said. "I'm bushed."

"Bed, huh," Maggie said. "I get fifteen minutes to say *how're ya doing*. Lucky me."

Rossiter followed Maggie into the kitchen, where she grabbed a flyswatter and started stalking flies.

"Why don't you get some fly strips?" Rossiter said. "Hang them around the house?"

"They get into my hair," Maggie said, whacking a fly in midair.

"Hang them higher," Rossiter said.

"They'll get into *your* hair," she said.

Rossiter rubbed his palm over the bristle on his head.

He opened the refrigerator, peered into the abundance of leftover food—Saran-Wrapped plates of cold meat and pale green vegetables, red-topped Rubbermaid plastic containers filled with week-old hummus, raw carrot sticks and raw celery sticks, whole cooked tomatoes in light sauce, homemade apple sauce—and grabbed a bottle of beer between his second and third fingers.

"Harry's got Friday going," Rossiter said, twisting off the bottle cap. "She's getting as nuts as he is."

"Why she doesn't leave his bony ass for your old pal."

"Plante? He's no pal."

"She should get married. Start a family."

Maggie whacked a fly on the wall.

"My helping Harry out time to time," Rossiter said. "The CO contacted Nightwatch, the city-wide commander. IAB's sniffing around."

"You going to lose your pension?" Maggie stopped stalking flies. Held the flyswatter upright like the Statue of Liberty's torch.

"I can't help Harry anymore," Rossiter said.

Maggie killed a fly on the window over the sink.

"IAB," she said. "Shit!"

She scooped up the dead fly with a Kleenex. It left a smear, which Rossiter wiped away with a thumb.

"What do we have for dessert?" Rossiter asked.

"You haven't had dinner yet," Maggie said, putting the flyswatter on the kitchen table.

Daintily, Rossiter picked up the flyswatter and tossed it into the sink. He spritzed the table with Fantastic and wiped where the flyswatter had been.

Maggie put a piece of homemade shortcake—with a biscuit, not angel food cake—in front of Rossiter.

Rossiter nodded.

"Six strawberries," he said. "You think it gives me a glow, helping to bust my best friend?"

"I think you'd bust me and the kid if you had the chance," Maggie said, slapping a fly on the kitchen table with her hand. Right next to her husband's shortcake. "I think you're the fucking Angel of the fucking vengeful God."

CHAPTER 98

The moon was high in the sky when the old-fashioned telephone on the stand at the top of the stairs rang.

A red light on its base blinked.

The telephone rang again.

Phil—in Vishnu-blue striped pajamas, glasses pushed up on his forehead, a forefinger keeping his place in the book he was reading: a World War I spy novel—hurried out of the first room off the upstairs hall.

"Why the hell don't they call my cell," Phil grumbled.

A dead ladybug lay on the stand. Phil crushed the bug between his forefinger and thumb. It made a satisfying crack.

Once more, the phone rang.

Phil looked at it and thought, Now that Harry's gone, we can get rid of this antique.

The top-of-the-stair telephone jack had been installed half a century ago.

The telephone rang a fourth time.

"Who?" Phil asked into the phone. "What?"

Phil ran a hand through his hair, which stood up

like a cockatoo's crest. He made a few mm-hmm's, tugged at the tip of his nose, and asked, "*Where* do you think he's going?"

Carol hurried out of her bedroom, tying the belt of her quilted bathrobe, holding the current *New Yorker* at her side.

"What's happening?" she asked.

"Harry's escaped," Phil told her, hanging up the phone.

Carol tried to hide a smile.

"They think he's on his way here," Phil said. "We better lock the doors."

"You really think he's dangerous?" Carol asked. "Give me a break."

"He's not dangerous," he said, "but he shouldn't be here."

"Why not?" Carol asked. "It's his home."

CHAPTER 99

Friday took corners at sixty miles an hour, skidding, throwing Harry against the passenger door.

Harry slumped in his seat.

"We're going . . . where?" Harry asked.

Friday turned left onto McKinley Avenue, skirting the park, the shortcut to Longmeadow.

"Turn the car around," Harry said.

Friday ignored him.

"I'm not going to Cotton's," Harry said.

"I tried Rossiter," Friday said. "He didn't pick up."

"Turn the fucking car around," Harry said.

Friday looked at Harry, her mouth open, her eyes stinging.

"Harry . . . ?" Friday said.

"Turn the car around," Harry repeated.

"You sound like Phil," Friday said.

He looked away from her, out the passenger-side window.

"Cotton kills this guy Pillette," Harry said. "I get locked in the loony bin. And *you* don't like the way I sound. Am I missing something here?"

"Yes," Friday said. Softly. "I think you are."

CHAPTER 100

Rossiter was crouched down in the back aisle of the convenience mart, a huge humped figure, trying to decide between Cape Cod Chips and Sierra Chips— why didn't Maggie tell him which kind she wanted when she sent him out on the errand—when he heard a young voice (he, at first, thought it might be a girl) tell the clerk, "Empty your cash register."

Rossiter eased his gun out as he peered through three other aisles, past cans of soup, pet food, boxes of pasta, at the kid in the gray hoodie holding an ancient Saturday Night Special.

"Sure," the clerk said. "Sure thing."

Still crouched, silently, Rossiter crab-walked his way toward the end of the aisle. Like many big men, he was light on his feet.

On the TV above the counter, Bruce Willis jumped from a helicopter onto the top of a speeding truck.

Distracted by the movie, the kid said, "Jesus."

The clerk, also distracted by the movie, said, "I seen it when it was in the movies."

"You think he uses a stunt double?" the kid asked.

"The sequel's not so good," the clerk said.

At the end of the aisle, Rossiter stood and shouted, "Freeze! Police!"

The kid dropped his gun as Rossiter's cell rang.

Keeping his gun trained on the kid, Rossiter, one-handed, answered his phone.

On the other end of the line, Maggie said, "Harry's escaped."

CHAPTER 101

"Pull in here," Harry said, nodding ahead at a motel.

Two of the letters in the neon sign—*Pilgrim Pines*—both capital *P*'s, were out. The *es* blinked and sizzled.

"This'll give me a chance to think," Harry said. "I've got to get out of town. Boston."

"Harry," Friday said, "you can't run away."

"Maybe New York," he said.

Friday angled in toward the office.

"How much money do you have on you?" Harry asked. "If they've got an ATM, max out your cards. No, any machine they'll have a low limit. Wait until we can hit a bank."

"You want me to get a room?" Friday asked.

The sizzling neon reflection made Friday's face look crumpled.

"Use cash," Harry said. "And a phony name. Why the hell didn't I ever get credit cards?"

"Yeah, Harry," Friday said. "Why? Can you remember?"

Friday opened the car door. She headed into the office, head ducked.

Harry glanced at the ignition.

When she returned, Harry said, "You afraid I'd leave you alone here?"

She buckled her seat belt.

"You took the car key," Harry said. "What's wrong with you?"

"The what?" Friday said. "I took what?"

"You think I'd leave you," Harry said.

"Leave? No," Friday said. "What are you talking about?"

"Anyway I can't," Harry said, "'till you get me some cash."

"Right," Friday said, setting her jaw and trying not to cry.

CHAPTER 102

Friday parked behind a two-story annex, eight units on each floor, hidden from the road. Half-a-dozen other cars were angled into the building.

Under the narrow roof that ran along the annex, two women in miniskirts and thin tops passed a crack pipe, the flame at the tip giving one of the women devil eyes. Beyond them, a guy in low-slung jeans, no shirt, and a back tangled with blue and red and green tattoos pissed into the woods. From a nearby pickup truck came a bass beat that Harry felt in his chest.

Harry fit the key into their room lock. He said, without looking at the pissing guy, "Why don't you turn up the music so we can all hear it, chief."

As Harry opened their door, the guy turned. Shaking his cock and stuffing it back into his pants, he said to Harry, "You got a problem, Mac?"

Harry nodded at the swastika tattoo on the guy's arm.

"Deutchland uber alles?" Harry asked. "Or White Men uber alles?"

"Huh?" the guy said.

"What are you doing, Harry?" Friday said.

The two women passed the crack pipe. The guy spread his hands waist-high, palms up.

"You don't like the music," he said, "go into your room and close your door."

"Tell your friend to put on his shirt," Harry said to the crack-smoking women.

"Harry . . . ," Friday said, plucking at his arm.

"We're not all enthralled by what he's done to his body," Harry told the two women.

The guy turned sideways, left foot forward, and shifted his weight back.

"People having a good time," he said, "minding their own business, you got to start some trouble."

"Let's just go in, Harry," Friday said.

"Nineteen forty-three?" Harry asked. "Which side would you have been on, chief?"

"You believe this?" the guy said to the women.

"You need a history lesson?" Harry asked.

To Friday, the guy said, "Your friend drunk?"

"I wish it were that simple," Friday said, stepping into the room.

"Or just to have the crap knocked out of you?" Harry asked.

"Aw, shit," the guy said.

"Nineteen forty-three," Harry said. "Berlin. A Nazi and an Italian Fascist are at the Adlon bar. The Nazi brags, 'We're going to kill all the Jews and dentists.' 'Why the dentists?' asks the Italian. The Nazi turns to his comrade and says, 'I told you no one cares about the Jews.'"

The guy with the swastika tattoo blinked at Harry.

"Dachau, Sobibor, Majdanek, Chelmno, Sachsen-hausen?"

"Huh?" the tattooed guy said.

"Mauthausen, Belzec, Treblinka, Ravensbruck?"

The tattooed guy scratched his head.

"Goebbels, Gehlan, Goering?"

The tattooed guy shrugged.

"Streicher, Strasser, Speer? Heydrich, Himmler? Murdered six million Jews. Twelve million, including Commies, Slavs, Gypsies, gays, Poles, astrologers? Extermination camps. Crematoria? Any of this ring a bell?"

The tattooed guy turned away.

"Nilch? Zap? Ixnay? No? Hitler?"

"Who the fuck are you?" the tattooed guy asked.

"Who the fuck am I?" Harry said. "I'm Captain Kidd, Jesse James, Stackolee! I'm Stormalong Jones, Pecos Bill, Joe Magarac, Popeye, Casey Jones, Honest Abe, and Johnny Appleseed. A Manhattan roarer! A subway Captain Blood! A Wall Street screamer! Half-Ferrari, half-piledriver, and all thunder under the counter. I'm a hundred and forty feet tall and can stride from the Berkshires to the Catskills in one step. Cross the Hudson, wade the Mississippi with a leap. Tie my shoe on the Rockies. And backflip from L.A. to Catalina. I can blow up a Brink's truck faster than you can spit! I can pick your pocket and make you thank me for the slap on the back! I can punch like a pneumatic drill, drink like a seven-hundred-pound sponge. I'm Jimmy Valentine with atomic fingers! I'm slick as Wesson oil and twice as slippery! I'm the Rhinebeck Strider! If you give me a dollar, I'll flush out the Erie Canal just for kicks! I can out-snort, out-smoke, out-snaffle, out-snatch, out-filch, out-scrounge, and out-mooch any sandbagger, racketeer, picaroon, Peterman, or Viking this side of the moon or twenty light-years beyond! I'm the Furious Crimper! The Thief of Baghdad! A panther-leather harpie! A Cock-a-Doodle-Desperado from Cemetery Alley! A hydrogen blazer! An atomic reactor! A particle accelerator! A maniacal mosstrooper! Angry as an Orc! Smart as Ulysses! Big as the Super Bowl! Loud as a supersonic boom! I'm Billy the Kid and Al Capone! I'm going to rob this continent blind and steal its white-tipped cane!"

"Speed fucking freak," the tattooed guy said to his girls.

"I'll drive you wherever you want to go," Friday said, crossing from the room doorway to her car.

She turned on the ignition. She started to back up.

Harry grabbed the passenger door handle, opened the door, and jumped in.

"I thought you were modest," Friday said.

"What have I got to be modest about?" Harry asked.

"I don't like this," Friday said, heading out of the parking lot. "I don't like you. Not right now."

Harry shrugged.

"I am who I am," he said.

CHAPTER 103

"Rossiter lives up by the river on Sumner Avenue," Harry said. "Back towards town."

Friday was silent.

"What do you think he is?" Harry said, thinking of the guy at the motel. "Thirty? Thirty-two? Mother gone? Father gone when he was a kid? Or Dad plays the tom-tom on Mom when he gets drunk? And Mom bitch-slaps Sonny-Boy, who stomps the dog, which corners the cat? Sits in school with earbuds pounding Death Metal or whatever the fuck they listen to now, doing a little coke, a little meth, a couple of oxys, shrooms on the weekend, doesn't so much drop out as drift off, flips burgers, chops firewood, cuts grass for rich weekenders before breaking into a house or two and boosting a Marantz PM8004 and selling the nine-hundred-dollar machine for sixty bucks' worth of crank, popping out a bastard or two or three. *How many kids you got, chief?* He blinks: *Me? Shit, seven, four, who the fuck knows . . .* Runs out of ideas for his new tattoo so he says *a big motherfucking eagle* 'cause he believes in the U.S. of A, though the Marines turned him down, mopery and flat feet, and the

Army doesn't want him, not after they cop to the track marks on his arms, and he can't even get a nod from the volunteer fire department, not that he'd apply, *too square, Jack, and I got other things going on on a Saturday night,* like boosting that sweet cherry-red 1995 Honda Civic, still the most popular stolen car in the country—which is useful knowledge, none of that 'who signed the Declaration of Independence,' that 'who started the Civil War' shit, as useful as knowing how to turn out some precocious fifteen-year-old with double-Ds and make some trucker's dreams come true while he's stuck waiting for a new spider gear set to get shipped thirty miles from East Bumfuck, the closest supplier with a clerk not too stoned to find the right part, while Little Baby Cheeks carburets on her glass pipe, so she'll be ready to go down, up, sideways, without remembering how many cocks she wilted, and her boyfriend, the Tattooed Wonder, wakes up one morning and almost pukes 'cause the mirror shows him his toothless, wizened father, and he thinks, *What the fuck?* And the calendar says he's somehow reached sixty and the last time he combed his hair was fifteen years ago when he thought he was going to get the job at the mill, which shut its doors and moved to China. And now, well, he's back to cutting rich people's grass and notices next to him some mook in a black hoodie with these pee-yellow cat eyes, cutting grass with a scythe and smiling as Our Tattooed Friend thinks, *Geez, my left arm tingles.* No one even sees him fall off the Craftsman seventeen five hp forty-two Shift-on-the-Go Lawn Tractor. RIP."

Friday glanced sideways at him.

"The guy just got under my skin is all," Harry said.

"I like your other stories better," Friday said.

"What other stories?" Harry asked.

A car approached, its brights on. Friday blinked her lights. The approaching car did not dim its brights.

"Keep your brights on," Harry said. "The son-of-a-bitch isn't dimming his."

"Anyway," Friday said, "there's no guarantee Rossiter *will* help."

"You want a guarantee," Harry snapped, "buy a toaster."

CHAPTER 104

"You forgot the chips," Maggie said as Rossiter came into the kitchen.

"Fuckin' Harry," Rossiter said.

"Like you said, you can't help him anymore," Maggie said.

Rossiter washed his face in the kitchen sink. Rinsed his mouth. The water tasted rusty. *Got to change the Britta.* From a cupboard, he took a bottle of Canadian Club, poured half a juice glass, and knocked it back in one swallow.

"That'll help," Maggie said.

Even the whiskey tasted rusty.

Maybe it's not the water.

He poured another. Drank it.

Maybe it's me.

"I'm going up," Maggie said and left the kitchen.

When Rossiter finished the bottle, he staggered over to the cupboard, fumbled out a fresh bottle, opened it, and once more poured half-a-tumbler's worth, which he drank in three swallows.

An hour later Chloe, up late, having finished her homework, clattered down the stairs in a search of a late-night snack, found her father sprawled, face-down, snoring into the cushions on the living room couch. One leg hung over the edge, his knee on the rug as if he were about to push himself up. But he was dead to the world.

"Is Daddy okay?" Chloe asked Maggie, who came into the room, clutching her robe at the throat.

"What are you doing up?" Maggie asked.

"Can I have Frosted Flakes?" Chloe asked.

"Go to bed," Maggie said.

"Do we have real milk?" Chloe asked, still looking at her snoring father. "Or that two-percent junk?"

"Your father's having a hard time at work," Maggie said.

"He loves work," Chloe said, heading into the kitchen. "More than us."

As her daughter passed, Maggie smacked her upside the head.

"Be nice," Maggie said. "Or tomorrow morning you can walk to school."

"That hurt!" Chloe said. "And if you give me olive loaf for lunch again, I'll barf."

After Chloe disappeared into the kitchen, Maggie crossed to her husband, looked down at him, and, sighing, touched his sweaty hair.

"This isn't working," she said. And called into the kitchen, "Chloe, get dressed. We're going to Grandma's."

CHAPTER 105

Cotton took plane tickets out of his suit coat pocket, checked them.

Brenda was putting on a black lamb's-wool coat, which looked as if it were made of Brillo pads.

Cotton punched in a number on his desk telephone.

"I want to confirm my reservations on the eleven-fifteen flight to Miami," he said into the telephone. "Uh-huh. Thanks."

He hung up and put the tickets back into his inside suit coat pocket.

CHAPTER 106

Rossiter's lawn was cluttered with a bicycle, a soft-ball bat, an old razor scooter. . . .

The house was dark.

Harry and Friday got out of the Tercel and headed up the front porch steps.

"Looks like no one's up," Friday said.

"So we wake him," Harry said.

Friday hesitated.

"He's a cop," Harry said. "It goes with the job."

Friday glanced at Harry, who rang the bell.

"If we prove Cotton had a gun," she said. "If we prove he shot Pillette . . ."

"They can't send me back to the hospital," Harry said.

"But can they reverse the drug?" Friday asked.

Harry looked confused.

"Do I seem that different?" he asked.

"Don't you *feel* different?" Friday asked.

Harry stopped, his finger suspended over the door-bell.

"Everything's the same," Harry said. "Except . . . except . . . Everything's so much sadder."

The porch light went on and Rossiter, a reindeer-patterned sweater over his pajamas, reeking of booze, opened the door.

"For a fugitive, you sure make a hell of a racket," Rossiter said. "There's an APB out for you."

CHAPTER 107

Cotton came into his library, carrying a small, fawn-colored, soft leather suitcase. Brenda followed with a knockoff Yves St. Laurent overnight bag. Cotton put the suitcase on his desk, swung the painting away from the wall, and opened the safe. Cotton and Brenda started taking bundles of bills from the safe and stacking them in the suitcase. After she had worked for a while, the tips of Brenda's fingers felt dry and sensitive.

When they were through, Cotton closed and locked the suitcase.

"One thing," he said.

Grabbing the suitcase, followed by Brenda, he headed through the foyer, the dining room, the butler's pantry, the kitchen, and the door down the stairs to the basement, where he snapped on an overhead light.

Spread out on sheets of plywood, thirty-three feet by thirty-three, was a miniature train diorama. HO scale. Two levels. Mainline run: 175 feet. Minimum radius: thirty inches. Minimum grade: 1 percent.

The lower level had an oval layout with a reversing

lock, eleven tracks in the staging area, eight tracks in the yard, two passing over branch tracks. The upper level: two concentric ovals with back-to-back switches to make a crossover. Both levels: three stations—urban, suburban, country. Buildings, vehicles, tiny people, four seasons . . .

Nineteen fifty-four.

Sha-Boom.

The last year anything made sense to Cotton.

Half to himself, Cotton said, "I just put in the new knuckle couplers."

"Where do you buy this stuff?" Brenda asked. "A dollhouse store?"

"I made everything," Cotton said.

"The trees?"

"Sagebrush, candytuft, and caspia."

"The pile of old tires?"

"Resin."

"You can see the treads."

"Wore them down in places spinning them on a drill."

"The lake?"

"Polyurethane," Cotton said. "See the corrosion on the battery boxes? I made that. The lamps and lights inside the buildings. Diodes. But the lights have working wall switches. The lamps' switches turn on and off. The softball lot, the sifted dirt—you bake it for two hundred fifty degrees for an hour to kill bugs."

"I like the commuter who just missed his connection," Brenda said.

"He missed a lot more than his connection," Cotton said. "That's my dad. I made his hat, his shoes, shirt, tie, his cuff links."

"Cuff links?"

"Real gold."

"Shit."

"I made everything," Cotton said. "The whole world."

From Hydrocal plaster, fine turf, coarse turf, underbrush, Static Grass Flock, polyfiber vines and undergrowth worked with Hob-E-Tac adhesive, scenic cement, foam nails, RIT dyes, PVC board, Flowering Foliage shaken from old McCormick spice boxes, ballast for the railroad ties and gravel roads, Polly Scale paints: Special Oxide Red, Pacemaker Red, Boxcar Red, Signal Red, Caboose Red, Oily Black, Tarnished Black, Rock Island Maroon, Prussian Blue, Reefer Orange, Boxcar Yellow, CSX Tan, Reading Green; Walthers, Atlas, Athearn rolling stock . . .

"And a new DCC system," Cotton said. "I installed the decoder chip in each engine myself."

"Well," Brenda said, "say good-bye."

Cotton started one of the trains, an Amtrak #242, Phase III engine, with a tail of rolling stock; some container cars; flatbeds, one carrying telephone poles; a dining car circa 1948, a little early for Cotton's setup, but matching the Pullman Car—the whole thing chugging around a mountain, entering a tunnel, emerging at a bridge, crossing a river, passing through a city, and starting its route again.

Cotton snapped off the overhead light, so the dark was illuminated only by the lights from the miniature world.

Leaving the train chugging, Cotton and Brenda climbed the stairs.

CHAPTER 108

Rossiter's kitchen was a disaster. The counter was covered with half-empty boxes of cereal, crackers, pretzels, pasta, and empty soup cans. In the sink, dishes soaked in greasy water. Dirty clothes—a sweat sock, a pair of Jockey shorts, a T-shirt with a cracked and faded picture of Bob Marley—were strewn over the floor.

Hung over the back of a chair was Rossiter's jacket and shoulder holster.

Rossiter poured hot water into three cups of instant coffee.

"Sorry about the mess," Rossiter said. "Maggie and the kid took off for her mom's."

He handed Harry a note.

"When'd she leave?" Friday asked.

"Tonight," Rossiter said.

"You made this mess since she's been gone?" Friday said.

Without reading it, Harry threw the note onto the kitchen counter.

"They'll be back," he said. "She says this weekend, she's taking the kid to Disney World."

Rossiter twisted up the corner of his mouth.

"Some guys lose their families to another man," he said. "I lose mine to a cartoon mouse."

"I didn't know you were having trouble," Friday said.

"We're not," Rossiter said. "Look, Harry, I should probably take you in."

"But Harry was right," Friday said. "Cotton *has* a gun. I *saw* it."

"Did you see Pillette's body?" Rossiter asked.

"They got rid of it," Friday said. "And compacted Turner. Marian Turner."

Friday hesitated, then added: "That's what they said."

"Tomorrow morning," Rossiter said, "first thing, we can send a car out to Cotton's house."

"And tonight?" Harry asked.

"Sorry, Harry," Rossiter said.

Harry grabbed Rossiter's gun from the shoulder holster hanging on the chair and aimed it at Rossiter.

"I'm not going back to the hospital, Rossiter," Harry said.

"Harry!" Friday cried.

"Sit on the floor, Rossiter. By the sink."

"Now, Harry—" Rossiter said.

"By the sink," Harry said.

"You know you're not going to use it," Rossiter said.

Harry didn't move. Still aiming.

"What the hell," Rossiter said.

He went known on one knee, used a hand to balance himself, then sat by the sink.

Harry used Rossiter's own handcuffs to lock him to the drainpipe.

"If Cotton hadn't knocked Harry out," Friday said. "If Harry had come up with some evidence. If Carol and Phil hadn't been so ready to lock Harry up. *If I'd believed Harry . . .*"

"A world of if's," Rossiter said.

A fly buzzed somewhere in the kitchen.

"'Where wast thou when I laid the foundations of the earth?'" Rossiter said. "'When all the morning stars sang together, and all the sons of God shouted for joy?'"

Unconsciously, Rossiter's eyes flicked around for his wife's flyswatter.

"Job," he said. "Thirty-eight." He continued: "'Canst thou bind the cluster of the Pleiades, or loose the bands of Orion? . . . Canst thou send forth lightnings? Doth the hawk soar by thy wisdom? Doth the eagle mount up at thy commands?'"

Harry tugged on, tested the handcuffs.

"That's what God said," Rossiter said, "when Job asked, *'Why me?'*"

"Is that this week's sermon you've been preparing?" Harry asked.

"God didn't give Job much to go on," Friday said.

"Job asks, *'Why me?'*" Rossiter said. "And God says, *'Why not?'* God says it's not up to us to question Him."

"Not the best answer," Harry said.

"I grew up on the Bible," Rossiter reminded Friday, who needed no reminder.

"When we were kids," Harry said, "you always had a passage ready."

Rossiter glimpsed a little of the old Harry in his friend's smile.

"Bases loaded," Harry said. "I'd strike out. You'd quote Leviticus, something."

Rossiter nodded.

"But it's the *only* answer," Rossiter said, searching Harry's face. "On the job, I get it every day. Why did my baby die? Why did my family die? Why AIDS? Why Afghanistan? Why did I lose my legs? Why did some punk shoot up a theater?"

"And God just says: *'Because,'*" Harry said.

Harry stood up, bumping the kitchen table, over-turning a bottle of beer, which foamed off the table onto the floor.

"That's it," Rossiter said. "Because He's God."

"That's not enough," Harry said.

The three of them looked at beer spreading in the dark across the floor like blood.

"I want to know why!" Harry said.

"Why pain?" Rossiter asked. "Why suffering? Why disease? You want to read God His rights?"

"Any twelve people would convict," Harry said.

"Lock Him up?" Rossiter asked. "And then what?"

Friday watched Harry's face.

"You fight with God," Rossiter said, "you better dance faster and punch harder than you been doing."

"If there is a God," Harry said, "I want him to prove He exists by—"

"Making sure the good guys win?" Rossiter said.

"*'Down these mean streets—'*" Harry started.

Rossiter interrupted. "I heard it," he said.

"You quote the Bible," Harry said. "I quote . . ."

Friday held her breath. This sounded like the pre-pill Harry.

But Harry shrugged. Dropped the gun into a drawer on the other side of the room. Picked up the almost empty beer bottle.

"It's you or me," Harry said.

"Never saw you put yourself first, Harry," Rossiter said.

"Maybe," Harry said, "it shows more self-esteem."

"That's one way to look at it," Rossiter said.

Harry started out the kitchen door.

Friday shrugged at Rossiter—and followed Harry.

CHAPTER 109

In the Tercel, Friday drove. Harry sat beside her, his hat on the seat beside him.

"Cotton's gun," Harry said. "You should have taken it when you had the chance."

"You sound angry," Friday said.

Harry didn't answer.

"It's the first time I've seen you angry," Friday said.

"It's the first time I've been in this kind of trouble," Harry said.

"What kind of trouble?" Friday said.

"*Real* trouble," Harry said.

"Oh," Friday said, "*real . . .*"

PART SIXTEEN

Confusion, and illusion, and relation,
Elusion, and occasion, and evasion?

—Alfred, Lord Tennyson
Idylls of the King

When Friday turned the corner onto Van Buren, Harry motioned her to pull over. Before the car had stopped, Harry was already opening the door.

"What's up?" Friday asked.

Harry was walking toward the deep doorway of a boarded-up movie theater, where a skinny mugger in a black watch cap and pea jacket was flashing a serrated bread knife at a young couple. The woman had dropped a yellow plastic shopping bag with a logo of an impossibly spiked boot and the words *Seven Inches to Heaven—Halavey Shoe Store*.

Half-blocked by the skinny mugger was a fat mugger in a ridiculous white cowboy hat, too-small black T-shirt, which revealed a roll of waxy belly flesh. He had a moon face and, instead of arms, flippers.

Harry braced the skinny mugger.

"Put the knife down, kid," Harry said to the skinny mugger, who stepped closer to the couple. Harry nodded at the fat mugger. "Back off, Fish."

"My name," Fish said, "is Aryell."

Friday approached.

"My mother named me Aryell, you fuck," Fish said.

"One," Harry counted.

"All I want is what's in her pocketbook," the skinny mugger said, his knife close to the woman's neck.

"Two," Harry said.

Holding the girl, the skinny mugger backed deeper into the old theater arcade.

"Drive away," Fish said, backing up next to and half-hiding behind his partner, "or we're all unhappy in the morning."

Harry kicked the skinny mugger in the balls and grabbed his knife hand by the wrist. He hip-checked the girl out of the way and slammed the ball of his hand into the skinny mugger's chin. The skinny mugger dropped the knife and collapsed onto the sidewalk.

Harry picked up the knife.

"We're not cops, pally," Harry said. "You're dancing with the stars now."

The two muggers scrammed.

Without saying thank you, the couple also ran. With the yellow shopping bag.

"You didn't give them fair warning," Friday said. "You never said *three*."

"Screw them," Harry said. "They're just street rats."

"This isn't like you, Harry," Friday said.

Harry said, "Let's get that fuck Cotton!"

CHAPTER 111

Cotton's house was dark. Trees rustled. The breeze smelled of cut grass. Harry and Friday sneaked up to Cotton's French doors. Carefully, Harry pried off a plywood panel, reached through, and let them into the library. The room smelled of ashes.

"Must have been burning evidence," Friday said.

"Whatever," Harry said.

Harry watched as Friday swung back the painting and opened the wall safe. She reached in.

"No gun," she said.

"Maybe you imagined it," Harry said.

Friday turned on Harry.

"*I'm* not the one who imagines things!" she said.

Cotton and Brenda entered. In one hand, Cotton carried his leather suitcase. In the other, his gun—which was pointing at Harry and Friday.

"You have this habit, Harry, of dropping in unannounced," Cotton said. "Brenda, wait in the car."

Brenda left.

"Friday figured out I was right," Harry said. "You *are* a shit!"

Cotton appraised Friday and told Harry, "Your

friend turns out to be a pretty good detective, after all."

Harry lunged.

Cotton shot him, shattering his hip.

But Harry's forward motion carried him into Cotton, who was bowled over backward.

Harry and Cotton landed in a heap.

Harry grabbed Cotton's gun as Cotton scrambled away. Harry tried to stand and collapsed in pain.

"Linda," he said through his teeth, "call the cops."

Cotton grabbed Friday with his left arm across her chest. With his right hand, from the desk, Cotton grabbed the shiv-shaped letter opener, which he held to Friday's throat.

"This isn't make-believe anymore, Harry," he said.

Harry lay on the floor, crippled, keeping the gun aimed at Cotton, who ripped out the phone wire and used it to tie Friday to a chair.

"You two have made my departure a little awkward," he said, picking up the leather suitcase. "I've got five million dollars in here."

"All the people you cheated," Harry said. "Marian Turner wasn't the only one, was she? How much do you have stashed in some off-shore account?"

Cotton crossed the room and stopped by the French doors.

"Too bad I can't buy time," he said.

"Drop the bag," Harry said. "Untie the girl. And stand facing the wall."

"You won't shoot," Cotton said.

He threw down the letter opener.

"Not when I'm unarmed," Cotton said. "Your code of honor—remember?"

Harry aimed.

"*No!*" Friday cried. "Harry, if you shoot him, it means—"

"What?" Harry asked.

"—you're just like the rest,". Friday finished.

"If I don't shoot him," Harry said, "he walks."

Friday begged, "Harry—"

Harry shot Cotton in the leg.

Cotton collapsed. Both men were equally—similarly—disabled.

"Oh, God," Friday sobbed.

Cotton touched his leg, came away with blood on his hand. Bewildered, he looked at Harry.

"What about your code of honor?" he asked.

"What do you think I am, Cotton?" Harry asked. "Crazy?"

CHAPTER 112

Outside Cotton's house, four police black-and-whites, two EMS vans, and half-a-dozen unmarked cars were parked on the street and in the driveway. The rotating bubble-gum lights on the squad cars flashed red and yellow on the fronts of the house and the bushes. A dozen neighbors—some in overcoats thrown on over pajamas—rubbernecked.

A uniformed cop led Brenda from the house to a patrol car.

Two EMS workers carried Cotton across the front lawn on a gurney. A couple of uniform cops walked alongside.

"You have the right to remain silent and refuse to answer questions," a cop told Cotton, who said, "I know. I'm an attorney."

The EMS workers slipped Cotton into the back of the EMS van.

Two other EMS workers carried Harry out of Cotton's house on another gurney.

Friday and Rossiter walked alongside.

"I should pull you in for resisting arrest," Rossiter told Harry.

"You were making me coffee," Harry said, "not reading me my rights."

"The pipe you handcuffed me to," Rossiter said. "It's got one of those new plastic couplers. Hand-tightened. I had it unscrewed before you were in the car."

"Why didn't you come after us?" Friday asked.

"Harry may be crazy," Rossiter said, "but he's never been stupid. Or dangerous. No matter what the court says."

Friday gave a worried glance at Harry.

"What *will* the court say?" she asked. "Now?"

"After all this?" Rossiter asked. "They're not going to give him a medal. But it'll be hard to stick him in a straitjacket when he was the one who caught on to Cotton."

CHAPTER 113

In the courtroom, Friday, Rossiter, Carol, Phil, and Bender sat on benches, watching the proceedings.

Harry stood before Judge Loomis, who was examining some papers.

"After hearing the facts presented by the defense and the prosecution," Loomis said, "and in view of the extenuating circumstances, I think justice would be best served by dismissing the criminal charges against Mr. Dickinson."

Loomis put one set of papers down and flipped through another set.

"In the related matter with respect to competency," he said, "given new evidence that Mr. Dickinson had some cause to justify his behavior at Mr. Cotton's house and office, the court will release Mr. Dickinson on his own recognizance."

Friday sighed in relief.

CHAPTER 114

Harry maneuvered down the courthouse steps on crutches. Friday and Carol, on either side, helped him manage. Phil trailed behind.

"Harry," Phil said, "I never thought you'd be a hero."

"Until a few days ago," Harry said, "I never thought I'd be anything else."

"So," Carol asked, "you're giving up the detective business?"

Harry stopped for a moment—looked around at the municipal buildings, the Court Square park, and, at last, across the common, to the windows of his office.

"It was a nice dream," Harry said. "While it lasted."

Phil opened the back door of his car for Harry, who shook his head no.

"I think I'll stop by the office," Harry said. "Figure out what I want to save."

"Your posters?" Friday asked. "Your mysteries? Police manuals?"

"Maybe it's just as well if Harry gets rid of them," Phil said. "Huh, Harry?"

"Yeah, maybe," Harry said. "See you at dinner."

On crutches, Harry hobbled across the common toward his office.

"He's as normal as I am," Phil said.

Friday didn't answer.

"Go away together," Phil told Friday. "A week, ten days. No murders, no mysteries."

Still, Friday didn't answer. She watched Harry with tears in her eyes.

Phil and Carol got into their car and drove off.

Bender came down the steps from the courthouse. He joined Friday watching Harry, who, swinging on his crutches, had crossed the common and was entering his office building.

"A fresh start," Bender said.

"The effects," Friday said. "Do they ever wear off?"

"The therapeutic benefits *may* vitiate in time," Bender said. "In a *few* cases—"

"How many cases?" Friday asked.

Bender hesitated.

"How many cases?" Friday repeated.

When Bender still hesitated, Friday said, "So Harry will be like this for the rest of his life?"

"Yes," Bender said. "And no." He shrugged. "He's the same Harry."

Friday shook her head.

"Yes," she said. "And no."

From the top of the courthouse steps, Rossiter watched the scene.

The sun cast a low light through the street from the river.

"'Where wast thou when I laid the foundations of the earth?'" Rossiter said. "'When all the morning stars sang together, and all the sons of God shouted for joy?' "

Rossiter was talking to nobody. Or maybe to God. Or maybe to himself.

CHAPTER 115

Harry entered his office and looked around as though he was waiting for something. Or as though he was trying to remember something.

He picked up a copy of *Black Mask*, leafed through it. And put it down.

He sat at his desk, aimlessly opened and closed drawers.

He took his bottle of bourbon from one drawer, thought about pouring a drink, decided against it, and put the bottle away.

He got up, turned on the record player. And stretched out on the couch.

Don't know why there's no sun up in the sky, Sinatra sang. *Stormy weather / Since my gal and I ain't together . . .*

Unseen by Harry, Friday entered.

"Life is bare" Friday sang with Sinatra. *"Gloom and misery everywhere . . ."*

Harry got up, hobbling on his wounded leg, and took Friday in his arms.

Awkwardly, they danced.

"Hold me tight, Harry," Friday said.

Harry did.

"Aren't you happy?" Harry asked.

Friday nodded halfheartedly.

"Well," Harry said, "let's go, Friday."

Harry grabbed his crutches and headed into the outer office.

Slowly, she realized Harry had just called her Friday.

She smiled.

And hurried after him.

The door closed behind them.

The office was empty, silent.

The door opened.

Harry reached inside, grabbed his slouch hat from the clothes tree, put it on his head, pulled it low over his right eye, and again closed the door—which read, in the frosted pebbled glass *Harry Dickinson—Private Investigations.*

AFTERWORD

HOW I CAME TO WRITE *FAST SHUFFLE*

1

When I was twelve years old, Rita Hayworth asked me to marry her.

I didn't know it was Rita Hayworth. I'm not sure I knew who Rita Hayworth was.

I was a kid actor, playing small roles—like John in *Life With Father*—and I used to detour backstage to my dressing room so I could peek into our ingénue's room. I don't remember her name, but she was often in her underwear; and, even though twelve was younger in the 1950s than it is now, I found the sight of her exciting.

One evening, around the half-hour call, when I passed the ingénue's room, I heard someone sobbing. Through the half-closed door, I saw a woman hunched over, head lowered, gasping, trying to stop crying. She was talking about a relationship gone bad. And, when she saw me, she said, "You wouldn't treat me like that. Would you, kid? Come here . . ." She reached out and pulled me to her. "You'd treat me right, wouldn't you, kid?" It was the first time I recall smelling liquor on an adult's breath. "You'd treat me right. Let's you and me get married."

Our ingénue introduced me to the upset lady, whom I assumed was another actress. Maybe a relative? A friend? Named Margarita Cansino.

Cansino may have had a stage name. Many actors did. But I was introduced to the person, not the actress.

"Come on, kid," Margarita said, "let's get married. . . ."

"I've got a show," I said, paying more attention to our ingénue in her underwear than to the drunk clutching me.

And that was the last time I thought of Margarita Cansino for three decades until I was on my way to my first TV writing job on *Hill Street Blues*. I was reading a history of Hollywood and came to a chapter about the Dancing Cansinos in which I learned that the drunk woman who pulled me to her bosom and asked me to marry her at the Valley Players thirty years earlier—Margarita Cansino—was Rita Hayworth. I'd written a novel a few years earlier and based a character on the ingénue. I'd left out Rita. I'd buried the lead.

On my way to Los Angeles to work in the Industry, this struck me as an omen.

2

My first day on staff, I arrived at the *Hill Street Blues* offices early. Too early. Seven o'clock. I wasn't due until ten. The parking lot next to the two-story building, which held *St. Elsewhere* on the first floor and *Hill Street* on the second, was empty—except for a new black Porsche. I pulled in next to the Porsche; and, nervous because I'd never worked on a TV show before, I crumpled the entire side of the new black car.

I backed up and parked across the lot from the Porsche, sat for a moment struggling with my conscience, and then reparked—more carefully—next to the ruined car.

I left a note on the windshield.

I had arrived in Los Angeles the day before, Sunday, and had checked into the Oakwood Barham in the Valley, where you could rent an apartment with anything you needed from TV to toaster, bedsheets to easy chair. As I checked in I saw a guy lugging a ripped black plastic garbage bag, trailing clothes, into another unit.

"Another poor sucker whose wife threw him out," said the old-timer, sinewy, mahogany-colored, sunning on a deck chair on a patch of lawn. "Check out the car." This one wasn't a Porsche, but it was expensive. I'd never seen a sleeker, lower, more feral-looking automobile. "Guy's got to be loaded," the old-timer said. "But he uses a garbage bag for a suitcase. They all do when they come here. Don't ask me why."

The old-timer had been a DP, director of photography, for decades. He'd been forced into retirement when work dried up.

"It's all contacts, kid," he told me, "and when your contacts start dying, you hang up your spurs."

I told him I'd been hired to be a story editor on *Hill Street.*

"That's who lives here," he said, "kids out from the East on their first jobs, *alta kockers* like me who read the trades and get lizard skin from the sun, and rich guys whose wives caught them with a little cooze on the side."

He'd forgotten the hookers—aging starlets who never made it—like the one who lived in the unit next to mine. Her bedroom wall was my living room wall. My first night—after driving over the hill to get a burger and malted at Mel's on Sunset—I was reading a *Hill Street* script from earlier in the season, written by Bob Ward, another novelist-journalist, who had gotten me the job on the show, when I noticed that the TV in the bedroom beyond our shared wall clicked off.

"See you in an hour, Ma," I heard, muffled, through the wall.

The next unit's door opened and closed. A beat. Through the wall, Sinatra came on the stereo. A beat. A knock at the next unit's door—which opened, closed. Muffled talk and laughter, getting louder as two people—the thirty-something failed starlet and her guest—came into her bedroom. A beat. And the *thump-thump-thump* of her bed's headboard bumping against our mutual wall. A beat. No more laughter. Some talk, casual, getting softer as the starlet and her guest left the bedroom for her living room. Her apartment door opened, closed. Sinatra silenced. TV back on. And, a little later, the door opening and closing and the starlet saying, "That's it, Ma, till my next one at eleven."

I hadn't unpacked. I was wondering if I could get out of my deal at *Hill Street*—which the next morning promised to be an easy enough thing to do, as I looked at the Porsche I had just ruined.

I went up to the *Hill Street* offices and wandered the empty halls until I ran into David Milch, who was running the show with Jeff Lewis. They had hired me. I had been in L.A. on assignment from *Playboy* and had stopped by the *Hill Street* offices to pick up Ward for lunch. When Ward introduced me, Milch asked if I was the guy who had written such-and-such a book. I said I was. And he asked if I wanted to write for TV. I liked Milch, was in awe of his work, wonderful scripts—he was TV's Chekhov. All of his shows—including a show he would create later, *Deadwood*—were compelling.

When I destroyed the Porsche, I sought out Milch. I took him to a window overlooking the parking lot and told him—showed him—what I had done.

"Find out who owns the car," I said. "It'll take me years to pay off the repairs, but I'll cover it—and if I have to I'll resign."

Around quitting time, Milch came into my office.

"I asked around," he said, "and no one claimed the car. It's gone anyway. Probably somebody who wasn't supposed to be on the lot. I wouldn't worry about it."

Later, I found out the Porsche belonged to Milch.

3

A few weeks after I had arrived in Los Angeles, I was invited to a dinner party by Everts Ziegler and his wife, Maryanne. Ziegler, one of the legendary agents, a graduate of Princeton and the OSS, was Hollywood royalty. I was new blood. My article on AIDS in *Rolling Stone* had just won a National Magazine Award.

I was from the East. I was a novelist. Those were my merit badges. There were three or four couples, Mary-anne, and me.

On my way to the party, I passed the La Brea Pits, where fossilized writers, trapped, tried to claw their way out of the tar.

"Now that you're inside the velvet rope," one of the other guests asked me, "now that you're making Hollywood money, what are you going to do? Get a place in Malibu? A Porsche?"

"For the first time in my life," I said, "I can go into a bookstore and get anything I want."

It was as if I had farted. It wasn't that anyone at the dinner was against books. But the small scale of my choice betrayed too little ambition.

4

The other Hollywood party I attended around the same time was thrown by Toby Rafelson, the wife of Bob Rafelson, the director. Jim Harrison—the novel-ist and poet—called her "Hollywood's Den Mother." Harrison and his agent, Bob Datilla, had taken me to Toby's, where maybe a hundred movie types mingled. Upstairs, Datilla told me, a group was playing strip charades. Bob said he had left when someone acted out "Sit on my face, Stevie Nicks." Downstairs, I found a corner in the living room. Doing the coke that was offered, I took in the scene. When I felt someone giving me a shoulder rub, I looked up and saw my masseuse was the model Iman, who was talking to someone else as she massaged me.

Jack Nicholson leaned across the coffee table and said, "Harrison says you're a smart guy. What do you know about Tesla?"

This was before the Tesla cult had gained momentum. I had happened to research him for a book I had written, so I was up on Tesla. After we talked for a while, Nicholson handed me a scrap of paper.

"Here," he said, "this is my private number. Maybe you could do a script about Tesla for me."

Back at the Sportsman's Lodge, where Harrison, Datilla, and I were staying—a hotel where Billy Wilder used to work on scripts, near Jerry's Deli—Harrison asked me what Nicolson and I had been talking about. I said he told me to call to work on a script with him.

"Well?" Harrison said.

"He was just being polite," I naively said.

"Shit," Harrison said.

We were all stretched out on deck chairs. I was in the middle.

"What are you doing?" Datilla asked me.

"Relaxing," I said.

"Then why are your knuckles white?" Datilla asked.

I was gripping the chaise arms. Harrison and Datilla each put a hand on the back of my chair and launched me, fully dressed, into the pool.

A few days later, back in New York, Datilla asked if I had called Nicholson. I repeated that he was just being polite. Datilla said, "He's the hottest actor in the business—he doesn't have to be polite. Call him!"

I didn't.

The opportunity seemed too extraordinary. There

had to be a hitch. I couldn't be that lucky. Also: I had a scruple—I didn't like the idea of using a social event to hustle business. I didn't understand how Hollywood worked.

Six months later, I joined Harrison and Datilla in San Francisco for a gallery opening of the paintings of Russ Chatham, Harrison's pal, who did the covers for all Harrison's books. It was Harrison's regular crowd, pals from Paradise Valley in Montana: Peter and Becky Fonda, the novelist Tom MacGuane, the singer-songwriter Jimmy Buffet (I think he was there: he usually traveled with this pack), Margo Kidder (Superman's Lois Lane), the publisher Sam Lawrence (I think he was there, too: my memory is uncertain, I was blasted on cocaine and pills and booze). One elegant woman, married to one of the celebrities, walked around with a little amber bottle plugged into a nostril. Every time she wanted a hit, she tilted back her head. Peter Fonda grabbed me and preached the evils of coke.

I ran into Nicholson, who said, "Smart guy, smart guy, you never called me. Here," he folded a piece of paper into my hand, "here's my new private number. Call me. We'll do the Tesla movie."

At dinner, Harrison said, "Jack says you never called him. Call him."

I didn't call.

I was embarrassed about not having called, still intimidated, and still not sure this wasn't just Hollywood schtick. Hollywood can love you to death. Everyone loves everything. No one ever follows up. Showbiz is all foreplay.

No—that's not quite true.

"You're going to get fucked," Tom Fontana (a legendary writer—producer, the creator of *Oz* and other series) once told me. "The question is: Do you get kissed afterward?"

"I love your work," a producer told me recently. "How can I get in business with you?"

"Offer me a job," I said.

"Seriously," the producer said. "I've been following your career ever since you started. How can I get in business with you?"

"Seriously," I said, "offer me a job."

"No, no," the producer said, looking over my shoulder at who just came into the party we were at and already beginning to edge away, "no kidding. How can I get in business with you?"

"No kidding," I said as she slip-slided away, "you want to be in business with me? Offer me a job."

But the producer was gone.

Another six months. Another party. Nicholson buttonholed me.

"Don't you like my pictures?" he asked.

"I love your pictures," I said—and quoted one of his famous speeches.

He quoted something back to me. When I looked baffled, he said, "That's from one of your books."

"I don't remember what I write," I explained. "I write to get stuff out of my head."

He gave me another piece of paper. With a new private number. I've noticed that stars tend to change their numbers regularly. For obvious reasons. But it tends to fill up an address book.

I've also noticed that stars often assume you don't know or like their work. When my daughter Susannah was nine years old, I took her with me to see a movie with Martin Sheen. At a diner after the show, during lunch, Marty realized Susannah didn't recognize him and he explained who he was. Susannah was at the *oh, Dad* stage and rolled her eyes.

And once, when I had just started working in Hollywood, she answered the telephone.

"Is David there?" the voice on the phone said. "This is Michael Douglas."

"Right," Susannah said and hung up.

I had a friend—John Henry Kurtz—who could imitate anyone. Once at Elaine's, we were sitting with Michael Caine and John Henry started speaking in Michael Caine's voice. For a long while, Caine didn't say anything about it. Then, Caine furrowed his brow. The dime dropped.

"You're doing me," he said. "You do me better than I do."

For the rest of the meal, they both did Caine's scenes from *Zulu!*

So, when Michael Douglas called, Susannah assumed it was John Henry pulling a gag.

Why on earth, she wondered, would Michael Douglas be calling her father? The phone rang again. Susannah answered it.

"Um," Michael Douglas said, "is David there? This is Michael Douglas."

"If you don't leave us alone," Susannah said, "I'm calling the cops."

When Michael Douglas finally reached me, he said, "I don't think your daughter likes my pictures."

After the party in L.A., another six months or so passed. Occasionally, Harrison or Datilla told me I was a jerk for not calling Nicholson. But, by now, I figured it would be so awkward I kept putting it off.

One night Toby Rafelson threw a dinner party. Nicolson was supposed to show up. I figured I'd say something when he arrived. But there was a power outage. Nicholson didn't come—although his friend Helena Kallianotes, who lived in the same compound that Nicholson shared with Marlon Brando, appeared. Not completely dressed.

"The lights went out," she said, "and I figured I'd come as I am."

That was one of the moments when I realized I loved Hollywood.

I never did call Nicholson.

Jack, if you are reading this and still want to make the movie about Tesla, offer me a job!

5

Hollywood can be hard to love. Most of the people I've met who work there—even people who have become stars—live in anxiety. Will I make it? Once I've made it, how long will I stay on top? When I start slipping, how far down will I go?

"Whenever I come to L.A.," a star once told me, "I feel diminished."

"You got seven years, kid," Nicholson told me the first time I met him. "Above the line, we all got seven years."

Knowing that, every five years or so, Nicholson has changed the kinds of roles he played. And has beat the odds. Being brilliant helps.

Every show's budget is divided into *above* the line and *below* the line.

Above the line are the boldface names, the celebrities, the power players.

Below the line are the union workers who make the movies.

Above the line: actors, directors, producers, writers . . .

Below the line: grips, gaffers, wardrobe people, hair and makeup . . . You can work forever.

The *line* separates the top section from the bottom section of every budget. It's Showbiz Apartheid.

It didn't take me long to realize the way to tell a happy production from an unhappy production is to map lunch. In a happy production, everyone eats with everyone else. The star sits down with the DP. The producer sits down with a PA. The director sits down with a grip. In an unhappy production, the star sits with the producer and the director. The co-star sits with the co-producer and the first AD. And so on and so medieval.

6

Ron Silver and I partnered to create a TV series *The Good Policeman,* based on a series of books by Jerome Charyn. We pitched and sold it at three of the then-existing four networks. During the third pitch, Ron noticed the pen I was using to take notes. When we left the room, he asked to see it—admired it and slipped it into his pocket. It was my lucky pen, given to me by Jeff Wachtel, who then was running Columbia Television and who now runs content at USA and associated channels. What the hell—I wasn't superstitious. I let it go.

Our last pitch was at CBS. Ron spent the pitch playing with the pen, an actor pulling focus, upstaging his partner. A pitch—like a psychiatrist's session or a tryst at a whorehouse—is a fifty-minute hour. And—like a psychiatrist's session or a whorehouse tryst—the important stuff happens in only five to seven minutes. Everything else is schmoozing and kibitzing.

The Good Policeman pitch at CBS was a stinker. My energy was low. My description of the premise was unfocused. As we walked out of the CBS office, Ron held the pen out to me.

"I guess," he said, "it's only lucky for you."

He hesitated.

"But it is a nice pen," he added.

Fox gave us the best deal. As we were driving to lunch to celebrate, we stopped at a red light near Universal Studios. I was driving. Ron was riding shotgun. On the side of the road, a haggard woman, who looked to be in her thirties, held out a sign: *We need food*. Three kids from five to nine sat by her feet in rags.

I took every bill in my wallet and gave it to Ron to hand through the window to the woman—why not; we'd just sold a show—who weepily turned to her kids and said, "We can stay in a motel tonight."

"It must be expensive," Ron said, "to be a Red Diaper Baby."

During the McCarthy era, my father had been the town Trotskyist in Springfield, Massachusetts, where

I grew up. He used to put me to bed with "Good-night, sleep tight, wake up bright in the morning light—come the Revolution, may it be short and bloody."

It was almost two decades before I heard a friend putting his own child to bed with the more traditional: "Don't let the bedbugs bite."

"Bedbugs?" I asked. "What about the Revolution?"

At a dinner Richard Dreyfuss and Chris Lawford and I had with some lingerie models, Richard referred to me as a Red Diaper Baby. Not understanding the term, one of the women suggested I use Preparation H.

7

This feudal attitude informs everything in Holly-wood, including driving. Less expensive cars tend to yield to more expensive cars: Later today, you might be pitching to the guy in the Maserati. Road rage is directed downward. Deference upward. A movie star who flipped his car and was hanging upside down as the Jaws of Life were getting ready to cut him out of the wreck was confronted by an angry cop who leaned over, read him his rights—and when he recognized him, shyly asked for his autograph.

Can I get out of the wreck first? the star asked.

When I first went to Miami to the set of *Miami Vice,* I asked Don Johnson, at that time voted Sexiest Man in the World, what it was like to be famous. He told me a story.

He was at a urinal. A man standing next to him glanced over, recognized him, and, turning, said, "You're Don Johnson"—and peed on Don's leg.

Fame, Don said: They know who you are and piss on you.

Don was easy to be with, smart, a thorough professional, fun, and self-deprecating: To protect his anonymity, he used to check into hotels under the name Richard Head.

Dick Head, he explained.

On the first show I produced—the Lou Gossett show *Gideon Oliver*, about a detective who was a cultural anthropologist—I arrived to oversee production of two episodes in Acapulco, under the helpful eye of an old-timer, Bill Sackheim. Bill had been in the business since 1945 when he wrote *Let's Go Steady* and through the golden years of TV in the fifties when he worked on *Lux Video Theatre* and *Playhouse 90*, but I knew him best as one of the producers on *The In-Laws*.

"Serpentine," I said when I met him. Quoting Peter Falk's advice to Alan Arkin when they're under fire—the most famous line from the movie.

"Serpentine," he said, smiling.

Within a few days, Bill was flown back to L.A. He'd suffered from dehydration, fallen, and cracked his head. I was alone with a Method director, who communed with his locations and a Mexican crew, which I discovered was not at all like an American crew. First of all, there seemed to be a lot of people on the crew list who didn't seem to exist. I could never pin down the facts. One night, while one scene was lit with a 10-k spot—a big light—I checked our equipment and suggested we pre-light the next location a little way down the beach using our second 10-k. But, whenever I went to locate the second light, it had just been moved. If it existed. Our "new" generators kept breaking down. When we had to shoot in a local jail, the building seemed as if it had not been thoroughly cleaned and disinfected. Lou refused to shoot. Under the heat of the lights, he pointed out, who knew what kind of bacteria would flourish.

"It's not just the actors in danger," Lou said. "We've got to protect the crew."

In his production report, the UPM, who seemed to have an old beef against Lou, wrote simply that Lou refused to perform, a damning statement without context. I wrote my own addendum to the production report, explaining the circumstances and saying I agreed with Lou. I brought it to the UPM and told him I was sending it in with or without his signature. He signed it.

Protect the star.

That is not only one of the commandments. In this case, it was also fair.

When Lou found out, he pulled me aside.

"When I go onto a new production I neither trust not distrust people," he said. "I wait and watch."

He decided to trust me.

We began telling each other jokes. Once I waited until the second before the AD called in the first team—the actors who were in the scene—to hit Lou with a punch line.

He walked onto the set, trying to suppress his laugh, which of course made it even harder not to laugh. Speed, rolling, action—the other actor in the scene gave Lou his cue and Lou exploded in bottled-up laughter. Reset. Speed, rolling, action, cue, laughter. Many takes later, I realized why a producer does not give an actor a punch line just before a scene.

Bill's son, Dan Sackheim, came down to help me. He was younger than I was, but had grown up in the business and was as sharp a producer as his father. Both were pacers. When they were together on the set, one paced in one direction while the other paced in the other direction, a double act. A few days after Dan arrived, we were shooting a scene around a hotel pool.

"What do you think?" I asked Dan. "Do we have enough gals in bikinis?"

There were only a handful of bathing beauties. We could use more. It always helps to dress a scene when you can with half-naked women—a Hollywood rule that goes back to Mack Sennett. Dan headed up the beach to the left. I headed up the beach to the right. Neither of us was in beach attire. I was in slacks, a jacket, and leather-soled shoes. Each attractive woman I came to I asked, "Would you like to be in a TV show?" I got the obvious answer. "Yeah," they would say, glancing at my brogans, "sure," and then turn over to work on their tan. I have never felt so foolish since.

Once, because of a crisis, Dan and I missed the transport to a location. We couldn't find our driver, so we started hitchhiking in the noonday sun. Sweating, hungry, and foot-sore, Dan turned to me, grinned, and said, "Ain't showbiz glamorous?"

The big set piece was a scene in the whorehouse district, La Zona Roja. We paid the whores and their pimps for a day's lost income. Figure twelve to fifteen hours. After lunch, no one could find one of our key crew members who, it was rumored, was lost in one of the whorehouses. After fifteen hours, the Method director was building a scaffold to get an unnecessary high-angle shot. I can't remember if we went twenty or more hours, but we went way over time and budget. The hookers and pimps were unhappy. The extras were nervous. I finally took the director aside and pulled the plug. But it was too late. The next day, after L.A. read the production report, they called and properly blasted me. Another lesson for a producer: Keep the director on time and budget.

When we had checked into the hotel, the manager had made a deal with the production not to charge the crew the one-dollar telephone connection fee. Since we were there for a while, it made the stay significantly cheaper. For me, too. I had stayed at the hotel with the crew, not at the resort up the hill with the rest of the above-the-line guys and gals. A legacy of my dad's radical politics. But, when we were checking out to make a company move to Mexico City, the hotel had reneged on its promise and charged everyone the extra dollar. I got in an argument with the hotel manager, which led to a fistfight, which led to me grabbing a stanchion for one of the velvet ropes and raising it above my head to clock the hotel manager—when Lou's stuntman and body double grabbed me around the arms and whispered in my ear, "Mexican jail, Mexican jail." After I calmed down, I went upstairs to Bill Sackheim, who had recently returned to the production, and told him I had disgraced the production and tendered my resignation.

"You stupid son of a bitch," he ranted. "You stupid son of a bitch—you should have called me. Together we could have taken that prick!"

8

At the end of the shoot, Lou said, "David, you're too nice to be a producer"—a judgment that followed me for better or worse throughout my career. Although my first year running a rump staff for *Law & Order* in New York, I was so terrified of the responsibility I became, for a while, a screamer. Years later, when I was meeting a staff on a new show, one of the writers gave me the fish-eye. When I asked him why, he said, "You made [so-and-so] cry."

I made the guy cry when we had forty-eight hours to turn around a script. We had half the outline done, but were stuck on the second half. Every time I came up with a suggestion my colleague ferreted out what was wrong with it—fair enough, except I had learned that to succeed as a scriptwriter you had to decide where you wanted to go and then *make it work*. Otherwise, you become paralyzed by choice: Any story can be told in hundreds of ways. It's like getting the ball in basketball. You've got to commit and move.

"Shut the fuck up," I shouted about 3:00 A.M. "Give me a chance to figure this out."

I don't like how I handled it, but it worked. As Michael Mann had taught me when he gave me the job on *Miami Vice,* I started at the end of Act Four—where I wanted to go—and worked backward, figuring out how scenes, beats, could be made to work logically and dramatically. The show turned out to be one of the best my partner and I wrote together. His dialogue was, as usual, crisp and funny and true. But he never forgave me for shouting.

When I got my first show-running job, Bruce Paltrow—Gwyneth's dad and Blythe Danner's husband, one of the great TV producers—called me into his office. Intimidated, I listened to him explain that on the first day I went into work as a show-runner, I should fire the most powerful person on the production.

"That way," Bruce said, "no one will fuck with you."

Not my style. I preferred to run a production the way Sidney Lumet did—he was loved. With him, people bent over backward to do their best work. When I worked with Sidney for two years on *100 Centre Street,* I realized you didn't have to be nuts to be in the business.

September 11, 2001, on the way across the Triborough Bridge to our studio in Queens—Hell Gate Studios, which Sidney built in one month with the help of his production designer Chris Novak—Sidney's assistant, Lily Jacobs, and I saw an explosion in one of the World Trade Tower buildings.

"Terrorists," I said.

"You're such a conspiracy guy," Lily said.

By the time we got to the studio, everyone was standing around a radio listening. People were calling home—trying to call home—to see if everything was all right with their families. Many wanted to go home. Sidney gathered the cast and crew and said he had been through a lot of tragedy and disaster in his life—

the Depression, Pearl Harbor, World War II, the Holocaust, Hiroshima and Nagasaki, the McCarthy era, Watergate, barbwire gun emplacements on the steps of the Capitol—and the one thing he learned is the worst thing to do in a crisis is to go home and brood. Anyone who wanted to go was free to go. But the best thing was to put one foot in front of the other, trust the future, and do your job.

He gave the most inspiring speech I have ever heard.

No one left work.

9

The best way to explain Hollywood is to tell you a fable.

This is not a true story. It does not involve a real female movie star. It is not about a real whorehouse. In his 1967 memoir, Garson Kanin described a brothel that operated in the Hollywood Hills in the 1930s: Mae's. The madam—who looked like Mae West—ran hookers who were doubles for famous movie stars: Alice Faye, Barbara Stanwyck, Irene Dunne, Joan Crawford, Janet Gaynor, Claudette Colbert, Marlene Dietrich, Luise Rainer, Myrna Loy, Margaret Sullavan, Paulette Goddard, and Ginger Rogers. The whorehouse piano player even looked to Kanin—like Teddy Wilson. Apparently, the place enjoyed a vogue for years before closing.

In 1989, a new whorehouse using the same gimmick opened on Mulholland near Coldwater Canyon. It was also called Mae's; and, like its predecessor, it was staffed by women who looked like famous stars from the past and present. Paulette Goddard was joined by Marilyn Monroe and Jane Russell. Irene Dunne by Sharon Stone, Janet Gaynor by Jessica Lange. Working at Mae's was—for the women—a kind of acting. It made them feel as if they were in the Business. Show business. That's all that mattered. One way or another.

A year after it opened, a movie superstar, Phoebe Allen—remember, this is not a true story, so the actress I'm calling Phoebe is no longer a star, no longer a regular boldface name on Page Six— heard about the whorehouse; and, one April night shortly after I had arrived in L.A., after a drunken dinner at a Japanese restaurant in the Valley, not Teru Sushi, she tracked down the place, introduced herself to Mae, and, as a gag, offered to play her own lookalike for a couple of hours.

People who know Mae—who have heard the story—are surprised that Mae agreed. Maybe Phoebe threatened . . . something. Two other big whorehouse scandals were brewing—one involving an S-and-M parlor on San Vicente. It wasn't the best time for bad publicity.

In any case, Mae did agree. And, for the next few hours, Phoebe pretended to be a whore who looked like Phoebe. She serviced two customers, one of whom asked for his money back, claiming that Phoebe seemed an imperfect counterfeit of the original. To avoid trouble, Mae gave him back his money—which she subtracted from what she paid Phoebe, who insisted on getting the same percentage as the other women.

Phoebe was recently divorced. Her second marriage. Her ex—let's say he was an art history major from Wesleyan—was raising her twelve-year-old son. She was between jobs, lonely, with a lot of free time—much of which she spent impersonating herself at Mae's.

For customers, before getting down to business, Phoebe acted out some of her most famous moments on the screen. One or two customers she refused to go with. Most she enjoyed and forgot.

A few weeks before leaving for Mexico to shoot a new picture, Phoebe met a surgeon—call him Dr. Boyle. He also is—of course—a fiction. Boyle had just been kicked out of a fifteen-year marriage. He had moved from his four-bedroom home in Brentwood into a week-by-week rental at the Oakwood near Warner Bros., where I met him. A friend in the movie business had brought him to Mae's. Since he had always been a fan of Phoebe's, he asked for her lookalike—not knowing, of course, that he was getting the real thing.

He was more lonely than horny. When Phoebe started to act out one of her movie scenes, he claimed he could do a better Phoebe imitation than she could. He tried. She was delighted and called in Irene Dunne and Myrna Loy to watch. Of course, Irene and Myrna didn't know Phoebe was really Phoebe. They thought she—like them—was a lookalike.

Irene and Myrna claimed it was the first time they saw Phoebe relax, the first time they saw her happy. Before Boyle left, Phoebe told him to visit her again.

During the following two weeks, Phoebe and Boyle met three times. Irene said Phoebe confided she was in love. After Phoebe left to start her new picture, Boyle stopped by Mae's twice a week looking for her. When told she was unavailable, Boyle would leave without choosing another women to take her place. Apparently, he, too, was in love.

Three weeks after arriving in Mexico, Phoebe left the production for a long weekend, claiming she had to see a doctor in Los Angeles—which was true. The doctor was Boyle. Phoebe went from LAX directly to Mae's, where she waited for Boyle to show up.

Early on a Saturday night, Boyle arrived. Phoebe disappeared with him for six hours. She returned to Mexico distraught.

She had finally found her true love—the man she believed was her true love—and she could not tell him who she really was. He believed she was a whore—and, apparently, was willing to marry her anyway. If she had been a whore, it would have been hard enough. If she told him she was really Phoebe—the real Phoebe—it would be, she was sure, impossible. Maybe he could love a whore, but could he love a liar, especially one who—he might think—had made a fool of him?

Drunk—possibly coked up—Phoebe arrived at Mae's again the following weekend. While she waited for Boyle, she sat in her room, drinking champagne and, later, cognac. Boyle arrived and disappeared into Phoebe's room. Forty-five minutes or so later, Mae heard a gunshot.

Mae rushed into Phoebe's room, where she found Boyle dead.

Phoebe couldn't have Boyle. But she couldn't stand

the idea of losing him. As Norma Desmond says in *Sunset Boulevard,* "Great stars have great passions." An old story: If Phoebe couldn't have Boyle, she decided no one would.

The detective who covered up the case for Mae—Phillips, not his real name because this is not a real story—claims that no one outside of Mae's place, not even Phoebe's agent, ever found out about the incident.

Phoebe returned to Mexico and finished the picture—a blockbuster, which put her in the running for an Oscar. As for Boyle, neither his ex-wife, nor his family, nor his friends, ever found out the truth. He just disappeared. In Hollywood, it happens all the time. Anyway, it doesn't matter, does it? He wasn't in the Business.

10

During these Hollywood years, I got jobs on dramas—grim scripts written and produced for adults. Because of the era, every year the stories got harsher. Darker. Bleaker. When they were broadcast, my daughter Susannah would leave the room.

"Everything you do is so unpleasant," she said. "Why don't you write something for me?"

Which is when I got the idea for *Fast Shuffle.*

What was the first shadow of a shadow of Harry? I was going to say *of the story,* but for me there is a difference between story and plot. The plot is the *what-comes-next.* The story is the mythic underpinnings of the plot.

For example, *Terminator 2*.

I have rarely come across anyone who disliked *Terminator 2*—even people who usually hate those kinds of movies. Why? The plot is straightforward: The T-800 Terminator, Arnold Schwarzenegger, comes from the future to alter the past—to protect John Connor, the future leader of the humans fighting the machines, from the murderous, shape-shifting Proteus: T-1000.

Interesting enough, but it doesn't explain the appeal of the movie.

During the movie, how does the Terminator-800 change? What does the machine from the future want? Why do we root for him?

At the end of the movie, the Terminator-800 sacrifices itself for Connor and the human race by melting itself down in a vat of molten steel—saying good-bye with a thumbs-up. The sacrifice and the good-bye are both *human*—not machine—gestures.

So much for the plot.

But beneath the plot is an American legend. Just as loggers had Paul Bunyan and sailors had Stormalong Jones and cowboys had Pecos Bill, steelworkers had Joe Magarac (who was first recorded by Owen Francis in 1931), a superhuman who ended melted into the steel he milled.

This is a story beneath the plot, part of the reason the movie hooks us—the archetype works on us on a subterranean level.

But such archetypal stories also have stories beneath them.

Before Joe Magarac, another half-human hero fit into a similar mythic niche: a being who starts mechanical and ends up becoming human. Joe Magarac and *Terminator 2* compel our attention because their story is the story of Pinocchio (the Carlo Collodi's 1883 tale).

And beneath—or beyond—Pinocchio (who is swallowed by a whale: *his* visit to the underworld) is Jonah. And beneath or beyond Jonah are all the tricksters—sacrificial figures going back to Ulysses and Gilgamesh, Dionysus and all the other heroes who are sacrificed and resurrected. We respond to *Terminator 2* for the same reason we respond to *ET.* They all tell the same story: the sacrificed hero who is reborn, the story of Jesus Christ.

When a plot has an atavistic story beneath it, beyond it, behind it, it can't help but move us.

Fast Shuffle—in its inception—touched something deep in me.

If I can identify the first moment I consciously started spinning the tale—and there are certainly many moments I am not aware of—it began at Du-par's restaurant at Laurel Canyon and Ventura in Studio City, where I used to stop for breakfast on my way to the *Hill Street Blues* offices on the nearby MTM lot.

One morning, a man entered, stood for a moment scanning the room from under heavy-lidded eyes. He was medium height, blocky build, and was wearing a trench coat, a baggy brown suit, suspenders hiking his pants high, a white shirt with a short wide tie, and a brown slouch hat. A forties look. His face was ruined in a good-looking way. He looked as if he had walked out of the pages of *Farewell, My Lovely* into a late-eighties world where people wore sneakers, jeans, baseball caps, and shirts with epaulets. When I asked Bob Ward, the pal who got me my first Hollywood job, why *epaulets,* he said, "Because we're in the Army of Entertainment." A year later, the fashion would change: writer-producers started wearing all black, assassin chic.

But there was something appealing about the man in the slouch hat at Du-pars—something satisfying about his rejection of contemporary style. Harry—he looked like a *Harry* to me—sat alone at a table, ordered and nursed a cup of coffee. By the time I left the restaurant, he had joined that Commedia dell'Arte troupe I carried around in my head. Every once in a while, I'd walk into a room—a used bookstore that in my fancy was a front for a blackmail ring, or Musso and Frank (where Faulkner used to hang out), or a greenhouse with orchids—and Harry would conjure himself into the scene, hat pulled low, a pint of rye in his coat pocket, and a toothpick in the corner of his mouth.

Five years or so later, on the Taconic from New York City to Columbia County, I saw a lean biker on a BMW followed by a short fat companion trying to keep up on an old Vespa motor scooter: Don Quixote and Sancho Panza. They enlarged and changed Harry's world. Harry was no longer just a Bogart phantom, but a contemporary Quixote who imagined himself as a previous generation's knight-errant.

Beneath and beyond Quixote was a tradition of stories going back to Apuleius's *Metamorphoses* or *The Golden Ass*—which, in turn, looks back into the early mists of humankind when the membrane separating human from animal, the shaman from the totem, was permeable.

A year or so after that, I was sitting at a picnic table outside a clam shack on Cape Cod, when a female biker stopped nearby: she took off her helmet and shook out her long hair and became Rosalind Russell in *His Girl Friday* in leather, body-checking my previous biker, Sancho, out of my imagination and becoming Harry's *nonbiker* companion, Harry's girl Friday.

I was inventing characters with mythic dimensions, which meant I was piecing together a story.

I saw—no, I heard—Harry and Friday talking. And like a picture in a pop-up book as I flipped through the tale, Harry's office rose off the page around them.

Almost immediately afterward, I heard—and saw—the final scene: Friday beaming, leaving the office, and Harry reopening the door, reaching in and grabbing his hat.

But I didn't yet have a plot—until I saw a photograph of a high school class in Chatham, New York, and noticed three boys who stood out from the other kids, clearly friends, and I had my teenage models for Harry, Rossiter, and Cotton.

The elements of the plot clicked into place like tumblers in a lock Friday was picking.

By the time I started writing about Harry and his world, the whole tale was formed, waiting to be teased out of the words that magicked them into being. What do I mean? The process was something like crossing a bog: put out a plank (start writing a scene), walk to the end of that plank, and put out another plank, walk to the end of that plank, and put out yet another plank—until you have crossed the swamp and are safe on the other side.

11

There is—at least—one more veil to penetrate.

There are probably many more veils. Many more realities behind and beyond each reality we discover.

Thomas Mann starts his *Joseph* books with "How deep is the well of the past. . . ."

The well is deep.

No doubt it keeps going down farther and farther. We never get to the end. Like the woman who told Bertrand Russell that the world was an elephant on the back of a turtle.

And what does the turtle stand on? Russell asked.

Another turtle, the woman said.

And—making a point about First Cause—Russell asked, What does *that* turtle stand on?

Oh, you can't trick me, the woman told Russell. It's turtles, turtles, turtles, all the way down.

Where did the impulse not to write *this particular story* come from, but the impulse to write *any story*?

The impulse to write.

I first thought of myself as a storyteller in first grade. On Yom Kippur. We lived on Washington Street in Springfield, Massachusetts, right across from my school: Washington Street Elementary School.

Since my parents weren't observant Jews, they sent me to school on Yom Kippur. My first grade teacher told me, *People like you don't come to school today. Go home.*

So I went home. Rang the front doorbell. And started to explain what had happened, when my mother, angry that I'd disobeyed her and had left school, slammed the door—on my thumb.

I was caught: a rabbit in a trap.

I screamed and cried. But my mother, thinking I was faking, refused to open the door. I watched the blood seep into my wool mitten. And after a while the blood crusted over.

My mother was unable to acknowledge what she had done. She may have even then been suffering from the mental disease that kept her in an asylum for the last decade of her life.

She told me she would open the door at three-fifteen, when school let out.

It was around eight-thirty in the morning. Almost seven hours to go.

I remember two things—two *thinks*—about being caught in the door.

First, I knew I had to protect my mother. I couldn't let other people know what she had done to me, so I crouched between the storm door—the bottom panel was sheet metal—and the wooden front door, so no one in the school playground across the street could witness my plight.

Second, at some point, I suppose just to pass the time and make it all bearable—I started describing to myself the situation I was in. Turning it into a story. As storyteller, I was outside the action. Safe. And—as storyteller—I understood that the more terrible the thing I was describing, the better story it would make.

I don't know if I'd been a storyteller before that. But, after that, I told stories—about myself and others—all the time. While I was experiencing something, I was at the same time describing it to myself. Trying to make the descriptions more and more specific. More and more accurate. If I smelled something, it couldn't just be sour. *How* was it sour? Was there a taste associated with it? A color?

Years later, I once spent a day and a half trying to figure out how to describe dawn—some quality I knew, but didn't know how to specify. I went around my apartment sniffing. Then, I went up and down Broadway sniffing. At last, I came home for lunch. When I cut into a cucumber—*that was it*: dawn. For me, for that scene, dawn smelled like the inside of a cucumber.

Plots are conflicts. My favorite plots come not from conflicts between black hats and white hats, but from conflicts between two incompatible realities.

Not from when a character gets in his or her own way and, by that, generates conflict.

But when the conflict comes from a double-bind. Not:

Take the job, Willy! (Death of a Salesman)

Not:

Tell him you love him, Cordelia! (King Lear)

But:

My mother killed my father, Agamemnon. The gods say I must avenge the murder with murder. But to avenge my father I must kill my mother, Clytemnestra! (Aeschylus' Orestia)

My father used to tell me there were only three plots:

A man or a woman against fate, nature, or God.

A man or a woman against another or others.

A man or a woman against himself or herself.

This *plot* is a toy Chinese finger-stall: The more you pull, the tighter your fingers are stuck.

The *story* is how your characters respond to being stuck.

12

Fast Shuffle has some shadows.

Terminator 2 is in there. And the Man in the Trench Coat at Du-par's. The biker with his sidekick. And Quixote and Sancho. Pinocchio and Dionysus. And Thomas Mann's Joseph and Sidney Lumet and Bill Cosby and all those who taught me not just how to write and produce stories, but also how to be an adult. How to try to be an adult. Because we *are* our stories. Our stories *are* us. Action equals character: What we do is who we are. There's no *deep down* as in *deep down that SOB is a wonderful guy.*

It's all a muddle we live every moment: good, cruel, surprisingly decent, absurdly nasty . . .

Maybe it can be explained by admitting we're primates: motivated by status and territory. Just that.

But I believe—not deep down, but on the surface where we behave—everyone is a radiant soul. And, as I once ended a novel, our only obligation is not *do unto others as we would have them do unto us.* That is a transaction. Mere moral commerce.

Our only obligation is: *Be kind.*

This book can't escape the grit I usually bring to my

yarns, because without the grit—without conflict, without the double bind, without rough reality—there is no tale. But on the whole I've tried to make it sunlit. Less grim than the tales I had been writing in previous novels, stories, TV shows, and movies.

This, my children, is a story for you.